# ANNOUNCING WITH PLEASURE THE FIRST PAPERBACK APPEARANCE OF

## *Outsider in Amsterdam*

"Should van de Wetering not write a sequel, I personally will bring him up on charges. . . . If *Outsider in Amsterdam* doesn't receive an award from somebody as the best first mystery of the year, we ought to sue on his behalf."

—*Soho Weekly News*

## Featuring

## Grijpstra and de Gier

"On foot or in their battered VW, the detectives hunt for clues among the city's ancient alleyways, and a steadily suspenseful narrative climaxes in some brisk action."

—*Publishers Weekly*

"One looks forward to more of Grijpstra and de Gier."

—*Detroit News*

**Books by Janwillem van de Wetering**

The Empty Mirror
A Glimpse of Nothingness
Outsider in Amsterdam
Tumbleweed

Published by POCKET BOOKS

# OUTSIDER IN AMSTERDAM

## Janwillem van de Wetering

A KANGAROO BOOK
PUBLISHED BY POCKET BOOKS NEW YORK

POCKET BOOKS, a Simon & Schuster division of
GULF & WESTERN CORPORATION
1230 Avenue of the Americas, New York, N.Y. 10020

ISBN: 0-671-81338-2

First Pocket Books printing March, 1978

2nd printing

Trademarks registered in the United States and other countries.

Printed in the U.S.A.

FOR JUANITA

# PREFACE

Once, some time ago now, I was a child and my parents would ask me what I wanted to be. I always gave the same answer. I wanted to be an Indian, and a cowboy in my spare time.

When fate, which according to Buddhist thought is the result of previous actions, brought me back to Amsterdam after a trip which took me to a large number of countries and lasted a long time, I received a letter from the army. The letter gave me an address and a name and a date and I found a middle-aged lady behind a desk who told me that I would have to be a soldier. I pointed out that I was over thirty years old but she wasn't impressed.

A little later I received another letter from the army. It told me that I would have to consider myself to be in "extraordinary service." The letter puzzled me and I put it in a drawer. Then there was another letter that told me that I would have to join the "civil reserve." I saw another middle-aged lady and told her that I didn't want to join the civil reserve, whatever it was. She told me to join the police. I told her that I already had a job. "In your spare time," she said.

The idea staggered me. I never knew that one can be a policeman in one's spare time.

But one can, and for several years now I have been a member of Amsterdam's Special Constabulary and serve the Queen in the uniform of a police constable. I have been in a number of adventures in the inner city of the capital and some of them inspired me to write this story. My imagination has, here and there, carried me away and the result is that the police routine as described in this book is not, in every instance, based on established police technique.

# OUTSIDER IN AMSTERDAM

# CHAPTER 1

The Volkswagen was parked on the wide sidewalk of the Haarlemmer Houttuinen, opposite number 5, and it was parked the way it shouldn't be parked.

The adjutant* had switched the engine off.

The adjutant hesitated.

He had arrived at his destination, Haarlemmer Houttuinen, number 5, and the high narrow gable house was waiting for him. He studied the gable house and frowned. The house had a body in it, a dead body, suspended. The body was bound to be turning slowly. Bodies, suspended by the neck, are never quite still.

The adjutant didn't feel like doing anything. He didn't feel like getting out of the car, running through the rain, watching a corpse move slowly, dangling, turning.

---

*Dutch municipal police ranks are constable, constable first class, sergeant, adjutant, inspector, chief inspector, commissaris. An adjutant is a noncommissioned officer.

"Hey," said sergeant de Gier, who sat next to adjutant Grijpstra.

"Hey what?" asked Grijpstra.

De Gier made a helpless gesture. Grijpstra could explain the gesture, the waving arm with its connected stretched-out hand, as he wanted.

But he still didn't move and adjutant and sergeant listened, peacefully and unanimously, to the fat raindrops that pattered from the heavy juicy spring sky onto the tin roof of the Volkswagen.

"Yes," the adjutant said, and got out of the car. De Gier had parked the car on the edge of the sidewalk and Grijpstra was forced to step into the street, a main thoroughfare, busy at all times of the day and the night. He didn't pay attention and a large American limousine approaching at speed had to turn suddenly to avoid the door of the car. The limousine, suddenly indignant, honked its powerful horn.

De Gier laughed and shook his head. He got out of the car as well, on the safe side, and locked the door carefully while the rain hit him in the neck. In Amsterdam nothing is safe, not even a police car, and this Volkswagen didn't look like a police car. No expert would recognize the VW as a means of transport reserved for officers of the criminal investigation department. Its radio set was hidden under the dashboard and the antenna was a mere twig, slightly rusty. No one would suspect that the back seat contained a well-oiled carbine, neatly wrapped in canvas, and complete with six magazines, or that the harmless nose of the car was filled with a complete collection of utensils that police officers think they need during the lawful exercise of their duties and including such items as a small suitcase full of burglar's tools, a powerful searchlight, a dredge, gas masks and a tape recorder.

But nothing was suspected and the officers looked as innocent as their vehicle. Grijpstra is a fat man, and de Gier neither thin nor fat, qualities they share with a large number of other men in Holland's capital. Grijpstra wore a badly fitting suit made of expensive English striped material, with a white shirt and a dark blue tie, and de Gier a made-to-order suit of blue denim, a blue shirt and a many-colored scarf neatly folded around his Adam's apple. Grijpstra's hair looked like a well-worn scrubbing brush and de Gier's curls were beautifully cut by a proud and highly trained coiffeur taking an almost personal interest in the glamor of his clients. De Gier's curls were so well shaped, in fact, that he could be mistaken for a woman, if viewed from the rear, and only his narrow hips protected him from attacks from that side.

A pedestrian, in a hurry to reach his parked car, bumped into Grijpstra and hurt himself against the large model service pistol that the adjutant carried under his jacket.

"Watch where you're going," the pedestrian mumbled ferociously.

"Yes sir," said Grijpstra kindly.

An ordinary car was parked on the sidewalk and two ordinary men ran through the rain until they reached the porch of number 5 and tried to catch their breath.

Their object achieved, a new period of inactivity began.

"Bah," Grijpstra said and read the sign on the door.

The sign said HINDIST SOCIETY.

Both men studied it. It looked neat, like the door. The text had been written in an unusual script as if the letter artist had tried to create a mysterious atmosphere. It seemed as if the letters had been drawn very quickly; the result was vaguely Chinese, far away.

De Gier produced a comb and arranged his hair while he looked about him.

The porch was old, and magnificent in its Golden Age splendor. It had been designed in the seventeenth century for a gentleman-merchant who specialized in expensive timber, imported from Africa and the Far East and stored in the first three stories of the tall house, while the merchant himself would have lived in the top three stories from which he could see the harbor and his vast stocks of cheaper timber, stacked in an area of perhaps a square mile. But that was long ago and the stones of the porch were cracked now and the beams supporting the gable house sagged a little. But the well-built house still retained a good deal of its original stately beauty and the present owner had kept it in reasonable repair.

A small window showed a number of objects and de Gier studied them one by one. Glass jars filled with health grains and brown and green tea and a substance that de Gier, after some thought, determined as seaweed. A sign in the window, showing that the same sort of lettering as the main sign, informed the visitor that the Society went in for a variety of activities. Grijpstra grunted and read the sign in a loud voice:

"Shop, open from nine to four. Restaurant and bar, restaurant open to nine, bar open to twelve P.M."

He looked at de Gier but de Gier was still studying the display.

There were several small cartons filled with incense and a gilded Buddha statue sitting on a pedestal, staring and smiling, with a headgear tapering off into a sharp point.

"A pointed head," Grijpstra said. "Is that what you get when you meditate?"

"That isn't known as a pointed head," said de Gier, using the voice of his lecture evening, once a month, when he taught the young constables of the emergency squad the art of crime detection.

"Not a pointed head," de Gier repeated, "but a heaven-head. The point points at heaven. Heaven is the goal of meditation. Heaven is thin air. Heaven is upstairs."

"Ah," said Grijpstra. "Are you sure?"

"No," said de Gier.

"You can ring the bell," Grijpstra said. "You have a nice index finger."

De Gier bowed from the hips and rang. His index finger was indeed nice, well tapered, thin and powerful.

Grijpstra, as if he wanted to avoid all comparison, had hidden his hands in his pockets.

The door opened immediately; they had been expected. Both men braced themselves.

"Suspected suicide," the police radio had said, a few minutes ago. "It seems that a man has hung himself." That was the message, and they had been given the address.

Grijpstra had repeated the address and had said that they would go there, and the female voice belonging to the constable first class of the radio room had thanked them and closed the communication.

And now they had arrived, but they knew no more than the radio had told them.

And now, of course, there would be a great commotion. Several people talking at once. White faces. Fearful eyes. Shouts and screams. Violence affects people.

But the face that looked at them, from the open space where the thick green monumental door had been, wasn't white but black, and it wasn't excited but calm.

The officers studied the man in the door.

"A Negro," Grijpstra thought, "a small Hindist Negro. Now what?"

De Gier hadn't drawn any conclusion. Like Grijpstra he had associated black with "Negro," but he was in doubt. The man was no Negro. "Who else is black?" de Gier thought but the logic line of his thoughts was interrupted by the inquisitive expression on the face of the dark man.

"Police," Grijpstra said and produced his wallet, a large leather wallet consisting of a number of plastic compartments and a notebook. He shook the wallet, the plastic compartments dangled and a small card hung in front of their host's eyes.

The man came closer and concentrated on the document.

"That's a credit card of the Amsterdam-Rotterdam Bank," the small man said.

De Gier laughed softly and Grijpstra looked at his colleague. It was a heavy look, full of criticism.

"I'm sorry," said de Gier.

Grijpstra dug in his wallet and after a while his square fat
fingers found his police identification with its blue and red
stripes and photograph of a much younger Grijpstra dressed
in uniform with the silver button of his rank on both shoulders.

The dark man bent forward and read the card.

"H. F. Grijpstra," he read in a clear voice. "Adjutant.
Municipal Police of Amsterdam."

He paused.

"I have seen it. Please come in."

"Extraordinary," de Gier thought. "Fascinating. That
fellow actually read the card. It never happens. Grijpstra
always shows his credit card and nobody ever notices anything. He could have shown a receipt from the electricity
department and nobody would object, but this chap really
reads the identification."

"Who are you?" Grijpstra was asking.

"Jan Karel van Meteren," the man said.

They were in the corridor. There were three doors on the
right, heavy oak doors. One of the doors was open and de
Gier saw a bar and several young men with long hair and one
elderly man with a bald head. Everybody was drinking beer.
He had a glance of another young man behind the bar,
dressed in a white T-shirt and decorated with a necklace of
colored stones. Van Meteren was leading the way and they
followed obediently. A staircase at the end of the corridor,
again made of oak and recently polished. The floor of the
corridor was covered with slabs of marble, cracked but very
clean. Near the staircase Grijpstra noticed a niche with an
upright Indian figure, made of bronze, life-size and with the
right hand raised in a gesture of solemn greeting. Perhaps the
gesture symbolized a blessing.

They climbed the staircase and came into a large open

space with a high ceiling made of iron, painted white and with a relief of garlands picked out in gold. This was the restaurant, occupying the entire floor. De Gier counted ten tables, six seating four persons and four seating six persons. Nearly every chair was taken.

Grijpstra had stopped while their guide waited patiently. He was admiring a statue, standing on a stone platform attached to the wall. It was a statue of a female deity, performing a dance. The noble head on its slender neck seemed to contrast at first with the full breasts and the lewdly raised foot and Grijpstra was surprised that this naked sexual figure represented divinity and that he accepted her divinity. Undoubtedly the figure was free, quiet, detached and powerful. Superior. The thought flitted through his head. Superior. And free. Especially free. The thought disappeared as he walked on. De Gier had seen the statue but hadn't allowed himself to be interested. He watched the guests without fixing any one of them in particular. A fixed stare is aggressive and invites attention. He didn't want any attention and didn't get any. The guests took him for another guest and thought he wanted to join them. One man took his hat and briefcase off a chair and made an inviting gesture. De Gier smiled and shook his head. He noticed nobody seemed to talk, perhaps they were listening to the music that came from several stereo loudspeakers and was hitting the room in waves. De Gier liked the music; it reminded him of a performance in the Tropical Museum. The heavy rhythmical cords would come from a bass guitar and the dry sharp knocks from a set of drums; he imagined that the wheezing high notes setting the melody itself would be a flute, a bamboo flute probably.

They were moving again, still following van Meteren. He led them through the restaurant and into a long narrow kitchen; through its windows there was a view of a garden full of red and pink rhododendrons. Two girls in jeans were busily stirring pots on a large stove. There was a sharp but not

unpleasant smell of weird herbs. One of the girls wanted to
object to the presence of strangers but stopped herself when
she saw van Meteren.

There was another narrow staircase and another corridor.
White walls and several doors. They passed three doors and
van Meteren opened the last, fourth, door.

De Gier had a feeling that they had now penetrated into the
secret part of the house; perhaps the silence of the corridor
motivated the thought. The music of the restaurant didn't
reach this lofty level. Grijpstra entered the room and sighed.
He saw the corpse and it moved, exactly as he had expected.
It would be the draft, of course, all phenomena can be
explained, but the slow ghastly movement chilled his spine.
De Gier had now come in as well and watched silently. He
noticed the small bare feet with their neat toes, pointed at the
floor. His gaze wandered upward and recorded the protrud-
ing tongue and the wide open bulging blue eyes. A small
corpse that had belonged to a living man. A little over five
feet. A thin man, well dressed in khaki trousers of good
cloth, nicely ironed, and a freshly laundered striped shirt.
Some forty years old. Long thick dark red hair and a full
mustache, hanging down at the corners by its own weight. De
Gier moved closer and looked at the corpse's wrist watch. He
grunted. A very expensive watch, worth a small fortune. He
couldn't remember ever having seen a gold strap of such
width and such quality.

Both officers froze and quietly looked around, noticing as
many details as possible. Almost automatically they had put
their hands in their pockets. They had been trained in the
same school. Hands in pockets cannot touch anything. This
silent room was bound to be full of indications, traces,
tracks.

They saw a large room, again with a high ceiling but not
made of cast iron but of plain sawn planks supported by
heavy deal beams. There were several bookcases, well filled.
There was a telephone on one of the bookcases, and an

expensive TV set and a new complete encyclopedia. The
furniture consisted of a low settee, a table and three chairs.
There were some cushions on the floor, embroidered. The
patterns were unusual. Eastern designs probably, de Gier
thought. There was a typewriter on the table with a letter in it.
De Gier bent down.

*Dear Sirs:*
*I thank you for your letter of the tenth and have to inform*
*you*

No further text. The letterhead looked expensive. HIN-
DIST SOCIETY, the address and the telephone number.

They saw a footstool, lying on its side, near the feet of the
corpse. They saw a gramophone, a stack of records and a low
bed covered with a batik cloth. The woven curtains were
closed but allowed enough light to filter through to see every
detail of the room.

"What's this?" Grijpstra asked, pointing at another low
table, covered with red lacquer and serving as a seat for a
fairly large statue, a rather fat bald-headed man sitting cross-
legged and staring at them with glass eyes.

"An altar of sorts," de Gier answered after some thought.
"That copper bowl filled with sand must be an incense
burner, and the brown spots in the sand are burnt-out incense
sticks."

Grijpstra raised an eyebrow. "You know a lot today."

"I visit museums," de Gier said.

Grijpstra sniffed.

"Incense?" he asked.

De Gier nodded. The heavy sweet smell gave him a
headache.

"Who discovered the body?" de Gier asked van Meteren,
who was standing near the door.

"I did," van Meteren answered. "I had to ask Piet something and as he didn't answer when I knocked, I went back to

my room. A little later I asked the girls in the kitchen if they had seen him and they said he had gone upstairs. I looked into the other rooms; one of them belongs to his mother, and another is the temple. He wasn't there. I thought he might be asleep and knocked again and then I opened the door and saw him hanging there. I telephoned the police and waited for you downstairs. Nobody knows anything yet."

"Why didn't you cut the rope?" asked de Gier.

"He was dead."

"How did you know?"

Van Meteren didn't answer.

"Are you a doctor?" Grijpstra asked.

"No," van Meteren said, "but I have seen a lot of corpses in my life. Piet is dead. Dead is dead. I could feel it. A dead body has no feel."

"Did you touch it?"

Van Meteren shrugged his shoulders. "I don't have to feel a corpse to know it is dead."

"So why didn't you cut the rope?" asked de Gier again.

"I couldn't do it by myself," van Meteren said. "Somebody would have had to hold the body. Besides, I wanted you to find it the way it was. Perhaps it will give you a lead."

De Gier looked again at the corpse. He had an idea that he had seen the man before and searched his memory. De Gier's memory was well organized and he knew his way around his files. After a while he knew that he hadn't seen the man before but that the strong chin, the long hair and the heavy mustache reminded him of a portrait he had seen in a museum in The Hague. A portrait of a Dutch statesman of the sixteenth century, a statesman and a warrior, on his way to do battle. The warrior had been sitting on a horse and had a sword in his hand. A leader. Very likely this man had also been a leader, a boss. A little boss in charge of a small society. Discipline, de Gier thought. That's it. This house and this room reek of discipline. Everything is neat and clean. The girls in the kitchen are clean too, reasonably clean. Van Meteren is clean. There would be some connection between the corpse and van Meteren. Perhaps van Meteren is an employee of the Society. But why do I observe this? de Gier asked. The answer came immediately. He hadn't expected cleanliness when he had read the sign on the door. HINDIST SOCIETY. He had associated the words with a mess. The new wisdom coming from the East is a messy business. He thought of the dirty doped vague shadowy people he had arrested in the street and interrogated at Police Headquarters. Petty theft, drug dealing in a small silly way, runaway minors, prostitution. All suspects stank. He had made them empty their pockets before locking them up and had been appalled at the dirty rags, the broken trinkets, the lack of money. He had seen the photographs they carried around with them. Pictures of "holy men," "gurus" or "yogis." Skeletons with long matted hair and crazy eyes. The masters preaching the way.

He had associated the word HINDIST with Hinduism or Buddhism. The religions of the East. Before he had begun to arrest the crazy tramps the words had had a different association. Peace and quiet, some form of detachment. Real wisdom. But gradually "messiness" had crept in.

And now he had to admit that this place, this nest of nonsensical imitation faith, was, after all, clean. And he had been surprised. De Gier's thoughts took a few seconds only and meanwhile Grijpstra had sighed again. The body was dead, no doubt about it, and they would have to cut the rope. They had to assume that the body was still alive. Only a doctor can determine death. He looked over his shoulder and nodded at de Gier.

"You can telephone headquarters, if you like."

There was no need to say it. De Gier was dialing the number already. He didn't have to say much. At headquarters the machine was already in operation. Within a few minutes they would be arriving. Doctor, ambulance and the experts.

While de Gier telephoned Grijpstra picked up the stool and put it right and climbed on top of it. He cut the rope with his switchblade, an illegal weapon that he carried against all regulations. The rope wasn't thick and the knife very sharp. De Gier wanted to catch the corpse but van Meteren was quicker. He put the corpse down, very carefully, on the bed. No one thought that Piet would start breathing again.

He didn't.

Grijpstra bent down and looked at the dead face. "Have a look."

De Gier looked. "Ach, ach," he said.

Van Meteren looked as well.

"A bruise," van Meteren said, "near the temple, slightly swollen."

"You saw that very quickly," de Gier said.

"He has been hit," van Meteren continued, "with a stick, or perhaps a fist. The doctor will be able to tell us."

"What exactly do you do in this house?" de Gier asked.

Van Meteren straightened his back and rubbed it. He thought. The low forehead became wrinkled and the nose seemed to flatten itself even more. Suddenly de Gier knew this man had to be. Not a Negro but a Papuan. He remembered the photographs in his geography book at school. Papuan sitting on the beach, sharpening spears. But not a fullblooded Papuan, the nose wasn't flat enough and the face showed other properties. Perhaps three-quarters Papuan or seven-eighths. That would explain the Dutch name. The Papuan's language was pure Dutch, impeccable, overcorrect even. De Gier knew the way the Dutch Negroes spoke and the Indonesians. Van Meteren's way of talking was more guttural.

"I live here," van Meteren said. "That's all. I do nothing here. Piet ran the Society. I think that the girls will take over now, or Eduard or Johan. But Johan is in the bar and hasn't been told yet and Eduard took the day off.''

''All right,'' de Gier said, ''in that case I will go down. For the time being nobody is allowed to leave the premises. The cars from Headquarters can arrive any minute now. They'll be sending more detectives and probably uniformed policemen as well. It'll be the usual hullabaloo.''

De Gier ran down the stairs. Hullabaloo was the right word. Day after day nothing to do but to drive around and look around a little and now suddenly two corpses in one evening. They had found the first corpse early that evening, or rather, they had seen a body change into a corpse. The woman was still alive when they found her, naked and bleeding in the shabby whorehouse at the canal. A knife in her belly. She died in the doctor's arms; he had come immediately answering de Gier's emergency call. The woman had been able to describe her killer, while she kept her hands pressed against her body in a vain attempt to stop both pain and blood. An aging whore, a reasonably sweet person. De Gier had found the young man under a tree, right opposite the whorehouse. The boy was resting his back against an old elm tree and was staring into the canal's murky water. The knife was still in his hand. He confessed at once. A pleasant boy, but not to be trusted with knives and middle-aged women who reminded him of his mother. They had taken him with them in the car and locked him up after they had taken his statement. Another job for the municipal psychiatrist. Most likely the boy wouldn't even have to face court but be taken to an asylum straight away to rot there for the rest of his life while he filled his time making feltdolls and swallowing pills. Or they might release him after a while and put him on national assistance and the state's money would buy another knife and another middle-aged woman would die.

The dead prostitute hadn't taken much of their time and

Grijpstra and de Gier had gone out for another ride hoping to be able to fill the rest of their night's shift with peacefully ambling about, with a cup of coffee in a quiet café somewhere. And now this.

De Gier strode into the restaurant. He found the amplifier and turned the knob the wrong way. The loudspeakers screeched and some forty startled faces stared at him. One of the faces, a heavily bearded one, lost its temper.

"Look here," the face said, "would you mind leaving that amplifier alone? We are listening to that music!"

De Gier walked up to the man and put a hand on his shoulder. "Never mind the music. I am a police officer. I have to request everybody here to stay put."

He raised his voice.

"Something unpleasant has happened in this house tonight. Please remain seated. My colleagues will be here any minute now and we will have to ask some questions. It's only a formality and we won't keep you long. If anyone knows anything about what happened upstairs earlier tonight or this afternoon he can come and speak to me."

The faces began to mumble to each other. The two girls came from the kitchen and approached de Gier.

"What happened?" the oldest girl asked. A beautiful girl with large green eyes and pigtails, she would be just over twenty years old.

"You'll be informed in due course," de Gier said.

"Is it about the money?"

"Has money been stolen?" asked de Gier.

"I don't think so," the girl said, "but Piet asked us this afternoon if we had been in his room. Johan had taken the shop's money to Piet and put it on his table at four o'clock and Piet counted it and it was less than he expected. He probably didn't count properly. Did you come because of that?"

"No," de Gier said softly, "we wouldn't disturb the joint

for a few guilders. Piet is dead. He was hanging from one of the beams in his room.''

"Oh," the girl said and covered her mouth with a shaking hand. The other girl, a fat little thing with glasses, began to cry.

"O.K., O.K.," de Gier said. "It can't be helped. Any of you two been to his room?"

Both girls shook their heads.

"No," the fat girl said.

"No," the beautiful girl said, "not after five o'clock this afternoon. I saw the money on the table when I went up with Piet. I only stayed ten minutes or so and then I returned to the kitchen to prepare for supper. In fact, he told me to go, he wanted to write some letters."

"He is the boss here, isn't he?" de Gier asked.

"Yes," said the fat girl, "he is the Society's director. The Society is supposed to belong to all of us members but he runs everything. And is he dead now?"

De Gier gave her his handkerchief and she rubbed her eyes.

He looked at the black stripes on the clean white cloth and realized dejectedly that they would never come out in the small washing machine in his apartment.

"You can keep the handkerchief," he said to the girl, "with the compliments of your police force."

Her tears didn't impress him. He had seen the glint in her eyes. Death is sensation. Apparently she liked sensation.

He heard the doorbell and went to answer it. There was quite a crowd on the sidewalk and four parked cars, not counting his own. The colleagues had come quietly, without flashing blue lights or howling sirens. The experts didn't believe in a mad rush.

He shook a few hands and spoke to a fingerprint man, a close friend. He showed them all the way. The doctor and the experts to the dead man's room, the detectives to the restaurant where they started their investigation immediately. All they needed at this stage were names and addresses. De Gier told them to spend a little time on the two girls and Johan the barman, and to ignore van Meteren, whom he reserved for himself.

"Ah yes," he said to the senior detective, "if you find an old lady leave her alone as well. She is the dead man's mother. We'll see her later."

"Who's 'we'?" the senior detective asked.

"Grijpstra and myself," said de Gier.

The senior detective looked impressed and de Gier grinned at him.

"You are a comedian," he said.

'The doorbell rang again.

"Sir," de Gier said when he recognized the chief inspector.

"Suicide?" the chief asked.

"Could be," de Gier said, "but he has a bruise on his temple."

"Hm," the chief said, and went upstairs. He left within a few minutes, and Grijpstra accompanied him to the door.

De Gier looked at Grijpstra.

"Usual behavior," Grijpstra said. "He looked around and grunted a bit. It's all ours."

Peace returned to the gable house two hours later.

Grijpstra and de Gier sat at one of the restaurant tables and smoked and looked at each other.

"Twice in one day," Grijpstra said.

"Too often," said de Gier, "twice too often."

"But what do we make of it?" de Gier asked. "Murder or no murder?"

Grijpstra blew some smoke out of his nostrils; de Gier watched the little hairs wave inside.

"Could be either of the two," Grijpstra said, "but it'll probably be murder. Somebody gave him a nice thump, using his fist, for I saw no possible weapon lying around and the bruise didn't seem very serious. Bam, Piet is on the floor, it doesn't need much to knock a small man over. He is unconscious or dazed. The rope is ready. Rope around the neck. You lift him up with one arm and put him on the stool. Other end of the rope on the hook in the beam. You kick the stool. You leave the room quietly. One minute's work. Half a minute maybe."

"One or two killers?" de Gier asked.

Grijpstra gave him a fierce look and shook his head.

"Why two killers? Two men? Two women? One man and one woman? Why make it involved? One killer, not two or three. Killers are very scarce in Amsterdam so why would we suddenly run into a whole bunch of them?"

"But it isn't an easy job," de Gier said carefully. "He had to be carried around, and put on a stool. It may be difficult if you are by yourself."

Grijpstra got up. "Come with me, we are going to do a little work."

They were busy for several minutes. De Gier stretched out on the floor and relaxed his body. Grijpstra pulled him to his feet, put him on the stool, slipped the noose around his neck.

They tried several times.

"You see?" Grijpstra said. "Nothing to it. Your weight is more than Piet's, you must weigh a little over seventy kilos while he probably weighed ten or twelve kilos less. A very thin little chap. Anyone who isn't a hungry dwarf could have done it."

"Yes," said de Gier.

But later he disagreed again.

"It wasn't like that," he said. "Pay attention."

"I am paying attention," Grijpstra said and opened his eyes as wide as they would go.

"Right," said de Gier. "This Piet of ours is a morose fellow. He wants to die. Life isn't what it should be, he thinks. He can't remember ever having given permission for his own birth. And now he finds himself here, in a room in an old ramshackle house in the Haarlemmer Houttuinen, director of a nonsensical society that isn't going well anyway and gives him nothing but a lot of work and debts. He goes on thinking and works out that he is now over forty years old and that he will soon be an old man who won't be able to look after himself. And it annoys him that he is a *little* man, and that he always has to look up at people. Here he sits, in his empty room. Everything is stale. His ideas are gone and proved wrong. All he has is his own loneliness. It frightens him. He wants to leave, through the white gate which can be opened with the silver key. And he does have the silver key."

"Beg your pardon?" said Grijpstra.

"Imagery from the East," said de Gier. "Comes from my reading and it fits the case for this is a Hindist Society. Death is the white gate and everybody has the silver key."

"Excuse me," Grijpstra said. "I wasn't very good at school and I never read anything. But now I understand. The rope is the silver key."

"Don't excuse yourself," de Gier said. "You are very clever. And books don't give any real information. Words, nothing but words. Hollow words. I read that too. The rope is the silver key but if you have the will to stop breathing for longer than two minutes you are also using the silver key."

"Fine," said Grijpstra. "Piet wants to leave. Through the gate. Or into the tunnel, that's even better imagery. Death must be like a tunnel, I think, a tunnel that leads to the inexpressible. But now what happens? In your story he is still considering."

De Gier got up and began to wander through the restaurant. "He makes up his mind. But that sort of decision takes some doing. We never really decide anything, we take life as it comes and it drags us where it wants to drag us. It's all a matter of circumstances, of powers that control us. But to commit suicide is a decision. He decides but he helps himself by taking a drink. He drinks a lot. He becomes very drunk. Now he has to attach the noose to the beam. He climbs on the stool and he falls. He hurts his head. But he insists. And he manages to hang himself in the end."

Grijpstra scratched the stubbles of his beard. De Gier was still wandering through the restaurant.

"I didn't notice any smell of liquor," Grijpstra said, "perhaps a whiff. A glass of sherry maybe. But I don't think he was drunk. I didn't even find a glass in the room. I looked out the window but I didn't notice any splinters in the street. I'll check when we go home. He may have thrown the bottle out the window. Drunks often do. But I don't think Piet would have thrown a bottle out the window. I think we agree on his neatness. Somehow I can't believe that a neat man, living in a clean room in a well organized house, and dressed nicely, with combed hair and a beautiful mustache, will commit suicide."

De Gier looked at the statue of the dancing Indian Goddess. "Yes," he said. "Suicidal people lose their self-discipline. They don't shave anymore and have meals at odd times. They have accidents, they drop things. They don't make their beds. I remember the psychologist told us about it at the police school. Could be. But I could imagine a neat man hanging himself using a good piece of rope knotted into a perfect noose, and hung from a strong hook, screwed tightly into a solid beam. Why not? Perhaps there are neat suicides, we'll have to look it up in the library and we can ask the chief. Psychology is his hobby, they say."

Grijpstra went on scratching.

"Yes. And you may still be right. Perhaps he didn't drink anything but used a drug. A drugged person can fall too. There were no marks on his arms and legs but he may have sniffed cocaine or taken a pill. He hadn't smoked, there was no ashtray and no ash in the wastebasket. I asked the girls; he didn't smoke at all, they said. Funny, I had the impression they were lying. Why lie about smoking?"

"Hash," de Gier said. "He probably smoked hash and they did too, and they didn't want us to know."

"Hash doesn't make you fall over and bump your head," Grijpstra said.

De Gier shrugged. "I'm tired. Let's find out tomorrow. I want to go home but we still have to talk to van Meteren, he is waiting for us in his room upstairs. I sent the girls to bed; if they have been lying we can grill them tomorrow. We have to find out about that money as well. Perhaps there is a connection."

## CHAPTER 2

"Would you like some tea?" asked van Meteren.

"Coffee," said de Gier and Grijpstra in one voice. They were facing him, sitting on a low bed, with their heads leaning against the wall. It was close to midnight now and de Gier was exhausted; he had visions of his small but comfortable bachelor's flat in the south of the city. He felt the hot water of his shower streaming down his back and the foaming soap on his shoulders. The old gable house with its endless corridors and nooks and crannies began to get on his nerves and the imitation Eastern atmosphere stifled him, although he had to agree that van Meteren's room exhaled a pleasant influence. It was a fairly large room, with whitewashed walls and the floor was covered with a worn but lovely Persian rug. On a shelf along the width of one entire wall van Meteren had displayed a number of objects that interested de Gier. He studied them quickly, one by one, the strangely shaped stones, the shells, the dried flowers and the skull of a large animal, a wild boar perhaps. Van Meteren sat on the floor, on a thick cushion, cross-legged, relaxed and patient, the black

21

hard curls framing his flat skull silhouetted against the white wall, lit up by a light placed on the floor opposite him.

Van Meteren pursed his lips.

"I have no coffee here. The bar will be closed now. The bar is the only place where coffee is served. To drink coffee is really against the rules of the Society. Piet always said that coffee excites."

He poured tea from a large thermos flask, decorated with Chinese characters. Grijpstra and de Gier were given a small cup each. They sipped and pulled faces. Van Meteren laughed. "It's an acquired taste. This is very good tea, perhaps the best we can buy in Amsterdam. It's a green tea, very refined, first choice. Tea activates but relaxes at the same time. To drink tea is an art."

"Art?" Grijpstra asked.

"Art. A man who knows how to drink tea is a detached man, a free man."

"Detached from what?" asked de Gier.

"Detached from himself, from his greed, his hurry, his own importance. His own suffering."

"That's nice," Grijpstra said. "Did you hear that, de Gier?"

Van Meteren waved a small black hand. "Your colleague heard. He is an intelligent man."

"Thank you," said de Gier. "Could I have another cup of your delicious tea?"

Van Meteren poured another cup, showing his teeth in a wide smile.

"And now tell us," Grijpstra said. "What exactly are you doing in this house? Who are you? What does this Society represent? Who was Piet?"

"Yes," de Gier said, "and do *you* like coffee? Or are you only refusing to drink it because it is against Piet's rules?"

Van Meteren gazed at them. "You are asking a lot of questions at the same time. Where shall I start?"

"Wherever you like," Grijpstra said. De Gier nodded contentedly. Grijpstra was using their usual tactics. De Gier usually asked the unpleasant questions and Grijpstra acted "father," the kind force in the background. Sometimes they changed roles. Sometimes they left the room and only one of them would return, to be replaced later by the other. They would do anything to make the suspect talk. The suspect had to talk, that was the main thing, and they could sort out the information as it came. And their tactics usually worked. The suspects talked, far more than they intended to. And very often they confessed, or served as witnesses. And then they would sign their statements and the officers could go home, tired and content.

But de Gier's contentment was shortlived. Van Meteren wasn't the usual suspect. And he didn't say anything. De Gier observed his opponent. A weird figure, even in the inner city of Amsterdam. Small, dark and pleasant. Dark blue trousers and a clean close-fitting shirt with vertical stripes so that van Meteren looked a little taller than he was. Self-possessed. Conscious even. Do conscious people exist, de Gier asked himself. People who know what they are doing and who are aware of the situation they are in?

Grijpstra observed too. He saw a man of some forty years old, small and graceful. He had also classified the suspect as a Papuan. Grijpstra had fought in the former Dutch Indies and remembered the faces of a couple of professional soldiers who had joined his unit for an attack in difficult mountainous terrain. Papuans, very unusual types, contrasting with the much lighter-skinned soldiers from Ambon who had made up the bulk of Grijpstra's men. The Papuans revered a colored photograph of the queen, pinned up in their tent. Very courageous they were, but he never got to know them well. They were dead within a few days. They had volunteered for a sniping patrol and the Javanese got them after a fight of a few hours. Two Papuans who had killed nearly fifty enemies with their tommy guns. The Javanese had caught one Papuan alive, they had "tjingtjanged" him, cut him up with their razorsharp "krisses," starting at the feet.

"Your father came from Holland?" Grijpstra asked.

"My grandfather," van Meteren said. "My grandmother was a Papuan, a chief's daughter. My grandfather worked for the government; he was only a petty official, but a petty official is very powerful in New Guinea. My mother is also a pure Papuan, she is still alive and lives in Hollandia. I arrived here eight years ago. I had to choose in nineteen hundred and sixty-five whether I wanted to be an Indonesian or Dutch. I chose to be Dutch and had to run for my life."

"And what do you do for a living?"

"I am on the force," van Meteren said, and laughed when he saw surprise glide over the faces of his investigators. He had a nice laugh, showing strong, even, very white teeth under the small pointed mustache and the flat wide nose.

"Don't let it upset you," he said. "I won't arrest you. I am a traffic warden. All I can do is give you a ticket for parking your car on the sidewalk and you won't have to pay the fine anyway."

"Traffic warden?" Grijpstra asked.

Van Meteren nodded. "I joined the department five years ago. In New Guinea I was a real policeman, constable first class because I could read and write and my name was Dutch. I commanded thirty men. Constable first class is a high rank over there. But when I came out here they told me I was too old for active duty. I was thirty years old. They gave me a job as a clerk in one of their bureaus in The Hague. I kept on asking to be allowed to join the force and eventually they made me a traffic warden and assigned me to street duty. I have two stripes now and I am armed with a rubber truncheon. Every six months I apply for a transfer to the real police but they keep on finding reasons to refuse me."

"A traffic warden is a real policeman too," Grijpstra said.

Van Meteren shrugged his shoulders and looked at the wall.

"What exactly was your job in the New Guinea police?" de Gier asked.

"Field duty. During the last few years I served with the Birdhead Corps, in the South West. We watched the coast and caught Indonesian commandos and paratroopers sneaking in by boat or being dropped. We caught hundreds of them."

De Gier looked at the large linen map of New Guinea that had been pinned on the wall. The map looked worn and had broken on the folds. There were two other maps on the wall, a map of Holland and another of the IJsselmeer, Holland's small inland sea, now transformed into a large lake by the thirty-five kilometer dyke that stops the rollers of the North Sea. "Could I see your traffic warden's identification?"

The little document looked very neat. Van Meteren showed his New Guinea identification as well, yellow at the corners and spotted by sweat, its plastic cover torn right through.

Both Grijpstra and de Gier studied the documents carefully. A Dutch constable first class from the other side of the world. A memento of the past. They looked at the imprint of the rubber stamp and the signature of an inspector-general. They spent some time on the photograph. Van Meteren was shown in uniform, the metal strips had glinted in the light of the photographer's flashbulb. A strong young face, proud of his rank and his responsibility and of his Corps, the Corps State Police of Dutch New Guinea, part of the Kingdom of the Netherlands.

"Well, colleague," Grijpstra said, "and what do you think? Did anyone help Piet when he was being hung?"

Van Meteren's eyes were sad when he replied.

"It is possible. He may have fallen. I studied the room and I have thought about what I saw but it is always dangerous to come to a conclusion. Piet may have knocked his head against something. And there may have been a fight, it wouldn't be unlikely because he had a very short temper. His state of mind wasn't good, not lately anyway. His wife and child have left him and refuse to return. He has been depressed and he did mention the possibility of suicide. Man is free and has the right to take his own life, I have heard him say it at least three times. He knew he wasn't very well liked but he couldn't make himself likable. Perhaps someone came to see him, perhaps there was an argument, perhaps someone hit him and perhaps Piet was so upset that he hung himself after whoever it was left him."

"Who would have argued with him?" de Gier asked. "You?"

"No," van Meteren said. "I don't argue with anyone. Whenever Piet had one of his moods I avoided him. This is a very big house, there is always another room."

"Were you friendly with Piet?"

"Yes, but I wasn't his friend. I don't believe in friendship. Friendship is a feeling of the moment. Moments pass. I have neither friends nor enemies. The people around me are the people around me, I accept them."

"What are you doing in this house?" de Gier asked.

Van Meteren laughed. "Nothing. I live here. Piet invited me in. I was living in a small room in a boarding house. A cheap place although the rent was high. In a narrow street on the fourth floor, very little light and you can breathe the fumes of the street. The nearest tree was a mile away. I spent most of my free time walking around and had my meals at Chinese restaurants, as often as I could afford to. If I couldn't eat in a restaurant I would have a sandwich in a park. This place has a restaurant and I tried to have a meal here but they wanted me to become a member. I had to go to Piet's office and pay him twenty-five guilders and fill in a form. That's how we met. He seemed to like me straightaway and offered me a room, two hundred guilders a month including as many meals as I wanted."

"That's very cheap," de Gier said.

"Very," van Meteren agreed. "But he may have had a

reason. Perhaps he wanted a policeman in the house. I am not on the regular force but I do have a uniform and I am properly trained. There's a bar in the place, clients may be difficult at times."

"Did he ever make use of your services?"

"Once or twice," van Meteren said. "I have taken guests into the street but I didn't hurt anybody. The grips we were taught are either defensive or merely meant to transport a suspect without causing him any undue pain."

Grijpstra smiled, he remembered the textbook phrase.

"Was Piet a homosexual?" de Gier asked.

It was van Meteren's turn to smile.

"You are a real policeman," he said, "always assume the lowest motive and you are usually right. But perhaps you are wrong this time. Piet wasn't a homo. I have thought of it for he often visited me in my room, he was interested in my collection of stones and shells and wanted me to tell him stories about New Guinea. He wanted to know what Papuans eat and what our religion is and whether we used any herbs or drugs and if we danced. But he never bothered me. Whenever he felt that I wanted to be alone he would leave at once. No, Piet liked women even if they caused him trouble."

"Did they?" de Gier asked.

"Always. He wanted to own them, to dominate them."

"I thought women liked to be dominated," de Gier said.

"Yes. But not by Piet. He had little charm and tried to make them ridiculous, especially when he had an audience. So the women became bitter and attacked him and hurt him in his pride. He had a lot of pride. And in the end they would leave him."

"You don't make him sound a very nice person," de Gier said.

Van Meteren shook his head. "No no. He wasn't all that bad. He meant well."

"No friend, no enemy," de Gier said.

"Yes," van Meteren said. "I try to be detached, to keep

my distance. People are the way they are; it's hard to try to change them."

"And that's the reason you drink tea," Grijpstra said.

Van Meteren thought for a while. "I do other things as well."

"We are getting nowhere," Grijpstra thought, and asked for more tea. Van Meteren filled his cup, Grijpstra took a sip, breathed deeply and immersed himself again in the opaque sticky substance of an unexplained death of an Amsterdam citizen.

"And this Hindist business, what does it mean?"

Van Meteren felt through his pockets and found a pack of cigarettes. It contained one cigarette only. He offered it to Grijpstra.

Grijpstra shook his head. "It is your last."

"Never mind," van Meteren said. "I have some more somewhere, and if not I can get some downstairs in the shop, I have a key."

"Hindism," de Gier said.

"Yes," van Meteren said. "Hindism. I have been curious too, but I have never quite understood what Piet meant by it. Something between Hinduism and Buddhism perhaps. Piet's own homemade religion. It's quite intricate and bound up with right eating and tea and meditation. The room next door is a temple. There are cushions on the floor and twice a week people sit still in it for an hour or so. Piet is, or was, the priest and had his own special cushion, richly embroidered. He sat closest to the altar. Perhaps he really thought of himself as a prophet, a teacher who had something to show to the new people, the young offbeat types of today. But he was losing interest and he was running short of disciples. Hardly anyone showed up for the meditations and he had to put up with a lot of criticism from the people who work here. Nobody stayed long. The ones you have met, the girls and Johan, and Eduard, whom you'll probably meet later, are all newcomers, they haven't been here for longer than six months at the most and I think they only stay because they can't think of another place they want to go. They'll leave as soon as something turns up. Piet wanted to create an oasis of peace, a quiet place where people can get strength and where they can forget politics and money-making. Find their souls, their real selves. He had invented a special routine, the whole house has been redesigned for that purpose. The bar is an entry, people go easily into a bar. But finally they'll land up in the meditation temple, at least that was the general idea. The barkeeper would have to listen to the guests and direct them, tactfully and gradually to the higher regions, the restaurant with its clean food and pure fruit and vegetable juices, and the temple with its spiritual air. And Piet would be the divinity in the background, working through others and guiding them without showing himself much. Perhaps he really thought that way in the beginning but he must have lost faith and found himself weak. The arguments must have hurt him and his own lack of strength. I have listened to a long lecture he delivered once, the subject was that one should never eat meat. But afterwards he sneaked out and I saw him buying some hot sausages off the street stall around the corner.''

"Ha!" de Gier said. "But surely he can't have been that much of a failure. This place looks reasonably successful. It is clean for one thing and the restaurant was almost full. He must have been making some money and some people must have admired him one way or another."

"Sure," van Meteren said, "and the atmosphere here is quite pleasant. I have always been reasonably happy here and it would be a pity if it's all over and done with now. And Piet's ideas were all right, but he wasn't the right man to put them into effect. Perhaps if he had admitted that he was a beginner himself and had lost some of his pride. He wanted to be a great master and it must have been a shock to him when people belittled him. His own wife called him a lesser nitwit when she left, the others called him other things. He has been walked over a lot lately . . ." He didn't finish his sentence.

"Who else lives here?" Grijpstra asked.

Van Meteren counted them off on his fingers. "His mother, eighty-three years old, second door on the right from here, not altogether sound in mind."

"Old age?" asked Grijpstra.

"No, not just old age. A bit mad I would say. Then there is me, you know me. On the next floor there is Thérèse, the girl with the pigtails. Annetje, the other girl, sleeps in the servant quarters, on the other side of the courtyard. She shares her room with Johan. Eduard lives in the little cabin at the end of the garden. He had his day off today but he may have been here this afternoon, you'll have to ask him. Johan has been working, he had the shop today and has been barman during the evening."

Someone knocked at the door. Van Meteren called "Yes" but nothing happened. He got up and opened the door and the detectives saw a very old lady, tall and angular, dressed in a gown set off with lace, a thick woollen scarf hung over her shoulders. Two glinting sharp eyes stared at them. The aggressive nose reminded de Gier of a sparrow hawk's beak.

"What's going on?" the old lady asked. "What are you all talking about? I have been listening to the grunting of voices for hours now. It is half past one, I want to sleep."

Van Meteren put his arm around the old lady. "Come in, Miesje. These gentlemen are police officers. That's Mister Grijpstra and that's Mister de Gier."

The detectives shook the thin hand, dotted all over with dark brown spots.

She sat down, with a straight back, on the edge of the settee.

"So what goes on?" she asked in a brittle voice. "Are they your friends, Jan? Traffic wardens?"

"No, Miesje. They are regular police. There has been an accident. Piet has had a bad fall."

The old lady's eyes, which had been closing slowly, suddenly opened.

"He is dead?" she shrieked.

Nobody answered.

"He is dead," the old lady said and began to cry.

The sound of her sobs grated the detectives' ears. Her mouth dropped open and Grijpstra shuddered when he saw her tongue flapping and trembling with each fresh howl.

Van Meteren had rushed out of the room and came back with a glass of water and a very small white pill.

"Swallow this, Miesje." The old lady swallowed. The sobs stopped abruptly. She responded to the brief snappy command.

De Gier was grateful; the sudden silence eased his nerves.

The old lady began to talk. She spoke slowly: it seemed that the pill had given her a dry mouth.

"This afternoon Piet told me that I shouldn't complain so much and that the rhododendrons are in flower. But my eyes are so bad. What are rhododendrons anyway?"

Her voice was gathering volume again.

"Rhododendrons are flowers, Miesje," van Meteren said, still using his command voice. "Like tulips. And now you are going to your room and you are going to sleep. Tomorrow I'll come to see you before I go to work."

He pushed her out of the room.

"I can't stand old ladies," de Gier said, "and I most definitely can't stand them if they are mad."

"You'll have to learn to get used to them," said Grijpstra. "There'll be more and more of them. It's very difficult to find a doctor who'll let old people die nowadays. Haven't you been reading the papers? I wonder what was in that pill."

"An opiate," said van Meteren, who had returned. "It's called Palfium. The doctor prescribes it, she can get as much as she wants. She has been taking these pills for years now and she is hopelessly addicted to them. Piet knew but he didn't mind. It keeps her quiet. Without the pills she would have to go to an asylum and he preferred to keep her here. I'll telephone the doctor tomorrow; he'll probably have her taken away."

"Did Piet take those pills as well?" Grijpstra asked.

"Not as far as I know."

"But he could have taken them, his mother must have a bottle of them on her bedside table."

Van Meteren nodded thoughtfully.

"I don't think so," he said after a while. "Those pills are very strong. According to the doctor they will stun a horse but Miesje can take two at a time and stay on her feet. She hasn't got much of a stomach left. She has been operated for ulcers and I suppose most of the stuff goes straight down. If Piet had taken a pill he would have had to sit down and he probably would have gone to sleep. I have never seen him like that. He did drink a bit lately, he would come down to the bar and have a few whiskies. Three glasses would make him drunk enough to be able to laugh and talk to people. I take it you are suggesting that he took a pill today and that the pill knocked him over and caused the bruise on his temple?"

"Yes," said de Gier.

"Perhaps," van Meteren said, "but it would have been the first time that he took a pill. In my opinion anyway."

"Why do you call her Miesje?" Grijpstra asked.

"Ach," van Meteren said, "it's just a trick. Whenever she is hysterical she screams. I thought I might calm her down if I treated her as if she was a child. She was called Miesje once, when she was a child and wore laced boots and played hopscotch. When she behaves normally I call her Mrs. Verboom and when I think she will start one of her tantrums I call her Miesje. I take her on my lap and she'll talk quietly and sometimes I cuddle her a bit."

"Brr," said de Gier.

Van Meteren grinned. "Yes. It's quite ridiculous. Piet would do it too. I always laughed when I saw that tall skeleton sitting on his lap, he was such a small man. Perhaps it looks even funnier when she sits on my lap. But I have done other crazy things. I used to walk for miles with an Indonesian commando on a string. It was knotted in such a way that he would throttle himself if he tried to run away. I would hold the string with one hand and the carbine with the other. And now I have an old crazy lady on my lap and call her Miesje."

There was another knock on the door and a thin young man dressed in jeans and a T-shirt came in. De Gier looked at the long unwashed hair and remembered the barman.

"This is Johan," van Meteren said, and the detectives said, "Good evening." De Gier asked Johan to sit down and made room on the settee.

Grijpstra asked the usual questions but Johan could only shake his head. He hadn't seen Piet after he had given him the takings of the shop at four o'clock. Three hundred and fifty-six guilders and some cents. Piet had phoned him later on the house phone to tell him that there was a difference of some thirty guilders but Johan hadn't gone upstairs, he had been too busy getting the bar in order for the evening's customers.

"What do you think has happened?" de Gier asked.

Johan shrugged his shoulders and didn't reply.

Grijpstra grunted. He had been thinking that he had met the boy hundreds of times already. The inner city was full of duplicates of this boy. Well-meaning, unintelligent and knocked loose from their surroundings, full of protests and questions and wandering in a thin, almost two-dimensional thought-world where they could find no answers. "Maybe they don't really want to find anything," Grijpstra thought. "Maybe they wait for death, or a strong woman who will take them in hand so that they will find a daily routine again and start watching football on TV." He thought of his oldest son and studied Johan without much sympathy. Grijpstra's son wouldn't watch football either. He preferred to lie on his bed, dressed in a striped shirt and an embroidered pair of trousers and watch the cracks in the ceiling.

"Suicide, I suppose," Johan said after a few minutes of silence, which hung heavily in the room. "Who would want to murder Piet? He was a bit of a bore but he didn't hurt anyone. He couldn't if he tried."

Grijpstra changed his opinion. The answer had been cleverer than he had expected.

"You don't seem to be very upset," de Gier said.

"No," Johan said. "I am sorry. Perhaps I should be upset, but I can't generate any feeling. Annetje and I would have left next week anyway. This is a commercial enterprise where the goal is money. Piet wanted to make a profit and he wanted the profit for himself. He was the owner of the business. We intended to leave him and find some other place with a bit of idealism behind it, or maybe start one of our own. Piet crooked us. I don't really hold it against him. It's my own stupidity, I should have seen it. He made us work for the great purpose but all we worked for was his wealth. Did you see the gold strap on his wristwatch?"

Grijpstra nodded.

"There are other things as well. There is a new stationwagon parked outside. We earned it for him. He was a capitalist but he didn't tell us."

"You don't like capitalists?" de Gier asked.

"I don't mind them," Johan said. "It's a way of life. Free enterprise is a philosophy. It isn't mine. I am against fascism and I would fight it if I had to, but I wouldn't fight capitalism."

"So you think it was suicide?" de Gier asked.

"Yes."

"Enough," Grijpstra said. "You need some sleep. All of us do. Tomorrow is another day. Try and remember anything that may be relevant and tell us about it tomorrow. The peace of the citizens has been disturbed and we, criminal investigators of your police department, have to repair the peace again. And you have to help us. Such is the law."

He grinned, got up, and stretched his aching back.

Within a few minutes the detectives were walking toward their car. A late drunk came swaggering toward them, and de Gier had to jump aside.

"Out of my way," the drunk shouted and grabbed a lamp post.

"Bah," Grijpstra said. The drunk was pissing on the street and all over his own trousers.

"Watch it," de Gier shouted. The drunk had fallen over and rolled off the sidewalk into the street.

Grijpstra, who was getting into the car, grabbed the microphone.

"An unconscious man on the sidewalk of Haarlemmer Houttuinen, opposite number five. Please send the bus."

"Drunk?" the voice of Headquarters asked.

"Very," Grijpstra answered. "No need for an ambulance, the police bus will do."

"Bus coming," the voice said. "Out."

"We better wait," de Gier said. "I have pulled him off the street but he may roll over again. He is fast asleep."

"Sure. We've got nothing else to do."

They waited in silence for the small blue bus with its crew of two elderly police constables who dragged the drunk inside, cursing and sighing.

"Nice job," de Gier said, waved at the constables and started the engine.

"So have we," Grijpstra said, "nice and complicated. Murdered innocence dangling from a piece of string, surrounded by dear sweet people of which one is a black cannibal trained in guerilla warfare and another a crazy old female bag of bones."

"I hope his mother has done it," de Gier said.

"You love people, don't you?"

"I don't like jails," de Gier said. "I had to visit some of our clients in their cells this week. Cold, drafty and hopeless. Jail will get you if nothing else does. A day in jail means a year of crime."

Grijpstra turned his heavy neck and stared at his colleague.

"Well, well," he said, "have you forgotten how many people you have directed to the cold, drafty and hopeless cells?"

"Yes, yes," de Gier said and lapsed into silence.

The silence lasted until they entered their office and he had to help Grijpstra to phrase the exact short sentences that framed their report and that they both signed, mentioning in cool print that everything the report contained was the truth as they, officers of the Queen's law, saw it. Grijpstra typed, slowly, with four fingers, without making a single typing error.

De Gier didn't speak when he left but Grijpstra didn't mind. He had been working with de Gier for a number of years and they had never really fallen out.

# CHAPTER 3

The next morning de Gier was in his bed. It was eight o'clock, he should have been up and in any case he should have been awake.

He wasn't asleep either. He was applying a trick, a recipe he had discovered as a boy. Stretched flat on his back with his toes pressed against the iron bars of the old hospital bed that he had, some years before, picked up at an auction, he was maintaining, with some effort, a state of semiconsciousness. He was, in fact, directing a dream. His body tingled, not the unpleasant tingle of cold hands after coming into a warm room, but an exciting all over tingle that made his entire body glow. He was very close to being free, free from his daily routine, his responsibility, his planet-bound existence. Inside his tingling body his mind was at liberty to move, wherever he wanted it to go.

And, being a shrewd man, he was using his liberty for an immediate purpose. He made his mind go back to the room of the dangling corpse. He saw the Papuan again, and the old skeleton-woman, the restaurant and the guests, the kitchen and the girls. He didn't try to achieve anything, he merely tried to force his mind to go back into the day before and he was reasonably successful until Oliver jumped on his stomach and cut the thin film that separated de Gier from reality.

He woke up and, reluctantly, looked at his watch. Five minutes past eight.

"Yes," he said to Oliver and put the Siamese cat on the floor where it began to grumble and whine.

"Wait," he said and walked to the small bathroom, looking at his plants in passing.

If it is true that a house is a projection of the occupant's spirit then de Gier's spirit was not quite ordinary. He had furnished the little two-roomed apartment with a bed, plants, and bookshelves. No table, no chairs, no TV. A detachable shelf, screwed to the wall above the bed, served as a table if he wanted to write, which wasn't often. He ate in the kitchen, not much larger than an old-fashioned cupboard.

"Mmm," he said, stopping near the geranium, which had started as a seed no more than a few weeks ago and "Mmm," he said again when he admired his creeper, hanging down from a bookshelf.

"She grows," he remarked to Oliver, who wasn't interested, and began to splash cold water all over his chest and arms and poured hot water and lathered his face.

Oliver continued to grumble.

"We'll have breakfast together," de Gier said. "Go to the balcony and irritate the birds while I finish shaving."

He moved the protesting cat with his foot and opened the balcony door. A seagull swooped low, expecting to be fed, and Oliver chattered with fury.

A few minutes later the cat and the detective ate, chopped heart and scrambled eggs. Then they drank, water and coffee. Then de Gier went out to catch the bus, an hour late, and the cat stretched into the still warm blankets of the unmade bed, imitating his mater's trick of being asleep without dozing off altogether.

"You are late," said Grijpstra.

De Gier smiled, remembering the pretty dark-haired girl he had been sitting next to in the bus.

"I am often late," he said.

"That's true," Grijpstra agreed. "Here, read this, the doctor's report."

They were in their large gray room of Headquarters. Grijpstra relaxed into a plastic chair and watched his colleague reading. Grijpstra smiled. He was content. His wife had been asleep when he came home at 2:30 in the morning. She was still asleep when he left. He had breakfasted by himself, helping himself to more toast and more eggs without any contradiction or argument. And, alone in the detectives' room, he had watered the rubber plant and played drums on the set that, in a so far unexplained manner, had arrived in his and de Gier's office about a year earlier. Found perhaps, or confiscated. Put there for a purpose that had been conveniently forgotten. Grijpstra had wanted to be a drummer when he was still a young man with a sense of adventure, and he had some talent. He often came early, to hit the three drums and clash the cymbals. Very softly of course, which, in drumming, is the finer art. He had, during those many early mornings, specialized in the "rustle," the sweeping of the soft forklike instruments (which had come with the set of drums) on the stretched skin of the two smaller drums. Tsss, tsss and then BENG, but softly. And then a roll, a small roll, exciting because of its strict limitation. While de Gier read Grijpstra grabbed the sticks and sounded the small roll.

"Good," de Gier said, looking up.

"What's good?" Grijpstra asked.

"That roll. And this report too. So he had taken one of his mother's pills. Palfium, wasn't it? A trace of an opiate in the stomach. And the times fit. He must died around seven P.M. and we arrived at eight."

The telephone rang.

"Yes, sir," Grijpstra said and pointed at the ceiling with a thick index finger. De Gier got up obediently. Within half a minute they were between the cactuses of the chief inspector.

"And?" the chief inspector asked.

Grijpstra told his story.

"And?" the chief inspector asked again.

Grijpstra said nothing.

The chief inspector got up and paced up and down. The detectives stared, at nothing in particular.

The chief inspector stopped in front of a cactus that was nearly five feet high, a stiff giant noodle, pimply and dotted with sharp cruel hooks. He watched the plant with concentration. De Gier grinned. He had seen the chief inspector measuring the monstrosity, using a tightly wound measuring tape in a metal container, which could be released and sprung by pressing a button and which he carried in his pocket. De Gier knew that he carried the measuring tape at all times, for the pocket of his tailor-made expensive suit bulged. For years de Gier had suspected him of carrying a mini-pistol until he had seen the tape-measure one day when the door of his office had been open and its occupant had been indulging in his secret pastime. De Gier was sure that the chief inspector was sorely tempted at this very moment to produce the tape and measure the cactus, which should have grown another millimeter or so since the previous day.

The chief inspector turned on his heels and faced the detectives.

"A nut," he said. "A crazy nut who wants to improve the world. He goes to a solicitor and registers a society. To improve the environment. A religious society, it can't be less, and containing a religion that he has created himself, or combined from a lot of ill-digested rubbish he has read or heard about. He buys an old rackety house at the Haarlemmer Houttuinen, fixes it up a little and whitewashes all its walls. He buys a second-hand imitation of an Asiatic statue and puts it in the hall, lights an incense stick and sells health food. Unwashed tomatoes and grains. The kind that sticks in your throat. A rat couldn't digest it. And carrot juice.''

He interrogated the detectives with his eyes. Both nodded.

It was clear that the chief inspector had no liking for carrot juice. They knew what he liked. He liked Dutch gin, and shrimp cocktails, snails and peppersteak. Pineapple with whipped cream. And cognac.

''There's a bar as well,'' Grijpstra said.

The chief inspector looked surprised.

''A what?''

''A bar,'' repeated Grijpstra, ''downstairs, as you go in, on the right, a bar where they sell gin and beer.''

''Good idea,'' the chief inspector said. ''With a glass of jenever you can get through to the other nuts. And when you have weakened their defenses you can make them eat unpeeled rice.''

He thought.

''All right,'' he said, ''but there is no base to the thing. It will attract the odd misfits who will come to join the faith, eager to penetrate the emptiness of purity above. Valhalla on earth. Or Nirvana. Or whatever it is called. What the great man does is new and so he is admired. The society is a success. He is making some money. Before you get into his temple you have to fork out twenty-five guilders, because the joint is 'members only.' True?''

Grijpstra nodded.

''And later, if you pass the test, you are allowed upstairs. You can enter the meditation room. Have you been there?''

''Yes, sir,'' de Gier said. ''A large empty room with low seats of scraped pine topped with foamrubber cushions. And an altar. And a special higher seat with a cushion with an embroidered cover.''

"Sure," the chief inspector said, "for the chief nut. And candles of course. And there they sit, legs crossed. A row of holy men. Piet is the high priest, the illuminated sage. I have read a little about it. There are various degrees apparently, first degree of the silence, second degree of the silence and so on. The more silence, the deeper the whatever. Perhaps they were wearing funny robes. Did you see any funny robes?"

"No, sir," Grijpstra said.

"Probably hidden in a cupboard."

The chief inspector thought.

"And after a while the whole thing falls to pieces. The sage becomes transparent and you can see through him. He has come to the end of his new value. At first he blames the others, which is usual human procedure, but finally he grasps that he, himself, is the fool. A crazy man. And, worse, a silly crazy man. So he takes one of his mother's pills, falls over, stays on the floor for a bit but manages to get up and finish the job. And when you came he was dangling from a deal beam that had been created for a nobler purpose, namely to support a merchant's ceiling."

There was silence in the room, a nice noble silence. Perhaps a second degree silence, de Gier thought.

"Well?" the chief inspector asked.

"Perhaps," Grijpstra said, "but I would prefer, if you are agreeable, to look into the matter."

The chief inspector grunted. "You have suspicions?"

"No," Grijpstra said, "but I can't imagine how he got that bump on his temple. He wouldn't have got it from a fall on the floor. He must have fallen *against* something, if he did fall. There wasn't much furniture in the room. It's a pity the wound didn't bleed, we might have been able to find traces somewhere in the room. I keep on thinking that he was hit, and if he was there may have been murder."

"Homicide," the chief inspector said. "Murder is always hard to prove although we can try, it's the least we can do.

But the youngest silliest lawyer can convince the wisest judge it's been homicide, whatever we prove."

He sighed.

"And it might not even be homicide," resumed the chief inspector. "That Papuan of yours, is he really a Papuan? I didn't see him."

"Yes, sir," de Gier said. "His name is Dutch, van Meteren, but he is only one-eighth white, a rare specimen, an almost full-blooded Papuan in Amsterdam."

"There'll be others," the chief inspector said. "You can find anything in Amsterdam when you look for it. But I seem to remember that van Meteren pointed out that someone might have picked a fight with Piet and that Piet, after the fight, in a fit of depression, had committed suicide. You might work on that for a bit. Murders are rare in this city. A homicide, well. But murder . . . And your theory would point to a murder, what with a fist-fight and a noose."

He shook his head.

The detectives recognized the sign and knew that the meeting was over.


Coffee break was getting close. They were waiting in their room, the trolley would be due any minute now. Their normal patrol duty was suspended.

All available time could be spent on thought.

"We have a case," Grijpstra said.

De Gier nodded. The trolley's wheels squeaked near the door, he jumped to open it and smiled at Treesje, the coffee-and-tea girl, a mini-skirted nineteen-year-old. Grijpstra coughed; he didn't approve of the beaming contact de Gier and Treesje had built up over the last few months. But even Grijpstra had to admit that Headquarters' coffee had much improved since Treesje's appearance had put a glint in most of the officers' eyes.

They were busy for a while, tearing the little paper bags, pouring sugar and thick coffee milk, stirring.

A constable brought a thick file.

"Ha," Grijpstra said, "the interrogation reports. Let's see."

De Gier got up and looked over his shoulder. "Hey," he said.

Grijpstra cleared his throat again. "Nice, what?"

It was nice. The detectives had noted the names and addresses of the restaurant's thirty-eight guests. Nothing special with two exceptions. The two exceptions had been found in the Hindist Society's bar. Two drug dealers, one once-convicted, the other a suspect. The conviction had been minor for lack of substantial proof.

"I have heard about them," de Gier said. "Michiels of the Drugs Department was talking about them the other day. Big birds, both of them."

"Wholesalers," Grijpstra said and smiled. "Two nice juicy wholesalers. I'll spend a phone call on them."

The chief inspector wasn't easy to handle that morning and Grijpstra had to repeat himself twice. Finally he hung up and de Gier gave him a questioning look.

"It's all right," Grijpstra said. "We'll be given some help. And the chief inspector promised to look through the files."

The help arrived within ten minutes and Treesje was summoned for more coffee and another display of long tapered legs and rounded thighs. Grijpstra was forced into another coughing fit. The two drugs-detectives read the reports and listened. They said "yes," half a dozen times and left.

Grijpstra wandered toward his drums, sat down, and vibrated a stick.

"Right," he said. "They can be happy. Off to the bars and the cafés. I wonder how much money they'll spend, tax money, all of it. While we work."

De Gier looked morose.

"How many hours have you spent in cafés? Quietly? With half a glass of jenever on the table?" Grijpstra asked.

"Thousands," de Gier said.

"That's all over now," said Grijpstra.

De Gier half closed his eyes and dreamed. How many hours had he spent in bars? Listening, chatting, acting. And meanwhile the eternal search. Who knows something, who says something? Who knows whether the wholesalers were in contact with Piet? Piet who is dead now? Who knows Piet? Who knows the old gable house Haarlemmer Houttuinen 5? What happens over there? I don't mean the holy talk in the bar, the health food and the sitting-still in the temple room. What really happens? Would you like another drink? Shall I tell you another joke? Easy now. Talk to the girls. Listen to the girls. Wait for a little fight to break out, a nice argument. Stir it up a little. Whoever gets angry talks. Whoever gets jealous talks. Whoever's pride is touched talks. Or do you want some money perhaps? Here, have another drink first, there's plenty in the bottle. You name it you get it. A hundred guilders? Why not? If the story is worth it. You can tell me outside, on a bench in the park or under a tree in the square. And then you can drink as much as you like for a couple of evenings, or you can smoke something, or inject. Is there anything worse than the needle? The other stuff will release you, after a good fight, but when the needle has got you it keeps you.

"We'll do some work," Grijpstra said. "You go back to the house. Go right through it. It's a big house and we only saw a bit of it."

"And you?" de Gier asked.

"I am going to have a sniff at that Society. If you find anything important you can phone me and if I'm not here you can leave a message. And tonight I should be home."

"Car?" de Gier asked.

"You won't need the car. It's the right day for walking. You better phone the garage that the car is free today."

* * *

Grijpstra had looked through Piet's bookcase the night before and had found some files. One of the files contained bookkeeping and gave the name of a chartered accountant. Grijpstra had read a report, signed by the accountant, describing the Society's financial progress during the previous book-year. He had noted the accountant's name and address.

De Gier left. Grijpstra phoned the accountant.

"Police?" the accountant asked. "Certainly, I am at your disposal."

Grijpstra arrived ten minutes later. A beautifully restored house on the fashionable Keizersgracht, shadowed by elm trees, its gable elaborately sculptured and recently whitewashed. The accountant's secretary smiled and talked to him in a cultured voice. She took him to the oak-paneled inner office.

"Coffee?" the accountant asked. "If you please," Grijpstra said. "Cigar?" the accountant asked. "If you please," Grijpstra said.

The accountant knew. He had read the morning's paper.

"Were you surprised?" Grijpstra asked.

"Yes," the accountant said, and pulled a hand through his thick gray curly hair. "Yes, I was surprised. Piet wasn't the merriest type I knew, and he wasn't quite run of the mill of course, not very stable I may say, he had his moods. But suicide . . . ?"

He looked at Grijpstra's passive face. Grijpstra sucked on the cigar.

"Or wasn't it suicide?" the accountant asked.

Grijpstra shrugged his shoulders.

"Murder?"

Grijpstra shrugged again.

"What can I do for you?"

Grijpstra sighed.

"This Society, what exactly was it?"

"Yes, yes, yes," the accountant said. "It wasn't much. But we earned some money. The bar was a paying proposition, the restaurant definitely made a profit and the shop was all right. A small but profitable business. You know the sort of thing they sell in these shops. Cent buying, guilder selling. Very good margin. They sold some books and leaflets and statues of Buddha and holy men. And chopsticks, machine-made in Hong Kong, you can buy them by the ton for next to nothing and he was selling them at one ninety-five a pair. Not bad. And the cost of the operation was ridiculously low, of course. That was the main thing, perhaps. There is always a good margin between buying and selling in business but the money goes to costs and you still make a loss. But Piet had found the right way of doing it. He hired idealists only, made them members of the Holy Society and paid them a pittance a week. No social security, no minimum wage. He didn't even have to put them on the payroll. And if they didn't like it they could go back to the street, or the youth hostel, or the park. He always found others to replace them.''

"What was he making?" Grijpstra asked.

The accountant produced a ledger from a metal filing cabinet. "About two thousand guilders a week, I guess. A little more perhaps. He must have pocketed some as it came in.''

"Did he pay taxes?''

The accountant looked sly.

"Not yet. The Society was only three years old. He had copied it from a similar thing in Paris, I believe; I think he worked in Paris for a while. No, he never paid any tax, only purchase tax. Nobody avoids purchase tax unless they sell in the street and run when the coppers arrive.''

"No tax?" Grijpstra asked. "No company tax? No in-come tax?''

The accountant hadn't changed his expression. The sly look was still there. A professional slyness, a highly educated very smart fox who has made his lair in a gable house.

"No tax," he repeated. "Societies are very special, very

vague material. A proper society makes no profit, whatever it
makes it spends. It is allowed to form a slight reserve. If it
makes a profit there is trouble with the inspection. There
would have been trouble here and I have been warning Piet.
After all, I am a chartered accountant, not a bookkeeper he
could hire anywhere. I have a reputation to lose. I told him to
change his Society into a normal commercial company with a
balance sheet. I would have worked out his profit on the first
three years and he would have paid some tax. I also told him
that he could forget about my services if he refused. He might
have gone on for years, quietly pocketing the money and
improving his position. The inspection isn't very quick. But
they would have caught him in the end and fined him right
into bankruptcy.''

Grijpstra looked up.

''You said 'we' just now. If I remember correctly you said
'but we earned some money.' Do you mean that you had a
share in the business?''

The accountant laughed. ''I see I am dealing with the
police. No, no. Nobody is allowed to have a material interest
in a society. But an accountant always identifies with his
client and talks about 'we' and 'ours.' You can compare it to
a mother who tells her small child 'now we are going to do a
little whiddle' but the mother doesn't whiddle, the child
whiddles.''

Grijpstra grinned and told himself that he should remember to repeat the explanation to de Gier.

''So if Piet had continued on the way he was going he
would have been in trouble?''

The accountant made his fingertips touch and looked at his
interrogator from above, using his high seat and tall body to
advantage.

''Perhaps. The inspection is busy, and very slow. Their
servants are officials, nine-to-five men, moderately dedicated. With luck Piet could have gone on for years and years
and even if the inspection had become suspicious, well, there

would have been time. He could have sold out and run for it. He might have made a small fortune and retired, on an island somewhere. There are a lot of islands in the world."

"Piet was the only director?" Grijpstra asked.

"Yes. He asked me to join him but I refused. The Society's foundation was too rotten for me. His wife used to be a director but she never knew what went on. She left him anyway; you know that, don't you?"

"Yes," Grijpstra said, "and what did he do with the money?"

"Let's see," the accountant said and leafed through the ledger. "Here. The money wasn't spent. He invested some in the house, repairs and so on, improving its value considerably. There is a nice car in the Society, which Piet used, and he bought a small house in the South, in the country somewhere. A good buy, its present value should be three times what he paid for it. His own official income was six hundred guilders a month, plus free board and lodging. He paid income tax on the six hundred, which is next to nothing."

Grijpstra looked at the ceiling. The accountant waited patiently.

"So everything in the house, the stereo equipment, furniture, statues, inventory, stocks, were the Society's property?"

"Yes."

"And Piet could sell whatever he wanted to sell and pocket the money?"

"Yes," the accountant said. "In fact he *was* the Society. A difficult case, even for the inspection. If they had found out what he was doing they would have forced him to change it into a commerical company."

"To get a grip on him?"

"Exactly," said the accountant. "But what are you hinting at?"

Grijpstra smiled his special noncommittal smile and managed to put some human warmth in it.

"I don't quite know myself," he said. "I am gathering information, that's all. Who would benefit from Piet's death?"

"His wife," the accountant said, "but she ran away. To Paris I think; I seem to remember that Piet told me but I am not sure. If she is in Paris she can't have murdered him here. In any case, I know her and she is not the killing type. She is a rather lovely but very vague woman. She wouldn't hang anyone. And her little daughter is a toddler."

"Do you see any reason for suicide?" Grijpstra asked. The accountant sucked pensively on his cigar and began to cough. Suddenly he looked ferocious and the soggy cigar stub was killed with savage power.

"Bah. These cigars aren't what they are cracked up to be. Wet bags full of nicotine. Yagh."

Grijpstra waited patiently for the evil mood to pass.

" 'Suicide,' you said. I am no psychologist," the accountant said.

"I am asking you all the same," Grijpstra said pleasantly.

"I am an accountant. As an accountant I would say there might be a reason. I think I convinced Piet that his Society would have to disappear. He identified with the Society. Its death might mean his own death. And I think that the thought of having to pay a lot of money to the government upset him considerably. He might have had to pay as much as fifty thousand guilders, an amount he didn't have."

"Not in cash," Grijpstra said.

"Yes," the accountant agreed, "it wasn't all that bad. He could have raised the money on his property. I could have managed the mortgage for him, at a price of course. Mortgages are expensive these days."

"So he was upset," Grijpstra said. "He would have had to go to a lot of trouble to raise money to pay to the government."

The accountant put his fingertips together again and donned a pensive look.

"And there you may have your reason," he said suavely. "The government is the establishment and Piet fought the establishment. His Society was against the establishment. And now it looked like the enemy was winning."

"Aha," Grijpstra said. "And if his enemy would force him to change the Society into a commercial company he would have had to hire real staff and pay them real wages. It might have been the end of his small but profitable business."

"Quite," the accountant said.

Grijpstra studied the accountant, a tall wide-shouldered man, aged somewhere between fifty and sixty. A beautifully chiseled head. A chartered accountant, a man of standing, comparable to a surgeon, a bank director, an important merchant. An expensive office, an expensive image. Even an expensive name. Joachim de Kater. A "kater" is a tomcat. The tomcat watches how the others run to and fro, in the sweat of their brows, and every now and then the tomcat puts out his paw and flicks his nails and the others pay. A chartered accountant is a man trusted by the establishment. Whatever he says is believed and the tax inspectors talk to him as equal to equal. Grijpstra shuddered. Grijpstra is Dutch too and he feared the tax inspectors as the Calvinists had once feared the Spanish inquisition.

"Thank you," he said. "I won't take any more of your time."

"It was a pleasure to be of use," de Kater said, and stretched to his full length. His handclasp was firm and pleasant. His smile glinted in the dark room. Grijpstra studied the smile for a moment. Expensive teeth. Eight thousand guilders perhaps? Or ten thousand? The false teeth looked very natural, each individual tooth a work of art, and the back teeth all of solid gold.

\*          \*          \*

Grijpstra walked past the water of the canal, in deep contemplation. Fifty thousand guilders, payable in one go perhaps, but perhaps not. The tax people always appear to be reasonable. They don't like to slaughter the goose who lays the golden eggs. They might have been prepared to wait a bit. Perhaps he should go to see them.

But on the other hand . . . Perhaps Piet panicked. He might have been petrified with fear, fear of the possibility of losing his easy trick to make money. And fear might have forced his head into the homemade noose.

Would it?

Grijpstra thought of the small head with the abundant dark red hair and the beautiful full mustache. The small head with the large bump on its temple. He saw the little corpse again, the naked feet and the neat little toes, pointed at the wooden floor.

# CHAPTER 4

De Gier walked past the merchants' mansions on the Prinsengracht using the long strides that, he believed, prevent the common policeman's complaint of flat feet. His mind was clouded by anger. He was angry with everyone in general and with Grijpstra in particular. De Gier didn't want to walk, he wanted to drive. But the police are stingy, and Grijpstra didn't like to be an exception. Why use a car if there is no immediate necessity?

But it was a nice day and de Gier's anger evaporated. The image of a terrible, silly and stupid Grijpstra slid from his mind. Grijpstra had been punished anyway. He, de Gier, was walking, wasting the state's time. He could have taken a streetcar. De Gier had gone further than Grijpstra had intended him to go. He was even saving the state the price of a tram ticket.

De Gier smiled. He had analyzed his own thoughts. He now faced the conclusion with courage. He was a petty little man himself. De Gier always tried to analyze his own thoughts, trying to find the real motivation of his actions. And always he had to conclude that he, de Gier, was a petty little man. But the conclusion didn't discourage him. He shared his pettiness with all of humanity. He didn't have a very high opinion of humanity. He had, once, when they were drinking together, told Grijpstra about his line of thought and Grijpstra had nodded his heavy head. It had been one of the rare evenings when Grijpstra had been prepared to talk. Unwilling to meet his family, and after a long day, he had accepted de Gier's invitation to have a meal at one of the cheap Chinese restaurants and afterward they had found themselves in a small bar of the Zeedijk, the long spine of the prostitution quarter. The owner of the bar had recognized them as plain-clothes policemen and had filled and refilled their glasses, quietly and with a hurt smile on his cadaverous face. Grijpstra had done more than agree. He had finished his glass of jenever with one tremendous sip and raised a finger.

"You can," Grijpstra had said, "divide humanity into a few groups."

"Yes?" de Gier had asked, with his softest and most melodious voice. He had been almost breathless with anticipation. Grijpstra would talk?

"Yes," Grijpstra said. "Listen. First of all we have the big bounders. You know them as well as I do. Chaps with red heads and fat necks who drive large American cars and who smoke cigars. Their coats are lined with real fur. There are pimp-bounders and banker-bounders, but in essence they are all the same. The bounders have understood. They know what people want. People want to be manipulated and the bounders manipulate. They find out, or rather, they pay others to find out (bounders are surrounded by very intelligent slaves) what people want to have and then they buy it cheaply and sell it for the most ridiculous amounts you and I can imagine. The principle works for goods as well as services. Bounders always make money. They never join a queue and they often go on holiday. They own big yachts on the IJsselmeer and villas in Spain. Their mistresses are kept in the best apartments of the Beethovenstreet. They never have any problems and they never make any problems. Whatever crops up is taken care of quickly or rather, as I have already indicated, is taken care of for them. They pay very little tax. They are the first group."

De Gier listened with all the concentration he could muster. The man behind the bar refilled their glasses.

"The second group," Grijpstra continued, slurring his words slightly, "is the biggest group. This is the group of the idiots. You can, if you like, subdivide this group into a fairly large number of subgroups, but why should you?"

De Gier shook his head energetically, he didn't want to subdivide.

"Very well," Grijpstra said, "if they are idiots anyway why should you? There is this type of idiot and that type of idiot but their skins are always gray, they have a variety of illnesses, they stand in queues, they take a holiday once a year, they drive small secondhand cars that break down continuously and they buy the expensive rubbish the bounders sell to them, and they pay a lot of tax of course. It is taken off their pay so that they won't notice much. They do as they are told, not just what the boss tells them to do but also what advertising tells them to do, and the TV, and the newspaper, and anybody who has a loud voice and a few simple words. They'll even get into a cattle truck to be taken to a concentration camp, and when the camps go out of fashion, to Yugoslavia or a Greek island, on a charter plane. They visit dirty whores and drink jenever made in a chemical factory. Your health!"

He raised his glass unsteadily, spilling a little jenever.

"Your health!" de Gier said and raised his glass obediently.

"They do whatever the bounder wants," Grijpstra continued. "And when they have celebrated their sixty-fifth birthday they shake hands and go away and you'll never see them again but it doesn't matter for they reproduce faster than they disappear. They are fond of rubber stamps and forms and name plates on the door, with an indication of their rank or degree. They like medals and titles and privileges. But they never have any rights, only duties. The duty to save and to buy and never mind what they do, the bounders will make money. It matters little what type of political system you apply to them, they will stay idiots, and when the bounder drives past they shout Hurray. Keeping time and arranged in rows. Hurray hurray hurray!''

Grijpstra had shouted loudly and the other guests joined the cheering.

''You see,'' Grijpstra said, ''just as I have been telling you. But we still have the third group. It's a very small group. Do you know who I mean?''

''No,'' de Gier said, ''but please tell me.''

''The small third group,'' Grijpstra said, ''is the group of the well-meaning. The gentlemen. The idealists. They have good ideas and they are often very intelligent. They don't push and they never do anything out of turn and they give the impression that they don't manipulate and that no one manipulates them.''

''But that's very nice,'' de Gier said. ''So there are some nice people after all.''

''No,'' Grijpstra said, ''you never heard me say that. I called them the well-meaning. I meet them every now and then and I study them very carefully. Extremely carefully.''

''And what do you see?'' asked de Gier.

''Yes,'' Grijpstra said and rubbed his face with a tired hand. ''I don't know really. I don't see very much when I study them. But I don't trust them at all. These well-meaning people are no good either, I am sure of it.''

De Gier had often thought about Grijpstra's three groups and the older he became and the more he experienced, the more he believed in Grijpstra's theory. But he left some room on the side. De Gier didn't like theories that seemed to be watertight. De Gier believed in a miraculous surrealist world and he didn't want to give up his faith, mainly because the existence of this miraculous world seemed to be confirmed to him, and quite regularly, by the inexplicable beauty that echoed, he thought, in the perception of the half-conscious dreams he was subject to. It was happening again, right now, while he walked past the Prinsengracht's water. A seagull kept itself suspended above the hardly moving surface of the gracht, seemingly effortless, by the merest flick of its spread wings. A gable silhouetted sharply against a dark gray rain cloud, an old woman fed the sparrows throwing an ever-changing shadow-pattern on the cobblestones. A miraculous world, de Gier thought. Very beautiful. Perhaps the world is no good, but I am here. I walk here and I am doing something and although it probably serves no purpose, it's interesting. Fascinating even.

It was warm in the street and he was glad when he saw the Haarlemmer Houttuinen and knew that the coolness of the large house was waiting for him. But before he entered he had seen the car parked on the sidewalk, in the same place as he had parked the police VW the night before, and a little later he recognized the detective who greeted him in the corridor, a detective from the Bureau Warmoesstraat.

"Now what?" he asked his colleague.

"Breaking and entering," the colleague said and took him to the restaurant where van Meteren and the four helpers of the dead Piet sat quietly around a table.

"Hello," de Gier said to van Meteren. "Don't you have to work today? It's past eleven."

Van Meteren smiled. "You here again? No, I don't have to work. I took the day off because of special circumstances. I wanted to organize the removal of Piet's mother. But somebody broke in last night and I telephoned again."

"When was that?" de Gier asked.

"I don't know. I went to sleep after you both left. It must

have been between one-thirty and seven-thirty this morning. Someone kicked in the little cellar's door and they went all through the restaurant and the shop. I don't think they went upstairs for I should have heard them.''

"Anything missing?" de Gier asked.

The detective shrugged his shoulders. "Not much. The tape recorder that was supposed to have been here in the restaurant and the money box from the shop. According to the girls here it only contained small cash, they had given the notes to their boss. And the boss is supposed to have committed suicide yesterday, but you should know all about that.''

De Gier looked at his colleague and thought that he knew nothing at all. A corpse and now breaking and entering. Marvelous.

"Did you make your report?" he asked.

"Sure. The fingerprint man was here as well but there has been quite a crowd here they tell me, and you must have touched a lot of objects as well last night. I was on my way out when you came in.''

De Gier shook his hand and the detective disappeared, grumbling about the lack of staff and the impossibility of catching anyone nowadays. An old detective, close to retirement.

"Marvelous marvelous," de Gier said irritably to van Meteren, "and I came to see if we had overlooked anything yesterday.''

He realized that he was treating van Meteren as yet another colleague.

"Can we go now?" the girls asked.

De Gier nodded.

"Where do you want to go?"

"Don't worry," Johan said. "We'll stay in town. Eduard and I found a houseboat at the Binnenkant, opposite number 10. The ship is called *The Good Hope*. She belongs to my brother but he is on his way to India and he left me the key.''

De Gier noted the address.

"And what are you going to do?" he asked the girls.

"I am going with the boys," the fat girl called Annetje answered and moved closer to Johan. De Gier had to suppress an expression of horror, he didn't mind fat girls but if they were wearing dresses with flower patterns. . . He was sure that she was barefoot, and that her feet would be dirty. He dropped his pack of cigarettes and bent down to pick it up. Her feet were dirty.

"And you?" he asked the beautiful girl.

Thérèse stared.

De Gier repeated his question.

Thérèse began to cry.

"There there," van Meteren said and moved over so that he sat next to her.

"She is pregnant," he said to de Gier, "and she doesn't know where to go."

"It's all right," de Gier said to the girl. He had become interested and watched her closely. A lovely girl, long black hair, green cat's eyes, a tall rather thin girl but with a good full bosom. He dropped his matchbox. Her legs were long and well shaped and she wore sandals, and her feet were clean.

"Can't she stay here for the time being?" he asked van Meteren.

"I don't know. The place is closed. I sent a telegram to Piet's wife. Paris isn't far, she can be here any minute now. She used to be a director of the Society, together with Piet, and now she would be the only one in charge, I suppose. I never saw the Society's articles, perhaps the accountant can be of help. The house will probably be sold."

"But she could stay for the time being," de Gier insisted.

"I don't want to stay," Thérèse said. She had stopped crying. "It's the house of a corpse. And now they have broken in as well. I'll go to my mother."

She gave an address in Rotterdam and de Gier wrote it

down in his notebook. Johan, Eduard and Annetje said good-bye. Their bags were packed and had been stacked in the corridor, very neatly. De Gier touched Annetje's hand. Van Meteren got up as well.

"I'll see you later," de Gier said to van Meteren. "I'd like to have a few words with Thérèse."

When they were alone he offered a cigarette and lit it for her. She sucked on the Gauloise and began to cough. "Put it out," de Gier said, "it doesn't help. I wanted to ask you who caused your pregnancy."

"Piet," the girl said.

"Is that why his wife left?"

She shook her head. "His wife was used to it. Piet tried to make us all and sometimes he was lucky. I kept away from him at first but he insisted and it was hard to refuse him all the time. I lived here, and he could be rather charming at times."

"Was he really nice?" de Gier asked.

The girl stared.

"Was he?"

She began to cry again. "No. He was a bastard. With his insane health ideas. Why did I have to get involved in all this? Now I need an abortion if it isn't too late. And I don't want his child."

De Gier let her cry. Van Meteren showed himself in the open door but de Gier made a gesture and he disappeared.

"Did you have any fights with him?"

The girl wasn't listening. De Gier got up and held her by the shoulders but it complicated the situation for she allowed her body to drop into his arms.

"Hey," de Gier said and put her back, carefully, onto her chair. He repeated the question.

She nodded.

"Did you have a fight with him yesterday?"

She nodded again.

"In his room?"

"Yes," the girl said. "I shouted at him but he didn't

answer. All he said was that I could leave if I didn't like it
here, and that I was over twenty-one, and that he was married
already. I should have been more careful. After that he shut
up. I called him names. It has happened before. 'Karma,' he
said. Everybody has to accept the consequences of his own
actions. Karma is very useful. It teaches you things. Haha.''

"Did you hit him?"

"I threw a book at his head."

"A heavy book?"

"Yes, a dictionary."

"Did it hit him?"

She didn't answer. He took her by the hand and they went
upstairs. The dictionary was on the floor of Piet's room.
There were other books on the floor as well.

"Can you remember whether it hit him? Did he fall
over?"

"I don't know," Thérèse said. "I walked out of the room
and slammed the door. I never looked around."

De Gier rephrased his question in several ways but got
nowhere. She hadn't hung Piet. When he asked her she began
to laugh, through her tears.

De Gier tore a sheet of paper from a notebook on the table
and wrote a short statement. He read it to her and asked her to
sign.

"You don't really think I hung him, do you?" she asked.
De Gier didn't answer but telephoned Headquarters and was
connected with Grijpstra. Grijpstra played his drums and
spoke at the same time, the telephone hooked between his
head and his shoulder.

"I am coming," Grijpstra said.

"Take the car," said de Gier, "it's a long walk," and
hung up.

"The noose," he said to the girl. "Did you know that
there was a noose in the room and someone had screwed a
hook into one of the beams supporting the ceiling?"

"That hook has always been there," Thérèse said. "Piet

used to have a mask hanging from that hook but it frightened me when I was on the settee with him and then he sold it. And that noose is nothing but an ordinary bit of rope isn't it? We have a lot of that sort of rope in the house. Piet used to import foods from Japan and it would come in lovely little casks, wound with rope. We used to take it off and use it for decoration. The noose was made with it."

"Did you see the noose?" de Gier asked quickly.

"No," the girl said. "Van Meteren told me."

"You think he committed suicide?" de Gier asked.

The girl looked indifferent. "It wouldn't surprise me. He wasn't quite right in the head, I think. When his wife left him he complained terribly. Even to me, while we were in bed together."

"What else did he complain about?" de Gier asked.

"Anything you like to mention. The purpose of life, and enlightenment. He thought he wasn't enlightened. He should be, he said, for he had lived according to the rules, but nothing had happened."

"Enlightenment?" asked de Gier.

"Yes," Thérèse said. "It always made me think of light bulbs. Buddhists, and Hindus too, I think, claim that you will be enlightened if you live according to the right rules. You should do everything you have to do as well as you can and meditate a lot and gradually you will begin to understand all sorts of things you never did before and you'll have visions, I believe. I don't know anything about it really. But I thought that enlightenment meant happiness, and absence of problems, and I think Piet thought that way too from the way he talked. But he kept all his problems, he said. And he didn't know what he was doing wrong."

"Suicide doesn't seem to be very Buddhist to me," de Gier said, "or Hindistic, or what he called it. A man who commits suicide stops trying and if you give up trying you won't get anywhere. Or not?"

Thérèse had sat down on the settee and rubbed her eyes.

"Piet said that there had been Japanese, Samurai or monks, I can't remember what, who had committed suicide because they had found themselves to be in a hopeless situation. Then it's all right, he said. Admirable even. But you have to do it in the right way. First you have to clean your body and your spirit and then you have to find a quiet spot and meditate for a while and then, when everything has become very quiet and you have said goodbye, in your mind, to all you love, you can do it."

De Gier thought about the crease in Piet's trousers, the combed hair, the beautiful mustache.

"What did you think of Piet's religion?" he asked. "This Hindism?"

"Bah," the girl said, "it made me puke. He talked such a lot of rot. Nothing really exists. Everything is illusion, everything changes and comes to an end. Life is a dream and nothing matters. It seems real but it isn't."

De Gier thought.

"But that could be true," he said.

"It *is* true," the girl said, "but you shouldn't hear Piet saying it. If one really knows that nothing is important and that we are only here to perform some sort of exercise (he used to say that as well), then one doesn't behave the way Piet behaved."

"And how did he behave?"

"In a silly way," Thérèse said. "Boring, depressive. He was very attached to property as well. He always said that property was just an idea and didn't matter and that we only have things so that we can use them and enjoy them, but that we should always be detached from them. But he was attached to every bit of furniture in the house, every book, every record. If you borrowed from him you would have to return it almost immediately. I never had a chance to finish a book. And he never gave anything away. He gave me things when he was trying to make me but I had to give it all back to him later. A little statue, a few shells, a record. I might as well give it back, he said, then we could share it. And he was always cleaning and polishing his car. And every day he calculated the exact worth of the Society. He was the Society. We were members but we weren't allowed to really touch it. Even when we went to the little house he bought in the south he checked the food we took with us and if he thought it was too much he would take it from the bag and put it back on the shelf. But when he went himself he took all he wanted."

De Gier shook his head.

"But if you disliked him so much, then why did you go to bed with him?"

Thérèse began to cry again.

"I don't know," she said. "Why did I? He kept on coming to my room and I don't make contact easily with people. When a man smiles at me I never know what to do. And men are always so difficult, they flirt and make silly jokes and Piet didn't. He said he wanted to go to bed with me and asked me to take my clothes off. The first few times I said 'No' but one evening I did."

Not bad, de Gier thought. He had heard about the method but had never met it in actual life. Perhaps I should try it on the girl in the bus, de Gier thought. I look her straight in the face and I say "Miss, my name is Rinus de Gier. I want to go to bed with you. Here is my card. Could you come to my flat tonight? I'll be home from seven P.M. onward but don't come after eleven for then I am usually asleep."

"Are you listening to me?" Thérèse asked.

"Sure, sure," de Gier said.

"Can I go then? Or do you still think that I hung Piet?"

"You can go," de Gier said. "If anything comes up I'll phone you. I have your address and your number."

"What could come up?" Thérèse asked. "Piet is dead and I am pregnant and I must find a way to stop being pregnant."

Grijpstra had come in and de Gier told him what he had found out.

"Well, well," Grijpstra said, "throwing books, hey?"
Thérèse said nothing.

"Never mind," Grijpstra said. "Have a good trip to Rotterdam," and he gave the girl a kind look.

Together they searched the house again, room by room. They had plenty of time and worked slowly. They were disturbed by voices and went to investigate. The men from the city's health service had come to collect Mrs. Verboom. They were going to take her to a clinic for neuroses, near the coast.

Mrs. Verboom allowed herself to be taken away quietly. She didn't recognize the detectives. Van Meteren had given her another Palfium tablet and the old lady was only partly conscious and could hardly walk. Van Meteren carried her bag.

"How did you manage that so quickly?" de Gier asked when van Meteren returned.

"The physician helped. He wanted Mrs. Verboom to go to a clinic anyway and now that Piet isn't here to frustrate the idea it was very easy. She'll never be allowed to live in a normal house again. She is really mad, you know."

"In what way?" Grijpstra asked.

"Perhaps I shouldn't have said she is mad," van Meteren said sadly. "What is madness? She only thinks of herself, perhaps that is mad enough. And she can't look after herself. She is over eighty and needs opiates. An elderly drug addict. They won't cure her but perhaps they can keep her happy until she dies."

"You are right," Grijpstra said. "We live in a socialist country and suffering is prohibited by law,"

"Suffering," van Meteren said disdainfully.

"You don't believe in it?" asked de Gier.

"No," van Meteren said. "Suffering is very egotistic."

"Nothing is important," said de Gier, who had learned a lot that day.

"Come off it," said Grijpstra, who had had enough.

"This Eastern philosophy is all very well but we have work to do. We are dealing with a corpse, and with breaking and entering, and with theft. Maybe it isn't important but I would like to know who we have to arrest, just for the hell of it."

"That's all right," van Meteren said. "Work is all part of it. Do what you have to do, as long as you don't think it is important."

Grijpstra looked furious and van Meteren smiled and went up to his room.

A little later, in Piet's room, Grijpstra began to growl. De Gier recognized the sound, it reminded him of Oliver's growl when the cat was on the balcony and sensed the presence of the neighbor's Alsatian dog, separated from the cat by a thin glass plate. At such moments de Gier was frightened of his own cat, silly Oliver, suddenly transformed into a puffed-up ball of rage, with a thick sweeping and twisting tail, spitting pure hatred.

"Yes, adjutant, what is it?" he asked sweetly.

"This," Grijpstra growled and pointed at a file that he had found on one of the bookshelves. "Look at this. Piet Verboom mortgaged his house, a couple of weeks ago, for fifty thousand guilders. That's a lot of money, a year's wage of a well-to-do man. The house looks all right but it is rackety and three hundred years old. Fifty thousand is about the most you can get on a mortgage, I am pretty sure. The money has been paid into his bank account and he has drawn it out again, together with another twenty-five thousand he had to his credit. It was taken out in cash. Where is it?"

"Any money left on the account?" de Gier asked.

"About ten thousand. This means that he has drawn about everything the Society owned in ready cash. And we found nothing. If it is here it must have been hidden in an impossible spot. If it is here. It's probably somewhere else by now."

"Stolen," de Gier said.

Grijpstra nodded.

"Then we have the motive."

"Certainly," Grijpstra said, and sat down.

"And the opportunity. Everybody had the chance to kill him. Van Meteren for instance. He must have killed quite a few people in New Guinea and he could have used the seventy-five thousand. And Mrs. Verboom, she is mad of course. But would she have wanted the money? She is over eighty years old."

"Money is money," de Gier said. "Old crazy people like to use it just like everyone else. Perhaps she has it in her bag and plans to spend it on a cruise around the world or a year in a luxury hotel in Madeira. There's an English hotel over there that caters to rich old ladies. Somebody told me about it."

"Possibly," said Grijpstra. "I wasn't trained along the new lines like you were. Psychology and all that. Perhaps you should go and visit her in the clinic."

"Nice," de Gier said. "Any more bright ideas?"

"A suspect has to be interrogated, even if she is as crazy as the government."

"True."

"And then we have Thérèse, she didn't like Piet either. She threw dictionaries at him. And the boys, Eduard and Johan. Perhaps they got tired of being used and squeezed dry. Perhaps a joint venture of Eduard, Johan and Annetje. They worked for nothing for a long time and now, suddenly, rich! For seventy-five thousand you can buy a nice new houseboat and cover the floor with Persian carpets."

"Second-hand carpets," de Gier said.

"Sure."

De Gier scratched his neck. "Everybody could have nipped up the stairs. Perhaps the girls were so busy stirring the health food that they didn't notice. Or they were looking at the rhododendrons. You can't watch rhododendrons and a staircase at the same time. Anyway, why would they have watched anything? Any of the thirty-eight guests could have done it, but what I can't understand is the breaking and entering. Do you think they were looking for the money?''

Grijpstra sat up.

"They hung him, you mean, and they wanted to grab the money. But it wasn't there. So they came back later?"

"Came back?" de Gier asked. "Perhaps they never left. The breaking and entering was a little sideshow. They just went on living here, quietly."

"Not quietly. Criminals are usually rather nervous. Fidgety."

"Next?" de Gier asked.

"Let's look through the house again," Grijpstra said. "We haven't found anything but it doesn't matter. There are still plenty of detectives around, in spite of the shortage. Let *them* have a try."

He telephoned. Six constables arrived and searched the house. They knocked on beams, removed floorboards, unscrewed drainpipes and put hands into lavatories. Two went through the shop, like moles. White moles, for they upset some bags of flour.

De Gier watched them and smiled. He had been a mole too, some years back.

He was still smiling when he climbed the stairs.

# CHAPTER 5

He found Grijpstra in Piet Verboom's room, reclining on the low settee, hands folded on round belly, a belly that had lately formed itself, bulging over Grijpstra's slipping belt, and that was being kept in some check by irregular gymnastics in Headquarters' sportsroom.

Grijpstra opened one eye. "Ha," he said. "Did you come to help me?"

"Yes," de Gier said.

"With what?"

"With thinking," de Gier said.

Grijpstra closed his eye.

"That's all right," he said, "but try and be as quiet as you can. There's nothing worse than loud thinking. And sit down somewhere."

De Gier looked around. The chairs didn't look very inviting and Grijpstra had the settee. In the end he selected three cushions and arranged them close to the wall. He closed his eyes.

An hour passed. Grijpstra breathed deeply, his mouth had lost its usual energetic expression and drooled slightly. De Gier had slept for a while but his head wasn't properly supported and he had waked up again. He smoked, stared, and saw vague, ever changing scenes and pictures in which the images of Thérèse and the girl in the bus, in various stages of undress, recurred. Grijpstra's mouth opened a little more and suddenly a sorrowful and very loud snore broke through the peace of the room. De Gier got up and stretched his back. He considered shaking Grijpstra awake but changed his mind. He thought of a more subtle approach. A set of small bongo drums in a corner of the room suggested it. He picked up the instrument, tiptoed to the settee, sat down on the floor, looked at the relaxed and helpless head of his superior, and hit the right bongo drum with a strong movement of his flat hand while the other veered quickly on the left drum.

Grijpstra leaped from the settee.

"Sha," Grijpstra said, "bongo drums. Where did they come from?"

"Some search," de Gier said. "They were in the room. You must have seen them before."

Grijpstra thought while he rubbed his face. "True. I had them in my hands even, to see if there was anything inside them."

He put out his hand and de Gier gave him the drums.

Grijpstra studied the instrument with some distrust. He was used to the larger drums in Headquarters. He vaguely tapped the right drum, rubbed the skin, and hit it with his knuckles, near the edge. Slowly a rhythm was being formed, quietly, pleasantly even, consisting of dry short plocks. While he played he looked at de Gier, invitingly almost and de Gier understood. He felt in the inside pocket of his coat and found, in between his two ballpoints, wallet and comb, the leather case containing his flute, the flute he had been carrying since Grijpstra had begun to play drums again. De Gier had been a promising musician as a boy, playing the recorder in the school's orchestra and had even specialized somewhat in medieval religious music, but he had given it up in exchange for sports and hanging around at street corners in the company of pimply friends exchanging tall stories. At the police school he had thought of music again but had been stopped by the prospect of becoming part of the police band, parading in the rain. But when Grijpstra had found his drums de Gier had been inspired as well and had bought himself a secondhand flute and brought it out, after much hesitation, during an early morning solo in which Grijpstra had excelled in delicate rustles and taps, and he had blown a long thin note.

Grijpstra hadn't even looked up but he had heard all right and immediately the drums filled the space that the weaving flute left open and since then they had often played together.

Grijpstra didn't look up now either. De Gier's flute was neither thin nor hesitant now, but strong and free and Grijpstra had to go down to the depth of his heavy soul to find the inspiration necessary to follow his artful friend. De Gier was on his feet, bent slightly, shoulders hunched, he had closed his eyes. The bongo drums formed a well connected base, fairly loud and extremely simple, and the flute was now very courageous, shrilly wavering between two notes, shrieking almost. One shriek was so loud, and so breakable, that nothing could follow it.

Grijpstra paused and waited, very straight on the settee.

The flute came back, with a lovely round sound and the two little drums with it.

Neither of the two had noticed the opening door. They hadn't seen van Meteren come in and they hadn't seen van Meteren leave again. They didn't notice his second entry either and they were so far gone that they didn't stop when the third player hit his wooden instrument, a tree trunk, hollow and with a long split in its surface. The sound of the jungle drum was hypnotic, magical, deep yet sharp and fitted in and even became the center of the melody. Both Grijpstra and de

Gier played around the new sonorous vibration and raised the theme until they could go no further and until van Meteren, with a high-pitched yell and a final groan of his tree trunk, broke the interlinking sounds and they looked at each other, silently, and utterly surprised.

"What was that?" Grijpstra asked softly.

Van Meteren shook himself from his dream and looked at them with a laugh.

"I heard you both play so nicely and I thought my contribution might go with it. This is a drum from the forests of New Guinea. My mother's grandfather used it as a telegraph, to pass messages to the next village. It can also be used to make music. And our witch doctors have other uses for it. Whoever knows the drum well can create moods, influence others. You can lame the enemy with it but if you do you take a risk. A grave risk. The power may turn around and strike you down and you have to be well protected. The drum can kill its owner, or drive him mad, and you rush off into the jungle, hollering and beating your chest."

"You're not serious," de Gier said.

"What do you mean?" van Meteren asked.

"This influence, this power," de Gier said.

Van Meteren smiled gently.

"And what about you? What about your flute? What about the adjutant and his drums? What do you think you were doing? Making music?"

"Sure," de Gier said, "we were making music. Nothing to it. Boom boom, Squeak squeak. Lots of people do it. To amuse themselves."

"But then you are changing your mood, aren't you?" van Meteren asked. "You are creating something, surely. Something new I mean, something that wasn't there before. Perhaps this new something is innocent. But you might, with the same effort, create something dangerous, a little evil force, which sneaks away from you and does what you intend it to do."

Grijpstra laughed.

"You are in Holland, van Meteren. Cheese, butter and eggs. Tulips. Windmills keeping the swamp dry. Nice crumbly potatoes and thick gravy. Gray porridge, so thick that you can hardly stir it. But all right, if you like we will be sorcerers and witches. We'll catch the murderer by creating a vibration."

"Yes," de Gier said, "and the vibration will rush off, and suddenly, hàts, it will catch him and bring him to us. And when he is close enough we'll hand him the ballpoint and he'll sign his confession."

"In his own words," Grijpstra added, "and clearly enumerating all the elements of the crime as it is listed in the law."

Van Meteren relaxed.

"But the music was O.K., wasn't it?" he asked.

"Yes," de Gier said, "rock group The Bopcops," and he looked at his watch. "Six o'clock. I'll have to go home. To feed the cat."

"You'll have to take the bus," Grijpstra said. "We have no car."

"Bah," de Gier said. "It's rush hour. The buses will be full. Bodies sweating all over you."

"Where do you live?" van Meteren asked.

"In Buitenveldert. Why? Do you have a car?"

"No," van Meteren said, "the parking police pay modest wages. But I do have a motorcycle."

De Gier wasn't enthusiastic. He detested the motorized bicycles cluttering the capital's streets by the thousands but he didn't want to offend his incongruous colleague.

"That'll be very nice," he said, "if you can spare the time."

"As long as you'll be back soon," Grijpstra said. "I am going to have dinner at the Chinese restaurant on the Nieuwedijk, next to the bare-bottom cinema. I'd like you to be there at seven-thirty. Can you make that?"

De Gier nodded and followed van Meteren.

They crossed the busy thoroughfare and van Meteren led the way into the large court of the monstrous Land Registry Office opposite the Haarlemmer Houttuinen.

"They let me park her here," he said. "They wouldn't have anything to do with me when I asked them but it was all right when I showed them my police card."

"Must be a new bicycle," de Gier thought, "a Kreidler, I suppose, with a fifty cc engine. Half a dozen of them are stolen every night."

They found the Harley-Davidson under a corrugated iron roof.

De Gier stopped. He recognized the model, a 1943 Harley of the Liberator type, which he had seen for the first time when the Allied armies rushed into Holland. He had been a twelve-year-old boy, waving at the side of the road, and a large American military policeman had waved back at him, firmly in the saddle of the gorgeous monster guiding a dozen halftracks loaded with cheering troops. The motorbike seemed to be in prime condition, spotless, white, its chromium plated exhaust gleaming in the sparse light of the large dark court.

"You like her?" van Meteren asked.

"Beautiful," de Gier said, and meant it. "Where did you get her?"

"From a junkyard, for a couple of hundred guilders," van Meteren said.

"We used them in the New Guinea police and I was trained on a similar machine, many years ago now. When I bought the wreck she was in very sad shape and it took me almost two years to strip and rebuild her again. The spare parts are very expensive so I tried to use all the old parts, but it was a lot of work. The gearbox was the worst part of the job, I had to replace it in the end, after having wasted a month on the bastard. And the leather sidebags are new, of course, or rather, unused. I bought them from an army dump and the leather had dried out and begun to crack. I must have used kilos of fat to restore them."

He kicked the Harley off her standard and began to push her out of the courtyard. The machine was so heavy that it was quite an effort to push her up the slight elevation toward the street.

"A little patience now," van Meteren said. "I'll start her up."

De Gier followed he process with interest. The clutch had to be kicked down. There was no spring to the clutch so that it couldn't resume a neutral position but would have to be adjusted continuously. On the tank an airstopper had to be unscrewed and pulled up. Choke. Regulation of the ignition by turning the left handlebar. Gas pushed back by turning the right handlebar. Kick the starter four times, giving a little gas each time, to suck petrol into the two cylinders. Turn the key on the tank. Push the choke back but not quite back.

"Now," said van Meteren.

He kicked the starter again and the engine came to life, with a soft but powerful gurgle.

"Do you have to do all that?" de Gier asked surprised.

"Yes," van Meteren said. "If you forget any of the movements you can kick the starter till your sweat fills your shoes. I can do it a lot more quickly but I saw you watching me so I went slowly. It can be done in a few seconds, and even a few seconds is a long time in New Guinea, especially when someone is firing at you with a bren gun."

He made an inviting gesture and de Gier climbed on the back part of the double saddle, van Meteren slid onto the front part and the machine took off at once. De Gier looked at the old-fashioned gear lever attached to the tank and thought of the BMW he once used to ride himself and the easy footgear that he could move with a flick of the toe. But van Meteren handled the cumbersome gear with the same ease.

De Gier was frightened. A motorcycle gives no protection. Only the skin envelops your life, the merest touch of a car or a lamppost and your leg is gone, your shoulder crushed or your skull split.

But his fear went when he realized that this was the best trip he had ever made through the city of Amsterdam. Van Meteren chose the grachts and sidegrachts and rode, without the slightest shock, through the narrow streets. He took no risks and the machine slithered through the rush-hour traffic. At every traffic light they were the first to take off and the Papuan never seemed to use his brakes, approaching the stoplights in gear and guessing the exact moment when the lights changed. A car that ignored their right of way was avoided in a supple curve and de Gier, pressed against the small body of his host, felt no irritation with the thoughtless or offensive driver who had endangered their lives. An obstacle, skillfully passed, no more.

When, at the end of the Beethovenstreet, the heavy traffic thinned out, van Meteren allowed the Harley to pick up speed and de Gier saw, when he looked over the Papuan's shoulder, that they were doing almost a hundred, but there was no danger, there were no sidestreets and de Gier watched the fat reed-plums, bordering the canal, flashing past him as a solid curtain and felt free.

The Harley slowed down and de Gier pointed at the large block of flats that contained his small apartment. Van Meteren changed into neutral and turned the key. The motorcycle approached the front door in silence. The Harley was in very good repair indeed, de Gier thought. He couldn't detect the slightest rattle or squeak anywhere in its complicated engine.

"Very nice," de Gier said. "Thanks a lot. Only the motorcops ride like that but they use BMW's and Guzzi's. I wonder if they could duplicate your performance on a Harley."

"Of course they can do that," said van Meteren. "I have ridden other makes when I was with the New Guinea police.

Each brand has its secrets, but you can solve them within a week and if there are any faults you can make use of them. The Harley is a little slow but makes up for it by its reliability. You can risk all sorts of maneuvers on the Harley that you shouldn't even think about on another cycle.''

"Come in a moment," de Gier said. "I have some beer in the fridge and you can drink it while I feed Oliver, but be careful with the cat. He isn't to be trusted and if he can't attack you straight away he'll wait for an opportunity and while he waits he looks very innocent, as if a mouse wouldn't melt in his mouth.''

He was glad he had warned van Meteren for Oliver was in a bad mood. De Gier had always kept the cat inside and Oliver had become neurotic. His twisted mind still loved de Gier but anyone else was considered as legal prey and of the few visitors de Gier had entertained lately at least two had left with bleeding ankles.

Oliver flattened himself when he saw van Meteren and began to growl, making his tail swell up at the same time. Van Meteren dropped to his haunches and scooped the cat off the floor, turning him upside down in the same movement. He caught the cat in his forearm and shook him gently, talking to the surprised animal in a gentle and smoothing voice.

"You are a sweet little cat, aren't you? A crazy silly animal? A crazy animal who hates large people, don't you?''

Oliver purred and closed his eyes.

"God, Christ Almighty," said de Gier. "He has never done that before.''

"He does it to you doesn't he?" van Meteren asked.

"Yes, but he has known me since he was eight centimeters long and white all over. He needs a lot of love, that cat, and he'll bite me if I don't spend half an hour a day stroking and fondling him, but so far I have been the only person who could really touch him.''

"Cats are marvelous animals," said van Meteren, who had put Oliver back on the floor, "great comedians."

Oliver tried again and attacked van Meteren's trousers, trying to gash a hole into the cloth. Van Meteren ignored him. The Siamese gave up and stalked into the kitchen, pawing the refrigerator and howling for his daily helping of chopped heart.

Grijpstra faced the chief inspector in the Hindist Society's restaurant. The chief inspector listened, while Grijpstra, limiting himself to the official language of a police report, summed up the events of the day.

"So you allowed her to go to Rotterdam?" the chief inspector asked.

"Yes sir," Grijpstra said.

"Let me see now," the chief inspector said and looked at the cast-iron ceiling of the restaurant, studying the golden garlands of stylized flowers. "She admits she hates him. She admits that she threw a heavy book at his head. You even have that in writing, nicely signed. A bruise, it could be attempted manslaughter. I'll have to look at the doctor's report again. And seventy-five thousand guilders are missing. And she is pregnant with Piet's child. And he never did anything for her and everything he gave her she had to return."

"Yes sir," Grijpstra said.

"Yes sir," the chief inspector repeated. He was still looking at the ceiling.

"Well, all right," said the chief inspector. "When we need her you'll be able to find her, I suppose. And we are short of cells. And she is pregnant."

Grijpstra said nothing.

"You still think it was murder?"

"I don't know, sir."

"There's no news from the detectives who are hunting the

two drug dealers. Or rather, there is some news. One of the detectives phoned me. According to the underworld there can't be any connection between the drug fellows and the murder. Nobody has ever heard of Haarlemmer Houttuinen number five."

"But that's the address where we found them," Grijpstra said in a flat voice.

"Yes," the chief inspector said. "Perhaps they were members of the Society. There must be a list of members somewhere. Did you see it?"

"No," Grijpstra said. "I think Piet pocketed the membership fees. I'll have to check with the accountant if the fees were part of the Society's income. Probably not. I did find a tearbook with membership certificates but there are no stubs. Piet just grabbed the twenty-five guilders each time and gave the new member his bit of paper. He didn't like to pay tax."

"Who does?" the chief inspector said. "Very clever man, our Piet."

Grijpstra grinned.

"Something funny?" the chief inspector asked.

"For a clever man he made rather a stupid picture, dangling from his own beam on a piece of rope."

The chief inspector grinned as well.

"So why would he have needed all that money?" he asked. "Perhaps he wanted to get away. The accountant claims that he might have had to pay some fifty thousand in taxes and fines. And according to the two boys and the two girls, and also to van Meteren, he didn't believe in the Society anymore. Perhaps he wanted to disappear and leave the Society as an empty hull, mortgaged up to the hilt and in debt to its suppliers. With seventy-five thousand he might have made a new start. He has lived in Paris so he must be adapted to living in other surroundings than Amsterdam."

"Possibly," Grijpstra said, "but he never left. He died, and the money is gone."

The chief inspector looked around the room.

"Funny atmosphere here, don't you think? Did you see the statue in the corridor downstairs? There are other statues as well. There is a proper Buddha statue somewhere upstairs."

"Very nice statues," Grijpstra said.

"A matter of taste. A chap sitting still all the time. So what? Is it recommendable to sit on your arse all day contemplating God knows what? Floating thoughts? Dirty dreams? One has enough of that, without sitting still."

He looked at his hands on the table.

"But it is a quiet pastime. Yes. Perhaps we are too busy. Perhaps we should have some of those statues in Headquarters, to teach a lesson to the colleagues who want to solve everything right away. Perhaps it is better to sit still and wait. Perhaps the right thought will bubble up. You can't trace where it comes from but it is there, right in front of you. Has it happened to you?"

Grijpstra thought and nodded, hesitatingly.

"Perhaps. A sudden spark, very fast. Too fast sometimes for it is gone before you can grab it. All you know is that you knew it, for a very short moment, but you have forgotten again."

"It'll come back later," the chief inspector said, "when you least expect it, sometimes."

"Perhaps," said Grijpstra.

"So what now, Grijpstra?"

"I am going to have dinner at a Chinese restaurant with de Gier."

"And where is de Gier?"

"Gone home to feed the cat."

The chief inspector laughed.

"Gone home to feed the cat," he repeated. "A clear motivation. I like that."

The mention of the word "dinner" made him finish the conversation. Grijpstra took him to the front door. A black Citroen was parked on the sidewalk, an impassive constable at the wheel. The chief inspector will be a commissaris soon, Grijpstra thought.

## CHAPTER 6

It was seven-thirty sharp when de Gier came into the Chinese restaurant. Grijpstra sat in one of the booths at the side, behind a glass of beer and his notebook. He was scribbling, connecting a number of circles. Each circle had a name.

"You see that I often come on time?"

Grijpstra mumbled something.

"And what conclusions is the master-mind drawing?"

Grijpstra connected two more circles.

"Well?"

"Ach," Grijpstra said, "what do I know? Bits and pieces, that's all I have. They all connect, but then anything does. I see the connections but I don't understand them. And what can I be sure of? The only fact we have so far is the book that girl of yours threw. The constables who are searching the house haven't found anything, except some dead mice. The search is still on. The detectives who are grubbing about in the underworld haven't found anything either. The theories we have come up with aren't very satisfactory. You helped me thinking today. Have you thought of anything?''

De Gier sat back and looked at the red lamps decorated with worn tassels. The owner had made use of the talents of a compatriot artist and there were some Chinese landscapes painted on the peeling plaster of the walls. One of the scenes was religious. A pagoda, or temple, inhabited by gods. Fat gods with bulging bellies, overpleasant smiles, bald heads and obscene female breasts. One of them had a thin beard. Fat tubby babies were crawling all over them.

''Well?'' Grijpstra asked.

''Bah,'' said de Gier.

Grijpstra looked up. ''I thought you liked Chinese food.''

''I do,'' de Gier said, ''but I was thinking. And I haven't come up with any good theory. The best one I have heard so far is the chief inspector's. We shouldn't think of murder straight off. Murders are rare in Amsterdam. It was suicide. A lot of the facts we have fit in, and the fact I like most is that he looked so neat.''

''Ah yes,'' Grijpstra said. ''I know what you mean. The Japanese suicide, wasn't it. You wash up and tidy yourself before you do it. You think he may have meditated a while in front of the little altar in his room, where we found the traces of burnt incense?''

''Yes,'' said de Gier, studying the menu. ''He may have been depressed for some time but he still needed a last push, and the girl throwing the dictionary at him set him off.''

''And the money?'' Grijpstra asked. ''The seventy-five red backs. Where are they?''

''Blackmail. Or somebody stole it *before* he committed suicide. Another reason to do it. Or, but perhaps that's too far-fetched, he destroyed the money to put suspicion on somebody else, somebody we would suspect of having murdered him.''

''Brr,'' Grijpstra said, ''no. Let's not be too subtle.''

''It could be, couldn't it?''

"No," Grijpstra said.

"Let's eat then."

De Gier had been given his beer and was blowing into the froth.

"Maybe you are right. I can't see him destroying money. Like putting it into one of these gray plastic rubbish bags we have nowadays and giving it to the garbage man. Nobody ever opens those bags. But Piet wouldn't destroy money. He liked money."

"But he may have been blackmailed."

"Seventy-five thousand is a lot of blackmail. What had he done? What can anyone do in Holland nowadays that he could be blackmailed for? Even murder will give you no more than a few years in jail."

"Ha," Grijpstra said. "Weren't you telling me the other day that even twenty-four hours in jail is more punishment than any man should take?"

"True, true," de Gier said. "Forget it. Let's eat."

They ordered and de Gier started eating the moment the waiter placed the food on the table. He tore the fried meat off the thin sticks with his teeth, broke a piece of shrimp-crackers and grabbed the noodles, all at the same time.

"Easy," Grijpstra said. "You are sharing this meal with me."

"You are right," de Gier said with his mouth full.

"Easy is the word. We shouldn't rush so much. This case will solve itself, all we have to do is sit around and watch it. That's what the chief inspector told me this . . ."

Grijpstra didn't finish his sentence and de Gier looked up.

"What now?" de Gier asked.

Grijpstra's face had frozen.

"Look behind you," he said.

De Gier looked around and froze as well.

"Shit," de Gier said, and jumped. Grijpstra jumped at the same time. They both pulled out their pistols and they were both running toward the door but de Gier got there first.

Grijpstra had run into the waiter, and the waiter and his tray were still falling when Grijpstra got into the street and saw de Gier running after their victim, a tall Chinese by the name of Lee Fong.

Poor Lee Fong was having very bad luck that day, the culmination of a lot of bad luck that he had had to put up with during his short stay in Holland. Ever since he had deserted his ship he had nothing but misadventure. He had lost at gambling and been arrested for pushing drugs. He had wounded a guard while escaping from jail. He had quarreled with the acquaintances who had hid him. This was the day he would leave the country. He should have stayed in hiding until the last minute but he had risked a short walk in order to buy a last good meal. And now he had run into two plain-clothes policemen.

He shouldn't have hesitated when Grijpstra looked at him.

There are a lot of photographs policemen have to remember and Chinese look very much alike to a Dutchman. But he had hesitated and touched his knife, a long nasty blade that he kept in a special pocket in his jeans. That one movement had caused Grijpstra to act. And now Lee Fong had de Gier after him and de Gier was gaining.

Lee took a corner and found himself in an alley, called the Ramskooi. The Ramskooi is a cul de sac. Lee thought he had no choice. He stopped, turned and pulled out his knife. De Gier stopped too and kicked. A good kick from a long leg will remove any knife. De Gier had learned at least three grips to disarm a knife fighter but they were all complicated, consisting of several movements. And he would have had to drop his pistol. He preferred holding on to the pistol. Lee Fong put up his hands as Grijpstra came panting.

The Ramskooi is a short alley and there are three bars in it. The bars' occupants were spilling into the street.

De Gier handcuffed Lee Fong and the crowd stared, and muttered. Grijpstra entered the first bar and telephoned the central radio room. Within seconds a siren began to whine. Within two minutes a white VW turned into the alley. Within three minutes it had left again, carrying de Gier and Lee Fong. The crowd was still muttering and Grijpstra dabbed at his forehead with a large dirty handkerchief. The crowd stopped muttering and returned to the bars and the next flood of beer.

"Sir," a small voice said.

Grijpstra, on his way back to the restaurant, looked down. A seven-year-old boy was walking next to him. A Negro boy, very black.

"Yes friend?" Grijpstra said.

The boy grinned, flashing large, white teeth.

"Are you a policeman, sir?"

"I am," Grijpstra said pleasantly.

"Can I see your gun please?"

"Guns are not for showing," Grijpstra said.

"No," the boy said smiling, "they are for shooting."

"You are wrong there, you know. Guns are for keeping in leather holsters, here." Grijpstra patted the holster under his jacket.

"What had the man done, sir?"

"Fighting," Grijpstra said. "He is a bad man. He fought with a knife and he hurt somebody."

"I fight too," the boy said.

"With a knife?"

"No sir. With my hands." The boy showed his small fists. "But my brother fights with a bicycle chain. He says he will teach me. It's very difficult, he says."

Grijpstra stopped and faced the boy.

"My name is Uncle Hans," Grijpstra said. "Now you go and tell your brother that he shouldn't fight with a bicycle chain. It isn't difficult and it isn't nice. If he wants to fight he should learn judo. You know what that is? Judo?"

"Yes sir," the boy said. "I have seen it on the TV. And

my teacher at school is a judo fighter. He has a brown belt but he want a black belt. He practices all the time."

"That's good," Grijpstra said. "Maybe you can learn from him. You know wh    judo fighters do before they start fighting?"

The boy thought, then he smiled.

"Yes, sir, I know. They bow to each other."

"You know why they do that?"

The boy thought again, a little longer this time. "They like each other? They've got nothing against each other?"

"Right," Grijpstra said. "Run along now."

"Goodbye, Uncle Hans," the boy said.


A minute later Grijpstra found himself cursing. The curses, strung together shaping an eight syllable malediction of some force, mildly surprised him. He had stopped in front of a small display window, part of a shop halfway between the dead end alley and the Chinese restaurant. He wondered what might have caused this sudden burst of harsh and indecent verbal violence. The objects in the small shop window? He identified the objects: three sets of dentures on a shelf, guarded by a fat cat, asleep and heavily motionless on a second shelf, placed above the first. But he knew that the unexpected appearance of false teeth would be unable to upset him. He owned a set of false teeth himself and the daily early-morning sight of them grinning from the waterglass on his washstand had never yet unnerved him, on the contrary, he thought his teeth to be both handsome and useful. The cat perhaps? But Grijpstra liked cats, even if he wouldn't admit the fact to boastful and sentimental cat-keepers like de Gier.

It was his attempt at education, he thought, and pushed his solid shape into motion again. The small boy he had lectured just now hadn't really been impressed. He had probably been frightened into agreeing. The display of firearms, the running feet, the suspect's knife, de Gier's kick, the handcuffs, the siren of the patrol car, the uniformed constable grabbing the prisoner. It's the war all over, Grijpstra thought. The kid will have his bicycle chain and join the free fight. Just give him a few more years.

Grijpstra was back in the restaurant. Their food was still on the table. The waiter smiled uneasily.

"Hey you," a fat woman said.

"Madame?" Grijpstra asked.

"You know what you did?"

"Yes," Grijpstra said. "I ran into the waiter. I am sorry."

"You a policeman?" the fat woman asked.

"Yes."

"That fellow you went after, what happened?"

"A criminal," Grijpstra said, "on the run. His photograph is in all the police stations. Dangerous. Armed with a knife. Had to grab him."

"Did you?"

"My colleague has got him. He is on his way to the cell now."

"You made a mess of my clothes, you know that?"

Grijpstra got up and looked at the woman's dress. It was stained badly.

"A whole plate of noodles. And my husband here got an egg roll on his head. And the girl over there got soup all over her. And you should have seen what you did to the waiter. He had to change his jacket."

"I am sorry," Grijpstra said again.

"You should pay something, maybe," the woman said.

"Ah, don't listen to her," the husband broke in. "She is having you on. The dress had to be dry-cleaned anyway and I got the egg roll on my hair, it's thick enough still."

"Are you all right?" Grijpstra asked the girl who had got soup over her.

The girl smiled shyly. "Yes."

"Women," the husband said. "A policeman got shot last

year. Dead he was. And she is talking about her clothes. You might have been shot too."

"He only carried a knife," Grijpstra said.

"Or knifed. Maybe that's worse."

"It's O.K.," the fat woman said. "But next time run around the waiter. He's a small chap, you could easily have avoided him."

"Women," the husband said.

"Shut up," the fat woman said.

"Yes dear," the man said.

"Would you two like a beer?" Grijpstra asked.

"Yes," the woman said and smiled at him.

The waiter brought the beer and refused payment.

"On the house," he said and smiled. He still looked very nervous.

"I wonder what he is hiding," Grijpstra thought. "No papers, that's for sure. And a friend of Lee Fong." He looked at the waiter's face, trying to remember it. Perhaps he should drop a hint at the Aliens Department. Perhaps he should not.

"There's enough trouble in the world," he thought.


Ten minutes later de Gier came in. The waiter brought a fresh plate of noodles and some fired vegetables.

"So?" Grijpstra asked.

"It's O.K. They've got him in the cell. A lot of charges against him now. The fool shouldn't have drawn his knife. I phoned the chief inspector and he seemed pleased for once. He asked me to congratulate you."

"Me?" Grijpstra asked.

"Don't be modest," de Gier said. "I can't stand it. You spotted him, didn't you?"

"Ah, yes," Grijpstra said, "and then you caught him. Because I told you to."

"You never told me anything."

"I would have," Grijpstra said, "If I had had a little time."

"Well," de Gier said and smiled nastily, "you got the waiter."

"It's the little things in life that give us our pleasure," Grijpstra said. "You pay the bill."

"I paid last week."

"Four rolls and two cups of coffee," de Gier said. "Six or seven guilders. This must be over twenty."

"You are the youngest," Grijpstra said, "don't argue."

"No," said de Gier, and paid the bill.

"Got anything yet?" Grijpstra asked, addressing a young constable who was moving casks in the cellar of Haarlemmer Houttuinen number 5.

"Perhaps," the young constable said. "These casks contain some sort of paste. I believe it is called mizo and they make soup with it. I ate it once in one of these health-food restuarants. The taste isn't too bad if you don't eat too much of it. Innocent stuff anyway but this is different. I picked it up on the floor."

He showed a few crumbs of a sticky dark brown substance. "It looks like mizo but it is harder. I think it is hash."

"You roll your own cigarettes?" Grijpstra asked.

"Sure," the constable said. "You want some cigarette paper?"

Grijpstra mixed a little of the substance with cigarette tobacco, cutting it up with his stiletto. De Gier lit the cigarette for him and Grijpstra took a deep puff and exhaled the smoke. They all sniffed.

"Hash," they said simultaneously.

"We'll send it to the lab to make sure," Grijpstra said, "but it's hash all right."

"Good work," de Gier said to the constable, who looked pleased, but he didn't think much of the find. A few crumbs of hash on the floor meant nothing. Of course these people would smoke hash. Johan, or Eduard, or the girls, or Piet himself, or van Meteren perhaps. And they might drop a little on the floor. Why not? To smoke hash is hardly punishable. To stock and sell it is a crime. If they could find a cask full of the stuff...

"You opened all the casks?" he asked.

"All of them. We had to cut the ropes and pry the lids open with a knife. Nothing but soup paste in there. We prodded them and took samples from the bottom and the sides. Soup, that's all."

"Anything else?"

"Nothing," the constable said, "but it's a hell of a mess here. Dirty. Dead mice and all. And they call it a restaurant. Bah."

"You are still young," Grijpstra said. "The world is held together by dirt. Don't think of it or you'll never eat again."

Before leaving the cellar he stopped and turned around. "I'll tell you something else. Female bodies can be very dirty too. Did you ever think of that? If you would only consider . . ."

"I don't want to know," the constable said.

De Gier laughed and climbed the stairs. A detective tapped him on the shoulder.

"You got a minute?"

De Gier followed the detective to the restaurant. "You found something?"

The detective shrugged. "Perhaps."

"So?"

"Well, you'll have to decide. You are in charge, aren't you?"

"Grijpstra is in charge."

"That's what I mean," the detective said. "You and Grijpstra, same thing."

"Oh yes?" de Gier asked irritably. "I am a separate entity, you know. We aren't a Siamese twin, you know."

"All right," the detective said. "You are separate. You want to hear what I have to tell you?"

"Please," de Gier said.

"In van Meteren's room, that Papuan gent, we found some funny things."

"I know," de Gier said. "I saw the room. A wild boar's skull, a jungle drum, a collection of twigs and shells and stones and some funny dolls."

"Exactly," the detective said, "and a Lee-Enfield rifle, well kept and wrapped in an oiled cloth, but no ammunition."

"Hey," de Gier said, "he shouldn't have that."

"Right," the detective said, "but the fellow is on the force and he had no ammunition. He told me that he used to be with the New Guinea state police and that he kept the rifle as a souvenir, when the Indonesians took over. He didn't want to surrender his weapon. A patriot. He took it apart and smuggled it in, and the customs didn't notice. Now do I grab him or not? To own a firearm is a crime nowadays. It'll cost him his job and maybe his unemployment benefits. He'll have to pay a fine and his name will be in the books forever."

"What have you done so far?" de Gier asked.

"I told him to report to the armory at Headquarters and ask them to pour aluminum into the barrel, then he can keep it. But I also said that the final decision rests with you. So I can still grab him if you give the word."

"O.K." de Gier said, ."let's do it your way. But tell him to report to the armory this week. If he hasn't been there in seven days' time we'll still grab him."

"Yes, boss."

"And write an unofficial report with a copy for the armory sergeant."

"Yes, boss."

"And don't call me boss."

"No, boss," the detective said.

\*     \*     \*

Grijpstra came into the restaurant, accompanied by a young woman and a little girl.

"Allow me to introduce you."

"De Gier," de Gier said. "You must be Mrs. Verboom."

"Mrs. Verboom has come straight from the airport," Grijpstra said. "This is Yvette. Yvette is very tired, aren't you?" The little girl smiled.

"We mustn't keep you, then," de Gier said. "Can we take you anywhere? Do you have a place to sleep?"

Mrs. Verboom smiled sweetly.

"Don't worry about us," she said. "My father is downstairs with the car. He'll take Yvette home and I'll go there later. I thought you might want to see me right away."

"Yes, that would be a good idea," de Gier said. "This officer will take your daughter down to the car."

The detective took the little girl by the hand. "You want to come with me, dear?"

"Are you a policeman too?" the girl asked.

"He is a very nice policeman," de Gier said. "Aren't you?"

"Yes, boss, the detective said.

Grijpstra and de Gier studied the young woman. Piet's taste must have been excellent. Thérèse was a good looking girl but this woman, although at least ten years older than her husband's mistress, and worn out by the trip and possibly tension, was a beauty. De Gier admired the long thick blond hair and the sensual, well-shaped mouth. Mrs. Verboom crossed her legs and produced a cigarette. De Gier smiled and lit it for her. She smiled back.

"I hope you don't mind if I am not sad. I didn't love Piet, not for a long time, and I am not really concerned about his death. I didn't want him to die but if he did, well, then he did."

"I understand," de Gier said.

"And I didn't kill him," she said calmly. "I couldn't have

if I had wanted to for I was in Paris. I can prove it easily. I'll give you my address in Paris, so you can check it out."

She wrote the address down and de Gier copied it in his notebook. He would have to ask the chief inspector to contact the French police.

"You are now the only director of the Hindist Society," Grijpstra said.

"Some society," Mrs. Verboom said sarcastically, "some nothing. The house is empty and everybody has left, except van Meteren, I hear, and he was never part of the Society. And he is leaving as well, he tells me. And I saw through the Hindist nonsense a long time ago. Piet converted me when I married him, when I still thought he had something to teach." She looked at the policemen.

"But I am interested in the money, I have to look after my child."

"I am sorry, Mrs. Verboom," Grijpstra said, "but I don't think there is any money. Your husband mortgaged the house and I don't know what happened to the money. There's still a chance we may find it but right now there is no trace of it. Perhaps you can sell the house and make something out of it but I think you should contact Joachim de Kater, your husband's accountant."

Mrs. Verboom looked out of the window.

"The bastard," she said. "For years and years I sweated on this house. I even plastered some of the walls and did carpentry. He made me carry bricks, right up to the top floor, he was too stingy to install a proper hoist. And it wasn't just me. We were all idealists, we were going to improve the mental climate of Amsterdam and make people happy by introducing them to the 'real peace.' We were detached! Ha."

The detectives smiled understandingly.

"And now he has blown the lot. What did he do with the money?"

"I wish I knew," de Gier said. "Then we might also know

if your husband was murdered and if so, why. But we can't find anything. Would you know perhaps if your husband ever dealt in drugs?"

"Hash?" Mrs. Verboom asked.

"Hash, heroin, cocaine, speed, pills, any drug at all." Mrs. Verboom shook her lovely head and allowed her cape to slide down from her shoulders. She wore a thin cotton blouse underneath, with the three top buttons undone. She bowed down a little. De Gier saw her breasts, first one, and then, after a charming twist, the other.

"Hmmpf, hmmpf," he said slowly.

"I beg your pardon?" Mrs. Verboom asked.

"No, nothing," de Gier said. "I said hmmpf hmmpf. I have been saying that a lot lately. No specific meaning. Maybe I work too much."

"May be the warm weather," Mrs. Verboom said and laughed. "Drugs you said. Perhaps he did. He had no morals, I know all about his lack of morals. But he wasn't very courageous and drugs is a risky business . . . I don't know. We did have hash here, a big tin full of hash. He must have bought it wholesale for there was quite a lot in it. But he never sold any as far as I know. We used to have parties with it, he called it concentration exercises, and he would play special music on his gramophone and we had to be quiet. I enjoyed those parties. Once we had some tomatoes on the table and they were very beautiful. It was the first time I saw what a tomato really is like. Or, rather, that's what I thought at the time. The next day it was just another tomato. Hash is very relaxing, you know."

"You still use it?" de Gier asked.

"No. I gave it up when I went to Paris. Nobody offered me any and I felt no need to start rushing around to see if somebody would give me a stickie. I never smoked much of it. Perhaps we had six parties in all. Anyway, I have to work for a living now. I live a very dull life."

"Why in Paris?" Grijpstra asked.

"My mother is French and we have relatives over there. French is my second language. When I left Piet I wanted to make a complete break."

"So your husband gave people the opportunity to take drugs. But did he ever sell any?" de Gier asked.

"I am not sure," Mrs. Verboom said. "We never sold stickies over the bar or in the restaurant. But perhaps he dealt in it in a big way. Some strange types used to come and visit him and he would receive them in his room and lock the door. Perhaps they were dealers."

"We didn't find the tin you mentioned," Grijpstra said.

"Perhaps somebody took it; van Meteren told me downstairs that somebody broke in during the night after Piet's death."

The detectives went on asking but Mrs. Verboom began to repeat herself. She mainly talked about Piet. Grijpstra became very sleepy.

"That'll be all Mrs. Verboom," he said. "You must be tired. I am sure you would like to go to your parents." He knew, by now, that Piet had not been the most charming person in Amsterdam.

# CHAPTER 7

Saturday morning, nine o'clock.

De Gier was asleep.

The alarm had gone off, as always, at six-thirty. And de Gier had got up, groaning, and fixed himself coffee and drunk the coffee on his balcony, while he looked at the large lawn behind the apartment building, a very neat lawn, with roses in the middle. He had listened to the many thrushes, admired the seagulls and the lone crow, and frowned at the pigeons.

"Why don't you catch yourself a couple of pigeons?" he had asked Oliver who had come out on the balcony too. "Pigeons shit too much. Look."

One of his geranium plants had been hit and showed a patch of slimy acid excrement.

De Gier went inside, got a pair of scissors, and snipped at the plant.

He looked at the lawn again, now populated by a dachshund. The dachshund couldn't make up his mind where to sit down, the lawn was too big. Acres and acres of grass and just one small dachshund.

De Gier finished his cigarette, grinned at the dachshund, patted Oliver on the head, and got into bed again. He grunted with pleasure as he pulled the blanket over his shoulder. Another hour, two hours maybe. A long pleasant day.

He dreamt.

It was a dream he had known before.

Some kind of warship sails through the bend of the Herengracht, Amsterdam's most aristocratic canal. It looks a little like one of the police vessels used to patrol the capital's waterways, a flat, smooth, powerful boat, gray and low for it must be able to pass under the bridges.

But the ship isn't manned by the bluecoated Water Police. Its crew consists of a large number of small square men, armed with old-fashioned tommyguns, dating back to the days of Al Capone, short blunt weapons with round cartridge-drums, fastened to the barrel.

De Gier is on the bridge, looking down. This is the moment when the underworld will take over. In a minute the boat will moor and send patrols into the city. The first will make for the city hall and arrest the mayor and the aldermen and the second will shoot its way into Police Headquarters and grab the chief constable.

De Gier is all by himself, and unarmed.

But he isn't nervous, he knows his power, the power of a municipal criminal investigator in a democratically governed country.

He studies the enemy and notes that all the small square men have the same face, and that every face is watching him, slyly from under the rim of its bowler hat. He sees that all these small parts, who, together, form the enemy, are dressed in striped suits, model Grijpstra, and in gray ties, model chief inspector.

But this is very logical, de Gier thinks. The enemy is the

perversion of official authority, so it will have to resemble official authority.

It's very early in the morning. The city is empty. The seventeenth-century gables frame its emptiness.

The ship is moving closer, now it's underneath de Gier.

He leans over the railing. He spits.

The white fluffy flake of spittle, moved by a weak breeze, floats down slowly and finally lands on a bowler hat. There is an explosion. The ship catches fire and begins to sink, the small square men jump overboard and drown. Only one bowler hat, afloat by itself, remains.

De Gier woke up. He sighed. All's well that ends well. He had had the dream before, it didn't end well that time. That time he got caught. He was tortured. And, worse, ridiculed. The small square men had made fun of him. He had been on his knees.

"I am improving," de Gier thought happily. "I can direct my dreams. A man should be able to direct his own dreams."

"Hello, Oliver," he said to the Siamese cat who was asleep on his legs, its wide head flattened comfortably, its mouth curved into a contented half grin.

Oliver squeaked sleepily.

"Don't squeak," de Gier said. "You are a cat, you aren't a mouse."

Oliver squeaked again.

"All right, you are a mouse."

He jumped out of bed, sweeping the blanket back and Oliver, suddenly folded into an untidy ball, flew against the wall and got mixed up with the sheets.

De Gier laughed. "You are a clumsy mouse."

Oliver liberated himself and rubbed his smooth body against de Gier's legs, purring.

De Gier was on his way to the kitchen when the telephone rang.

*     *     *

"Morning," Grijpstra said. "I am not waking you up, I hope."

"You didn't. I have been up since six o'clock, going through the files."

"Good fellow," Grijpstra said. "I am proud of you, you know that, don't you? Sit down, will you, relax."

De Gier sat down and lit a cigarette. "I am relaxed."

"Right," Grijpstra said. "Now listen. I have a nice little job for you."

"No," de Gier said. "No. I've got the day off."

"A policeman," Grijpstra said patiently, "never has the day off. Especially not when he is working on a homicide. And this job is nice, I am telling you. Do you remember that lovely Mrs. Verboom?"

"I do," de Gier said and thought of the breasts that had been presented to him, one by one.

"You sound much better now," Grijpstra said. "I am still looking for the right motive."

De Gier sighed. "You've got a good motive. Seventy-five thousand is a good motive."

"Yes. But what do you think of this? Van Meteren and Mrs. Verboom have an affair. We know that Piet was always on the make, and with some success. So the marriage must have been a failure, which means that Mrs. Verboom must have been frustrated. Frustrated women need company. Nature doesn't like gaps, it fills them up. Black is beautiful. She grabs van Meteren."

"Black is beautiful refers to Negroes," de Gier said, "not to Papuans."

"I don't know," Grijpstra said. "If I were a woman I would prefer a Papuan. Negroes, nowadays, are too civilized, they watch TV and football and make nice conversation. They are boring. But Papuans were cannibals, one generation ago. Just one generation ago. Imagine. Long pig for dinner, and feathers on your head, and dancing in the full moon, and pointing the bone."

"Hmm," de Gier said dreamily. "We used to do it too, you know."

"We did it a hundred thousand years ago. We have forgotten."

"I think you are right again," de Gier said. "I thought you knew nothing about psychology."

"No psychology," Grijpstra said, "just dreams. Imagination. The reason she took van Meteren was because she had him in the house. He could have been a Chinese, or a man from Rotterdam."

"No," de Gier said, "not a man from Rotterdam, she wouldn't have done that. She wouldn't have."

"A frustrated woman may do anything."

"Go on," de Gier said. "You excite me."

"So she took the Papuan," Grijpstra said.

"He is only seven-eighths Papuan."

"Stop interrupting me," Grijpstra said. "I have things to do. And seven-eighths of a Papuan is a complete man."

"What things to do? It's Saturday. You are free."

"Free!" Grijpstra exclaimed. "Free, ha! I have to take my children to the beach and it's late already. They are all packed, buckets, spades, sunhats, thermosflasks, the lot."

"O.K. Go on then."

"This van Meteren is a special man, have you noticed?"

"Of course I have," de Gier said. "Didn't I tell you how he rode that Harley-Davidson of his, and how he treated Oliver?"

"You have," Grijpstra said. "So he is a special man, and Mrs. Verboom is a beautiful intelligent woman. They get on well. But they have no money. Van Meteren has a minimal wage and Mrs. Verboom waits on her husband's customers and slaves in the kitchen for a penny a week. Meanwhile Piet makes a fortune, on drugs. Van Meteren knows about Piet's racket, maybe he is part of it. Perhaps he knows that Piet has seventy-five thousand ready to buy a large quantity. Heroin maybe, or cocaine. Or a big load of hash. He tells Mrs.

Verboom that he will get the money. She wants to help him but van Meteren realizes the danger. If we had found Mrs. Verboom in the house at the time of Piet's death we might have discovered the affair. She had to go.''

"Right," de Gier said, "so he told her to leave her husband, and to make the break complete, to leave the country as well. It would absolve her of being suspected of complicity. So what happened then?''

"I am glad you can follow me," Grijpstra said, "so early in the morning. Now the good part comes.''

De Gier looked out of the window and saw Oliver, who had climbed into the geranium box and was chattering at the seagulls.

"Ho," he shouted, "hold it. Oliver is in the flowerbox again. He fell out last week and nearly broke his jaw. He bled for days. I'll have to get him out.''

Grijpstra sighed.

"I got him," de Gier said, and sighed as well. "Damned cat. I should have bought a canary. Go on. What's the good part?''

"Piet becomes depressed," Grijpstra said. "He really misses his wife and child. He mentions suicide. Van Meteren eggs him on. Piet is an unbalanced type and capable of doing away with himself. Van Meteren spreads the rumor that Piet is very depressed and getting worse. Everybody in the house believes it.''

"Ha," said de Gier, who had become really interested. "But Piet is full of cheer, in spite of missing his family. He is busy on the biggest deal of his life. He is buying heroin or whatever, which he can sell immediately to the drug dealers who come to his bar, and who pass themselves off as proper Hindists. But the deal misfires and Piet is dead. How did he die?''

"Well," Grijpstra said, "simple. Van Meteren waits until Piet has the money in the house. Piet is waiting for whoever will bring him the drugs. But before the man arrives van

Meteren strolls into the room, knocks Piet out and hangs him. The money goes into his pocket and he hides it somewhere, outside the house perhaps. The world is large."

De Gier studied a discolored spot on his ceiling, a round spot. He remembered that he had dreamt about the spot. He had got into it and it led somewhere, but he couldn't remember where it led to when he woke up.

"Yes, yes," he said, "and van Meteren could make use of the fight Thérèse picked with Piet that day. He came in just after she had stalked out of the room, found Piet in a dazed state, holding his head after he had been hit with the dictionary, and finished the job. And when we came *he* was the first to notice the bruise, to stress his innocence."

"You really think the girl hit him with that book?" Grijpstra asked. "Women never hit anything. They miss. But it doesn't matter."

De Gier began to laugh. "Doesn't matter," he repeated. "You talk like a Hindist. You've been converted?"

Grijpstra laughed. "I have been converted years ago. The police may not teach much and I may have a thick head but I did notice that nothing is quite as important as it seems. But never mind, maybe it doesn't matter who the murderer is, we'll catch him all the same."

De Gier made a face at the telephone. "Just for the hell of it, what?"

"Hell, or heaven, or purgatory. Whatever you like. And if we don't succeed we'll keep on trying. And if we never succeed it'll be a pity, but not too much of a pity."

"Yes," de Gier said, "then what happened?"

"Van Meteren phones Mrs. Verboom in Paris and tells her he had made a neat job of it. She can come. She'll have to come for she has to show some interest in the inheritance."

"Why?" de Gier asked. "She might have stayed away. But she'll want to see van Meteren. But all right, maybe she should have come or we would have worried about her. Pity she came, I would have liked to have visited her in Paris. But now what do you want of me?"

"Yes," Grijpstra said, "glad you remind me. I want something of you. It's a nice day and you have nothing to do. I want you to date her. You were very impressed with her yesterday, she must have noticed. And you have thought about her all night. Tossed in your bed. Nothing wrong with that, you are a bachelor. So phone her and make a date and take her out."

"What if she refuses?"

"She won't," Grijpstra said persuasively. "You are a detective and charged with the case. She knows that and she is curious. And you are very handsome, you know. Two good reasons for her to welcome your company. And then you can listen to her. She is sure to drop her guard. Let her talk."

De Gier got up, stretched, and grunted.

"You do it," he said. "You are a great actor. Act the fatherly type. If your theory is correct I'm of no use to you. She'll be in love with van Meteren. I have a blotched pink skin, not a shining black one."

"I've got to go to the coast now," Grijpstra said. "Good luck and good hunting. Give me a ring tonight, any time, and tell me what happened."

"HEY!" de Gier shouted.

"Yes?" Grijpstra asked.

"A car. I need a car, you don't want me to take her on the luggage carrier of my old bicycle do you?"

"No," Grijpstra said. "There'll be a Mercedes waiting for you in the police garage next to Headquarters, at two o'clock this afternoon. There'll be fifty guilders in the glove compartment. The doorman will have the keys. Tell me what you have spent on Monday and give me the change, and the dockets."

He rang off.

*    *    *

He telephoned Mrs. Verboom. Her mother answered.

"This is Rinus de Gier. Could I speak to your daughter please?"

"A moment," the mother said. He heard her call, "Constanze."

"Hello, Constanze," he said in his smooth sexhunt voice. "This is Rinus de Gier. We met yesterday."

"How do you know my name?" she asked, surprised.

"The police know everything," de Gier said in his normal voice.

Constanze laughed, a very natural laugh.

"Grijpstra is wrong," de Gier thought. "The poor thing isn't connected with the case at all. She is the corpse's wife, that's all. However. . ."

"Are you phoning me as a detective, or as a man?"

De Gier picked up a little courage. The response was free, welcoming even.

"Well," he said. and hesitated, "as a man really. I thought you might be free this weekend and I am free too. I wanted to come and pick you up this afternoon. Perhaps we can go for a drive and have dinner in town, and so on."

"So on what?" Constanze asked.

"A beer after dinner, or a glass of wine somewhere."

"All right," Constanze said. "My parents are only interested in the child anyway. And they talk about Piet's death. I'd like to get away for a bit. Come and fetch me if you like. What time?"

"This afternoon? Two thirty?"

"No," Constanze said. "I have something to do this afternoon. A little shopping. Would you like to come around seven?"

"Seven o'clock," de Gier said.

"All right, Rinus, I'll be waiting for you," her voice had dropped. There was a hint of a promise in it. She rang off.

*       *       *

"Ha," de Gier said and looked at Oliver. Then he picked up the cat and rubbed its head against his face. "You wouldn't know," he said soothingly. "They cut it all out of you. But I had to ask them to do it. You would have gone mad in this place, jumping about and tearing the curtains and dribbling. You've seen me jump about sometimes, haven't you? You should be glad I had you treated."

He sang while he shaved and dressed.

Oliver whined, and rolled on the carpet.

"Shut your Siamese howler," de Gier said. "We consist of lust, you and I. Different sorts of lust. When one is satisfied the other rears its ugly snout. Let's eat."

They breakfasted together, on the balcony.

"Now watch it," de Gier told the cat. "I am going to leave the balcony door open. Try and stop yourself from falling off the flowerbox. I am going to the library to get all the books I can find on Papuans and then I'll come home and read them. And I'll get us some food. So watch it."

He picked up the Mercedes at 6:30. The car was almost new, with an open roof. The tank had been filled.

"A car of the Investigation Bureau," de Gier thought, "but they don't investigate. They just follow people and snoop. And then they call us and we make the arrest. Why didn't I apply to join them? I would have qualified. I could have spent my life in the best bars and the best nightclubs. And the best brothels. All at the state's expense. All for the good cause. And what do I do? I walk around and get flat feet."

But he was grateful, and guided the car carefully through the Jacob van Lennepstraat where Constanze stayed with her parents. The Jacob van Lennepstraat is a long, narrow, lightless ditch. There are no trees in it. The scenery consists of crumbling brick walls and dented unwashed cars.

"It wasn't my sexy voice that made her say yes," he

thought. "Nobody wants to spend any time here. Not in these stuffy small rooms, full of furniture and clammy air."

The mother asked him to come in for a minute. She laughed shyly, almost submissively. A very fat woman, with moist spots under her arms. Yvette ran into him in the corridor and remembered who he was. She gave him a little kiss and called him uncle. The mother pointed at a chair, he sat down and the child climbed onto his lap. The mother laughed again and complained about the hot weather. She spoke with a marked French accent.

"Meet my husband," she said and de Gier put the child down and got up stiffly. They shook hands. The father was fat as well and the hand he shook seemed swollen and a little rotten.

"I am on sick pay," the father said. "My nerves, you know. You work for the city as well, I hear."

"Yes sir," de Gier said. "I am with the police."

"Nice work," the father said, "better than mine. More exciting, I am sure. I work in the Land Registration Bureau. I put files away and when I have put them away I look for them again. And every time I show anyone a file because some builder or architect or prospective buyer wants to see what's what, the city earns six guilders and fifty cents. Of that I get about ten cents. I worked it out once. It must have got on my nerves. But I don't know how it got on my nerves. What has it got to do with me? Do *you* know?"

De Gier withdrew into a polite silence.

"My daughter will be here soon. She is painting her face and fluffing her hair and fiddling about. All unnecessary work. She is a nice doll. Of course I shouldn't know, I am her father. But I think she is a nice doll, even when she flops about in the morning with curlers in her hair. She shouldn't have married that little mangy squirrel. But he is dead now. That's better."

"You didn't like Piet Verboom?" de Gier asked.

"Of course not," the father said. "nobody did. He didn't like himself. A slimy slicker first class. He never talked to me because he thought I was too stupid. And I never talked to him for I thought he was a bore. He talked about himself only. I also talk about myself; it limits the conversation after a while."

De Gier broke his polite silence and laughed. The father laughed too.

"That's nice," he said. "I can be amusing, in spite of my nerves. You want a cold beer?"

De Gier got his beer. Constanze brought it, on a tray. Two cold tins, two glasses. She poured the beer. The father studied de Gier over his glass and smiled. "You like football?" he said.

"No sir," de Gier said.

The father sat up suddenly, nearly spilling his beer. "You are serious?"

"Yes," de Gier said. "I am probably crazy but football bores me. I often had to watch it, as a young cop guarding the field. I saw some of the famous matches, Ajax against Spain, and Ajax against that other club, I forgot the name, but all I see is a lot of striped men chasing a little ball. It means nothing to me. It doesn't just bore me, it irritates me. I think it's a waste of energy."

"You hear that, wife?" the father shouted.

De Gier had to say it all over again. The father's face split open in a wide grin.

"Against that other club," the father repeated. "I forget its name now. Hahaha."

"You made him happy, sir," the mother said. "He thinks he is the only one in town who doesn't enjoy watching football and he worries about it."

"Yes, damn it," said the father, who was still sitting on the edge of his chair, "I am ashamed of it. It's like I am different from all the neighbors, and the chaps at work. And now you are just the same. Ha."

"What *do* you like?" de Gier asked.

The father pointed at the floor. De Gier saw a long row of gramophone records. He got up and looked through them. All modern jazz and mainly piano and trumpet.

The father was watching him unhappily. "You like that sort of music?" he asked.

De Gier felt a chill going down his spine. It amazed him. He had had it before, at moments of deep emotion. This fat puffy man might share his own spirit. He tried to control himself but his enthusiasm and bewilderment won.

"Sir," de Gier said, "sir, I really like that music. I have the same records as you have, not all of them maybe, but most of them. And I listen to them, once, twice a week. I put the cat on my lap and switch the lights off and open the balcony door when the weather permits, and light a cigar and I listen. For hours. And then it all stops, you know, it stops."

He wanted to continue but the father interrupted him. "Christ will keep my soul," he said softly.

The mother touched de Gier's arm. "Maybe you cured my husband," she said softly. "He isn't alone anymore."

"I never have to see you again," the father said. "I'd like to of course, but it isn't necessary. As long as I know that you sit there, somewhere in the city, and listen to your music. This is a good moment. They happen at times. You don't expect them and they happen. When you do they don't happen. Mother! More beer!"

The mother brought more beer. Constanze had sat down, very gracefully. "She wants me to look at her," he thought, "but I prefer watching her father."

"You have had these moments before?" he asked.

"Yes," the father said, "as a child. I never quite understood them. Something occurs, you notice something, and suddenly the moment is there. You can't explain it, maybe you don't want to explain it. I remember when it happened for the first time. I saw a hornbill in the zoo. Some people call them rhinoceros-birds. It looked so weird that suddenly my whole life changed. I saw my life differently. I knew it would change back again and become boring again, ordinary, everyday life. But that moment it was all different. The logic had been knocked out of it. The 'this happens because of that and that happens because of that.' All gone. I never forgot. Now I sometimes go to the zoo to see the hornbill. I walk straight up to its cage and watch it for a while and then I walk straight to the gate. I don't look at the other birds and animals. Just a glance at the camels. They are weird too, but the other animals all can be explained. Not the hornbill. Nobody can explain a hornbill to me. That's the beauty of it, maybe.''

"You aren't drunk, father?'' Constanze asked. She turned to de Gier. "When he talks about the hornbill he is usually drunk, very drunk. We'll have to carry him to bed. He is heavy.''

"No, dear,'' the father said. "You go to town with the gentleman and enjoy yourself. I am not drunk and I won't get drunk. Not tonight anyway.''

De Gier said goodbye and waited for Constanze to go through the door. He looked around before he left the room but the father was gazing out of the window, with a peaceful expression on his flabby face.

"That was nice of you,'' Constanze said and leant against de Gier. "You should come again. Nobody can cheer him up anymore. He isn't too bad tonight. Sometimes he groans and doesn't know his own wife. He keeps on saying that everything is black and then he begins to mumble. He can curse for hours. He isn't angry then, he just repeats the curses. Over and over again. I couldn't live in this house anymore. When Yvette is here he gets a bit better. He took her to the zoo this morning.''

"To look at the hornbill,'' de Gier thought. "Join the navy and see the sea, join the police and see the soul. I must tell

Grijpstra, this would have interested him. Maybe Grijpstra should have a look at the hornbill sometimes.''

"Is that your car?" Constanze asked.

"Yes," de Gier said. "I saved up for it. Tuppence a day, and I never stopped saving for a hundred years.''

"Really?''

"Not really. I borrowed it. I have a bicycle, an old bicycle. And when I'm on duty I drive a VW.''

"Oh," Constanze said, "you don't need a car to take me out. I am used to nothing. Piet had a car but he used it to take his girlfriends out. I worked in the kitchen and looked after the child.''

"Don't you have a friend with a car in Paris?" de Gier asked. "You are a beautiful woman. You can't tell me the men in Paris haven't noticed.''

Constanze was quiet for a while. "I only left Piet some months ago. In Paris I have to work. My mother's brother owns a wholesale company and he gave me a job. I lived in his house for a while and they are very strict people. I only got a little flat last week, and when I leave work I have to pick up the child at a crèche. I haven't gotten around to men yet.''

"Hmmpf, hmmpf," de Gier said.

"You said that last night," Constanze said. "Is it your war cry?''

"Yes," de Gier said, "a war cry.''

"Do you want to have me?" Constanze asked.

De Gier blushed and Constanze giggled.

"Who is trying to make who?" de Gier thought and went on blushing. He put his hand on hers; she didn't pull her hand away.

"Did you bring your sandwiches?" he asked, pointing at the plastic bag she had put between them.

Constanze blushed. "Yes," she said, "but not because I thought you wouldn't feed me. It's some bread and cheese my mother gave to my father when he went to the zoo this morning. He brought them back again. I was going to ask you to drive to the park later this evening. I always went there as a child and I would like to see it again before I return to Paris.''

"Are we going to feed the ducks?" de Gier asked.

"No," she said, "it's a secret. You'll see." He took her to the Chinese restaurant on the Nieuwedijk. The owner bowed behind his counter and the waiter smiled. Constanze noticed the friendly reception.

"Do they know you here?" she asked.

"They do. We made a bit of a mess here yesterday."

"What happened?"

"We arrested a man we were looking for and my colleague accidentally ran into the waiter. In fact, he ran over him. There were noodles all over the place." De Gier grinned. "Pity I was out on the street when it happened, had to go after my man."

"You can't be very popular here."

"It's all right. The police are never popular. But they'll still sell us a meal."

The owner served them himself.

"Shrimps," the owner said, "very nice. Very fresh. With fried rice. And special soup. Real Chinese soup, not on the menu. And a glass of wine. Wine on the house. Yes?"

"Yes," Constanze said, "that sounds nice."

The owner bowed and smiled. He lit Constanze's cigarette and snapped his fingers at the waiter. The waiter ran to the kitchen, ignoring the other customers.

"You get special service," Constanze said. "How does it feel to be powerful?"

"I don't feel powerful," de Gier said. "A policeman is the public's servant."

"Ha," Constanze said.

"It's true, you know. I learned it at the police school. I believed it then. Later I forgot. But I learned it again. It's quite true."

"You are serious, aren't you?" Constanze asked.

"Yes."

"Let's not be serious."

"All right."

"Are you ever in uniform?"

"Yes," de Gier said. "Maybe once a month for a few days. When they are very busy at the stations and short of sergeants. Come and see me at the Warmoesstraat."

Constanze laughed. "I am having dinner with a police sergeant."

"Not now. I am just me. The Chinese owner thinks I am, and the waiter thinks I am, but I am not. I am a man who is having dinner with a woman."

She changed the subject and they chatted for a while. De Gier steered the conversation toward van Meteren. She talked easily.

"Oh, he's nice. He was the only one in that house I could rely on. Always gentle and pleasant, and always busy with something. He never hung around. And he wasn't part of the house, he kept his distance but he would always help if anyone wanted help."

"Busy?" de Gier asked. "Busy with what?"

"He studied."

"At the university? Did he take evening classes?"

"He would have liked to, I think," Constanze said, "but he didn't have the right qualifications although I am sure he is very intelligent. He read history, Dutch history. He used to borrow books from the library, he probably still does, and the librarians were helping him, telling him what to read and finding books for him."

De Gier shook his head. "History?"

"Yes," Constanze said. "Why? Why not history? He knows everything about Holland there is to know, I think. And he has been everywhere. He knows every city and every village. He planned trips and then he would go out on his motorcycle. Weekends, and holidays and all the time he could get from his boss. He wasn't enjoying his job much, I think, although he didn't complain."

"Did he ever take you with him?"

"No," Constanze said, "he never asked me but I wouldn't have gone anyway. Motorbikes scare me. I had a boyfriend who had a motorbike when I was a girl and we had an accident on it. I walked on crutches for months. Never again."

"Did you like him?"

Constanze looked at him, eyes half-closed. "Why? Are you jealous? Or is this an interrogation? Like last night?"

"No," de Gier said.

"Did you think I had something with that Papuan?"

De Gier didn't answer.

She put down her fork and looked at him. Her eyes were wide open now.

"I am sorry. I shouldn't have said that. I have nothing against color. Van Meteren was always very good to me. But as a man . . . I don't think I ever thought about him that way."

De Gier felt her foot against his.

A few minutes later she mentioned van Meteren of her own accord.

"Yes," she said, "a strange man. It must have been difficult for him to live here. He could never forget New Guinea, of course, and here he would never be accepted. People were nice to him, I think. But nice is not enough. They stared at him. Perhaps it would have been all right if he could have been a regular policeman. He would have had his self-respect. He has been a policeman all his life. Do you know he could tell stories? I laughed a lot about the story of the white official who had been sent to New Guinea as an assistant district commissioner. He had hardly arrived when they sent him on inspection and the very first time he went into a native village he ran into a tribal war. A tall thin lad, twenty-five years old perhaps, raised in a little Dutch city, and there he was with painted demons, dancing and yelling and clubbing each other. They never touched him. Maybe they left him alone because he was white. He had nothing to do with it. Big black hooligans with bones through their noses and feathers in their hair, and someone beating a drum. When it was all over the official was raving mad and they had to fly him back. He spent years in an asylum.''

"That's a funny story?'' de Gier asked.

"Maybe not,'' Constanze said and laughed. "You think the poor chap had come to maintain order. Doing his duty and so on. But I thought it was funny. Maybe you would have thought so too if you had heard van Meteren tell it. He acted both sides, the wild ones, and the official. He was really very good.''

"He acted the white fellow as well?'' de Gier asked.

"Yes,'' said Constanze, "ask him to tell the story, you'll see.''

"I will,'' de Gier said, and paid the bill. It was only half of what it should have been.

"I wonder what they are hiding,'' de Gier thought. "That waiter's papers won't be in order, that's for sure. Maybe there is something wrong with the owner as well. Or they were the fellows who hid Lee Fong.''

He wondered if he should mention the matter to the Aliens Department at Headquarters.

"Maybe not,'' he thought.


Constanze moved close to him in the car. "Let's drive to the park.''

He parked the car as close to the park as he could get. She guided him to a pond. "Crumble some bread and throw it in.''

"There are no ducks,'' he said.

"Never mind. Just do as I say.''

The crumbs hit the pond's surface and caused a strange spectacle. Great carp, some of them seemed more than two feet long, fought for the bread. The water foamed. The pond seemed full of carp. De Gier couldn't imagine where they had all come from. The smacking of their thick pink lips filled the air around him.

"Did you like that?" Constanze asked when he had finished the bread.

"Yes," he said. He thought the time had come and put his arms around her. She kissed him back and then pushed him away.

"Where do you live?" she asked.

"Five minutes from here," he said.

"Let's go there."

In the flat he asked her to wait at the door while he caught Oliver and locked him up in the kitchen. She slipped past him. He fed Oliver.

By the time he got into the bedroom she had little on.

He helped her take her panties off.

# CHAPTER 8

Grijpstra watched his wife, a formless lump under the blankets, and listened to the chief inspector whose loud voice hollered from the telephone.

The voice went on and on, connecting sentences, repeating itself. Mrs. Grijpstra's head became visible. She scowled. "Why," Grijpstra asked himself, "do curlers have to be pink? Why not brown? If they were brown they would blend with her hair, I wouldn't notice them so much, and I would be less irritated. I wouldn't have such a foul taste in my mouth. My stomach wouldn't cramp. I wouldn't have to worry about ulcers. My wife wouldn't forget to buy medicine because I wouldn't need to take medicine. I would be happier."

"Yes sir," Grijpstra said.

It was ten A.M., Sunday morning.

"No," the chief inspector said. "This 'yes sir' won't get us anywhere, Grijpstra. I don't see any progress in the case at

117

all. We aren't getting anywhere, Grijpstra. Complications, that's all we get."

"How do you mean, sir?" Grijpstra asked and changed the telephone to his other ear.

"By now we should have sufficient material to start sorting and shifting," the chief inspector said, "but we haven't sorted anything and we have more material. You said that you found another staircase, didn't you?"

"Yes sir," Grijpstra said, "another staircase and another door. The staircase leads to Piet's room. The door is locked but we opened it, the lock was simple. It wasn't rusty. Piet had a key to it and Mrs. Verboom used to have a key. Perhaps other people had or have keys as well."

"Yes," the chief inspector said impatiently, "so anybody could have sneaked up, without the girls in the kitchen seeing him. Or her. Mrs. Verboom could have used her key."

"She was in Paris, sir."

"So she says. But we have airplanes nowadays. She could have come in the morning and left in the evening. We'll have to check. Find out where she works."

"Yes sir," Grijpstra said and blew cigar smoke into the room. His wife began to cough, got out of the bed and stamped out of the door, slamming it.

"What was that?" the chief inspector asked.

"My wife closed a door."

"It sounded like a shot. Never mind. There is also the old Mrs. Verboom, do you know where she is now?"

"She is in Aerdenhout; the mental home is called Christian Freeminded Sanatorium for Neuroses."

"She is all that?" the chief inspector asked.

Grijpstra sucked on his cigar.

"Not funny, hey?" the chief inspector said and continued hopefully. "Perhaps we'll have an anonymous tip. Anything to give us a hint. A good hint. The commissaris is becoming impatient. He keeps on phoning me. You still think it is murder?"

"There is seventy-five thousand missing, sir," Grijpstra said.

"Yes," the chief inspector said, "very true. He may have paid someone. But who? I don't know. We'll have to go on, what else can we do? You go and see the corpse's mother in Aerdenhout. She is crazy but crazy people sometimes answer questions. She may speak the truth. Crazy people often do. Go and see her, Grijpstra. Today. Sunday is just the sort of day to visit a mental asylum. Do it today and you can do something else tomorrow. You have to go and see our two drug dealers. Monday is a good day to see drug dealers. They won't have much resistance after the weekend."

Grijpstra put his hand over the mouthpiece and sighed.

"Are you there, Grijpstra?"

"Yes sir," Grijpstra said. "I'll go to the mental home today. Goodbye, sir."

He rang off.

"Good hunting," the chief inspector had said but Grijpstra missed it.

His wife had come into the room again.

"You shouldn't smoke cigars in the bedroom," Mrs. Grijpstra said.

"It's a filthy habit," Grijpstra said and got off the bed. He dressed and clasped his gun holster to his belt. He took his time shaving.

"This'll be my only pleasure today," he thought morosely. "A good shave, a lot of very hot water, and a lot of nice frothy soap and a new blade. And after that a sea of trouble. A black sea. A sea. I should have become a fisherman. They sail around, early in the morning, on a black sea. And then the sun breaks, and everything becomes beautiful. But I joined the police." He cursed and wiped his face and went back to the bedroom to stare out of the window.

His wife brought a cup of coffee. He swallowed a little and made a face. "This is cold, and you forgot the sugar."

His wife stamped out of the room and slammed the door.

He stared out of the window again. The Lijnbaansgracht was dirtier than usual that morning. He counted three plastic dirt bags, a mattress, two chairs and some lesser and assorted rubbish, all floating slowly in the lazy current.

Grijpstra laughed, a dry hollow laugh. He had remembered article 41 of the General Amsterdam Police Ordination. "It is forbidden to dump any material, either on the public roads, or their adjacent precincts, or in the public waterways."

"Some article," Grijpstra thought. "The fine is probably ten guilders. I'll phone the municipality again tomorrow. They'll send a boat and two men. And there'll be other rubbish floating past on Tuesday. Dirt is like crime, the supply is endless."

He picked up the phone.

"Yes?" de Gier asked.

"I'll meet you at Headquarters," Grijpstra said, "in half an hour's time."

"No," de Gier said. "I have a date."

"You have," Grijpstra said, "with me."

He put the phone down and struggled into his jacket.

"You going out?" his wife asked in the corridor.

"Yes," Grijpstra said.

"Will you be home late?"

"Yes," Grijpstra said and slammed the front door.


De Gier was sitting at the wheel of the gray VW when Grijpstra strolled into the court. Grijpstra looked relaxed. The walk had cheered him up and he had remembered the truth of the proverb that says shared sorrow is half sorrow.

De Gier started the car as soon as his chief got in and drove off.

"Shouldn't you thank the doorman for opening the gate for you?" Grijpstra asked.

"No," de Gier said.

"In a bad mood?" Grijpstra asked.

"Not at all. There's nothing like duty. I had a date with Constanze Verboom and her daughter. We were going to the beach. Didn't you go to the beach yesterday?"

"Yes," Grijpstra said. "The beach was full. And the sea was dirty. And if you want to pee they charge you twenty cents. And the children wanted to build a sand castle and a fat German walked right through it. He couldn't help it, he had to walk somewhere. My son hit him with his little spade. He bled like a cow."

"Haha," de Gier said.

"Amused, are you?" Grijpstra asked.

"Very amused," de Gier said. "Got you into trouble, eh?"

"Yes."

"And where are we going?" de Gier asked.

"To Aerdenhout," Grijpstra said. "We're going to visit your girlfriend's mother-in-law. In the nuthouse."

De Gier stood on the brake and the car veered to the side of the road. Grijpstra had to extend a hand to stop his head from hitting the windshield.

"You aren't serious," de Gier said, "and if you are, why take me? You can go to the nuthouse by yourself, can't you?"

"I am not fond of old ladies," Grijpstra said, "and I am scared of mental homes."

De Gier tried to tear the plastic off a pack of cigarettes. "So why didn't you send *me*? I had to go and see Constanze by myself, didn't I?"

"It wasn't my idea," Grijpstra explained patiently. "It's the chief inspector's idea. And he told *me* to go. And I didn't want to go by myself. Two hear more than one, and you have to do what I tell you to do, and let's get going."

A motorcop stopped his gleaming while Guzzi motorcycle next to the VW and tapped on its roof with his gloved hand.

De Gier opened the window.

"It's all right, Sietsema. We are hunting criminals. Go and ride in the park, it's a nice day."

"Morning, sergeant," the motorcop said. "You are parked under a no parking sign. It'll give people ideas. Can't you park somewhere else?"

"Off, off," de Gier said. "We'll scratch your beautiful cycle."

Sietsema looked hurt and accelerated viciously The powerful Guzzi shot off.

"You shouldn't have said that," Grijpstra said. "See what you made him do? He went through a red light."

"Bah. He can ride his shiny monster, all by himself. Nothing to worry him. Free as a bird."

"Apply for a transfer," Grijpstra said. "Let's go."

They drove in silence. De Gier remembered the events of the night.

"How did it go last night?" Grijpstra asked.

De Gier nodded dreamily. "Very well, thank you. It was a good idea. But I don't think she had anything to do with it."

"Tell me," Grijpstra said.

De Gier told him.

"Is that all?" Grijpstra asked.

"Not quite."

"I thought so."

De Gier grinned.

"All right," Grijpstra said, "I'm glad you enjoyed yourself. I hope she enjoyed herself as well. But she could have done it. The constables found another door in Haarlemmer Houttuinen number five. It leads to a staircase and connects with the floor where Piet had his room. Mrs. Verboom, your Mrs. Verboom, is supposed to have a key to that door. And she may have flown in from Paris to pay a last call to her husband."

"We'll have to check with Paris to see if she did," de Gier said. "But I don't think so. Murderers are nervous people, very nervous. She wasn't."

*    *    *

"Where are you going?" Grijpstra asked.

"To Aerdenhout," de Gier said, "wasn't that where you wanted to go?"

"This road doesn't go to Aerdenhout," said Grijpstra.

"Ah yes. We'll take a turning to the left."

"There are no turnings on the left on this road."

"Then we'll turn around," de Gier said happily.

"You should watch where you are going."

"So should you."

They found the right road, they found Aerdenhout, but they didn't find the mental home. Eventually they found the police station and were shown the right way.

"If the civilians knew how silly their police are they would commit more crimes," Grijpstra said.

"They don't," de Gier said happily. He had reached the point of not caring. The day was lost and everything was going wrong but he only noticed the trees and shrubs of the lovely Aerdenhout gardens. Even the tarred roads seemed beautiful to him and a nondescript man leading a small dog on a leash sent a thrill of ecstasy down his back.

"What are you thinking about?" he asked Grijpstra, wanting to share hi feeling of sudden joy.

"I am thinking of my wife's curlers," Grijpstra said, "and of the missing seventy-five thousand. If somebody has lifted that money he must be spending it now. Maybe the Investigation Bureau boys will turn up something. Have they phoned you at all?"

"I phoned them," de Gier said, "early this morning, after Constanze left. They don't like being phoned early. There is a lot of money floating through town, black money, honestly earned by tax dodgers. The bars are full, the sex clubs are full and there is some gambling. Nothing unusual."

"And what is van Meteren doing?"

"Nothing special," de Gier said. "The detective who follows him phoned me of his own accord. Early this morn-

ing. He knows I don't like to be phoned early. Van Meteren
dined in a very cheap restaurant last night, the cheapest in
town, the municipal soup kitchen. He spent some thirty
guilders on the street market, buying a jersey and a pair of
jeans, and he took his time. The merchant lost his temper
with him, he had to see every article the poor fellow had on
his stall. Then he had two beers. He only paid for one, the
other was given to him by a drunk. The detective heard him
say to the bar keeper that he was going to spend today on a
long trip on the Harley."

"Anyone following him?" Grijpstra asked.

"No. I told him to forget it. It's impossible to follow a
motorcycle. Van Meteren would know within two minutes.
We waste enough time. I told the detective to take his
children to the beach."

"What's wrong with wasting time?" Grijpstra asked.

De Gier didn't answer. He was watching another nondescript man with a small dog on a leash.

"For God's sake," Grijpstra snapped, "pass that woman
in that silly little car. I have been looking at her for the last ten
minutes."

De Gier passed the small car.

"In a bad mood?" De Gier asked.

"Yes," Grijpstra said, "there's the mental home."

The mental home consisted of a number of buildings and
its roads were signposted.

Grijpstra read the signs.

"New Chief Building," he read. "Old Chief Building.
Now where?"

"New," de Gier said, but the building proved to be
devoid of human life and its doors were locked. They found a
kitchen with a young man in it, cutting vegetables. The
young man knew nothing. They wandered about and eventually found a young girl. The girl told them to come back in the
afternoon, during visiting hours. De Gier showed his police

card. The girl wasn't impressed. They still had to come back during visiting hours. De Gier insisted and used his charm and finally an elderly nurse arrived and took them to the director, a psychiatrist. They were shown into a stuffy little office and put on straight-backed chairs. The psychiatrist watched her visitors nervously, shifting a vase filled with dying flowers to have a better view, and managing to drop and break it.

Grijpstra explained the purpose of their visit.

"Foo," de Gier thought, "she looks like the chief inspector." She did, but her hair was shorter and her glasses dangled from a silver chain. Her hands were square, with short nails, and her dress seemed to be made of jute. The psychiatrist wasn't helpful.

"The lady has only just arrived," she said, "and we have her in observation. I haven't seen any reports on her yet."

"Would you mind calling the nurse in charge?" Grijpstra asked. "Perhaps Mrs. Verboom has said something. There has been a murder, you know. Mrs. Verboom may be connected with the murder. Murder is a crime that has to be solved."

Grijpstra didn't sound very pleasant; he was staring hard at the psychiatrist.

"Very well," she said.

The nurse came.

Had the patient said anything?

The patient had said a lot. She had screamed and howled and made a mess of her room.

"Why?" de Gier asked.

"We took her bag and her jewelry and locked her into a room. The windows of the room don't open."

"Is she that dangerous?" Grijpstra asked.

"Mrs. Verboom is under observation," the nurse said. "It's standard procedure."

"I see," Grijpstra said and looked at de Gier.

De Gier smiled. "We are never allowed to lock up a

person unless we have reasons to suspect criminal behavior."

"This isn't a police station," the psychiatrist said. "This is a mental home."

"I see," said de Gier.

"Did she mention the name 'Piet'?" he asked the nurse.

"She did," the nurse said. "Piet is her son. She blamed him for her stay here. She called him names. And she threw her breakfast at the wall and made a mess. I had to call a colleague and we gave her an injection. She slept, but right now she is awake."

"Can I take her for a walk in the park?" de Gier asked the psychiatrist.

The psychiatrist hesitated. "Do you think you can handle her?"

"My colleague is very good with women," Grijpstra said.

The psychiatrist's face cracked and showed some long yellow teeth.

"If I can't I'll bring her back at once," de Gier said, "but I would like to ask her a few simple questions that won't do any harm."

"All right," the psychiatrist said.

"Do you think Mrs. Verboom could have killed a man?" Grijpstra asked the nurse.

The nurse looked at the psychiatrist.

"Why not?" the psychiatrist said. "If she can throw her breakfast at the wall and fight with the staff she must be a violent person."

"Yes," Grijpstra said, "but here she is in a nuthouse . . ."

He looked at the psychiatrist. "I beg your pardon."

"It's all right," the psychiatrist said and showed her teeth again. "Go on, please."

"I mean to say," Grijpstra continued, "that here she may think that she can do anything she likes. She has nothing to lose. But when she was still living in Amsterdam her situation was different. She was restricted by more or less normal surroundings."

"Mad people have no brakes," the psychiatrist said. "They may fear other people but they will do anything if they get the chance. They wouldn't hesitate to kill, not if they are very aggressive as this patient obviously is. I am not saying that she is a killer, but she could easily be one. As you said, she has nothing to lose."

"She might lose her freedom," de Gier said.

"Did she have any freedom in Amsterdam?" the psychiatrist asked.

"No," de Gier said, "perhaps you are right. Her son kept her in her room, I am told. She never left the house."

"You see?" the psychiatrist said.

De Gier got up. "I'll take her for a walk now if I may," he said.

"Hello, Miesje," de Gier said.

The old lady turned sharply and looked at him with her small black glinting eyes.

"Who are you?" she shrieked.

"Jan van Meteren's friend, don't you remember?"

The expression on Mrs. Verboom's face changed. "Ah yes," she said softly. "I remember now. Parking police, aren't you? You made a lot of noise that evening. What are you here for?"

"I've come to take you for a walk in the park, Miesje," de Gier said and put on his best smile. "The weather is very nice. Are you coming?"

"There was a gale last night," Mrs. Verboom said grumpily. "The windows rattled. I couldn't sleep. It'll probably be a mess outside."

"Not at all. I'll show you. You come with me," he offered his arm.

"You see," Mrs. Verboom said a little while later, "it is a

mess. Branches on the ground everywhere. Quite a devastation.''

She seemed to like the sound of the word for she kept on repeating it.

''That's enough, now,'' de Gier said pleasantly. ''It's lovely out here, much nicer than inside in your room. Look, there's a thrush on the branch over there. Isn't he singing nicely?''

She wouldn't look and he held her head and twisted it.

''Look!''

''I *am* looking,'' Mrs. Verboom said. ''I don't like thrushes. Noisy birds. Piet used to have pigeons all around the house. Kuruku, kuruku all day long. They drove me out of my mind. I threw things at them but Piet told me I shouldn't.''

''But Piet looked after you very well, didn't he?'' de Gier asked.

''The little rotter,'' Mrs. Verboom said, ''he always was. He was a bore during his schooldays and he was a little stinker before he went to school. Like his father but his father left. Left me with Piet. I wanted to go on the stage, but I couldn't, had to look after Piet. I often told him to leave and live with his father, but he wouldn't.''

De Gier said nothing, walking next to her and holding her by the arm.

''Did you come to fetch me?'' Mrs. Verboom asked. ''I don't like it here. We eat in a nasty big room and there's an old woman at my table who lets everything go. She even vomits, right into her plate. Then I can't eat anymore.''

''Bah,'' de Gier thought.

''Did you come to fetch me?''

''No,'' de Gier said. ''Piet died and now you can't go home anymore, the house is empty.''

''Yes,'' Mrs. Verboom said, ''he is dead.''

She sounded pleased.

''Why did you kill him?'' de Gier asked.

Mrs. Verboom fought herself free and stopped. De Gier turned to look at her. The sharp glint had returned to her beady black eyes. The evil hit him and he felt himself tremble. Witches in the Middle Ages must have looked like that, old hags with shreds of hair hanging over their faces, suddenly appearing in an empty spot in the forest. A crow, muttering hoarsely to itself on a nearby branch, accentuated the scene.

Mrs. Verboom cackled. "Why are looking at me like that?" she asked. "You are nervous, aren't you? Just like me. I've always been nervous. That's why I am here. Maybe you should be here as well."

The moment passed. She suddenly changed and became meek and docile. He walked her back to the front door where the nurse was waiting for them. He tried a few more questions but she didn't reply, talking instead about the devastation the gale had wrought.

"Devastation," she said merrily, "terrible. What a mess!"

"Did she say anything?" the psychiatrist asked. De Gier shook his head. The psychiatrist had put on a jacket. "Lesbian probably," de Gier thought. "Women who wear jackets like that are usually lesbian. Would explain her heavy voice. Wrong hormones, I suppose. Took this job because she likes to have power. Everybody must do as she says, If she says you are mad you stay here for the rest of your life. Until she tires of you."

"No, madame," he said politely. "She said she didn't like her son and she seems to be pleased that he died but she won't say that she killed him."

"Of couse she wouldn't," the psychiatrist said. "A child won't admit to stealing cookies. It takes the fun out of the game."

"If you notice anything I would like you to phone us," Grijpstra said, and got up, "this is my card."

The psychiatrist opened the drawer of her desk, threw the card into it without reading it, and slammed the drawer shut.

"Never go mad," Grijpstra said while they tried to find a road leading out of Aerdenhout.

"I'll do my utmost," de Gier said.

Within an hour they had returned the car to the courtyard of Headquarters. De Gier bicycled back to his flat and phoned Constanze the minute he came in.

"She took Yvette for a walk," the father said.

"I'll ring later."

"Don't worry, boy," the father said. "She'll ring you as soon as she comes home. She'll go to see you tonight, she said so."

"Heaven is full of blessings," de Gier said as he put the phone down. "Stop sucking your tail, Oliver, or you'll finish up in Aerdenhout."

Oliver opened his mouth and the tail snapped back. Its end had been sucked into a point as sharp as a needle.

# CHAPTER 9

"Bah," de Gier said, "and bah and bah again."

He and Grijpstra were in a marked police car, a white VW complete with its blue light, siren and loudspeaker. They were on normal patrol duty.

"Three times bah," Grijpstra said. "Three is a holy figure, the bah of the father, the bah of the . . ."

"Don't," said de Gier, who was trying to worm his way between a streetcar and a parked tourist-bus.

Grijpstra laughed.

"One can't insult the great power above," he said. "He is there and whatever we say fits in with him."

"Who?" asked de Gier, who had got the car stuck and was waiting for the streetcar to move.

"God," Grijpstra said.

"Ah," de Gier said. "I see. You misunderstood me. I don't mind the blasphemous talk. I said 'don't' to the streetcar. It stopped and I wanted it to go on."

"But you should mind," Grijpstra said. "You are a policeman and a policeman has to do with the law, and the law has to do with religion. Don't you remember that lecture last month?''

De Gier remembered. A retired state-police general had told them about law and religion. First there was religion, then there was law. Don't misbehave for misbehavior displeases Divinity. It was only much later that the law came down to earth and bold spirits stated that misbehavior displeases humanity.

"But why are you complaining?" Grijpstra asked. "I thought that you would be pleased. Wasn't it your idea to apply for normal patrol duty today?"

"It was," de Gier said, "but we are still stuck. This is merely a diversion. I applied for normal duty today because I couldn't think of anything else to do and I didn't want to sit in the office. Tonight we go and see the drug dealers."

"Yes, we are stuck," Grijpstra said, "we have been stuck before. We'll be unstuck again."

The radio began to crackle.

A deep, slightly hoarse, female voice said the call number of their car.

"That's Sientje," Grijpstra said. "Let me talk to her." He took the microphone.

"One three," he said, "over."

"What's your position?" Sientje asked.

"Het Singel, close to the Jeroenensteeg, going north," Grijpstra said.

"Right, just where I want you. Please go to the corner of Singel and Brouwersgracht. There should be the dead body of a young girl or woman in one of the houseboats. I don't know which one."

"Crime?" Grijpstra asked.

"That's all I know," Sientje said. "Out."

"Lovely voice," de Gier said. "I wouldn't want to meet her."

"Why not?"

"She may be a disappointment."

Grijpstra settled back in his seat and held on. De Gier had switched the siren on and above them the blue light sparked silently. The narrow Singel's traffic tried to make way for them and the VW raced dangerously at forty kilometers an hour, two wheels on the sidewalk.

"Easy," Grijpstra said, and smiled.

De Gier looked ferocious, the top of his body stiffly erect, hands clasped to the steering wheel, jaws firmly closed and chin jutting out.

"A captain on a destroyer's bridge," Grijpstra thought, "plunging into the attack. A fighter pilot, zooming his powerful jet plane down into the desert to explode a row of tanks. A commando officer, all set to jump down from his helicopter hovering six feet above the ground, tommygun ready—and all the poor boy is doing is driving a little biscuit tin on the sidewalk, and he is armed with a thirty-two pistol loaded with bullets that will go haywire after fifty feet."

But de Gier enjoyed himself as he screamed through a red light. He regretted that he was so close to his goal. Just another few hundred yards.

The inevitable crowd was waiting for them, some thirty people huddled close together, muttering to each other. A narrow corridor opened and de Gier said, "Excuse me," and pushed through it.

The boat was old, a wreck, built from second-hand materials on the hulk of a small discarded river freighter. Its paint had peeled off long ago.

A youth waited for them on the plank that served as a gangway.

"A user," Grijpstra thought as he brushed past him.

Thin unwashed hair framing the face of a living skeleton dressed in a pair of torn jeans, rope-slippers and a shirt that had lost most of its buttons.

"Very far gone," de Gier thought, "hard drugs, heroin probably." He looked into the boy's eyes and saw the small pupils, contracted into black pinpoints.

"She is inside," the boy said. "Please go inside."

Grijpstra had switched on his flashlight. He couldn't see much. The curtains were drawn and the windows hadn't been washed for years. There wasn't any furniture. A small paraffin stove with a kettle, a few cups on the floor. A dirty carpet and some blankets. He bent down to study the small shape underneath the blankets.

The girl wouldn't be over nineteen, perhaps she was even younger. She was lying on her back, her mouth had fallen open and her dead eyes were staring at the rotten planks of the boat's roof.

"Who are you?" a voice behind them said.

"Police," de Gier said.

"Sorry," the brother-officer of the Municipal Health Service said. "I didn't recognize you, sergeant. It's dark in here. Just let me have a look at her."

Grijpstra made room for him and shone his torch on the girl's face. The Health Serviceman pulled the blanket down and grunted.

"Dead," he said. "Suffocated in her own vomit. Nice. If that clot had turned her over she would have been all right, but he probably didn't notice she couldn't breathe. Too busy, of course. You see, her pants haven't been fastened. Must have covered her up later, when he saw that there was something wrong."

"Stretcher," the officer said to his mate.

De Gier didn't hear. He was outside, in the street, leaning against a lamp post and trying not to be sick. Grijpstra joined him.

"I can't stand that sort of thing," de Gier said.

"Who can?" Grijpstra asked.

"I'll never get used to it," de Gier said.

"Who will?" Grijpstra asked.

"Did you see her arms?" de Gier asked.

"Of course. Pricks all over, what would you expect? Probably has three or four shots a day. Doesn't eat anymore, just drinks a bit. Thin as a rake. She would have died anyway, another year at the most." The Municipal Health men maneuvered past them, very carefully, and carried the stretcher toward the ambulance that blocked the street.

"Where are you taking her?" de Gier asked.

"City hospital," said the officer who had talked to them before. "We left her bag in the boat; perhaps there'll be some identification in it. Your doctor happens to be in the city hospital; the post mortem will probably be done before you get there."

De Gier waved and the ambulance started. They didn't use their siren; a corpse has all the time in the world.

"Let's get on with it," Grijpstra said and put a hand on the boy's shoulder. "Come into the boat with us, we'd like to ask a few questions."

They asked the usual questions and the young man answered, but on another level, perhaps from another dimension. He talked in circles and commented on what he said. De Gier remembered another boy he had arrested once in the middle of Leidse Square where he was jumping up and down, waving, shouting and disturbing traffic. In the station he had chased something, something invisible and had run with his head against the wall and collapsed bleeding. Whatever he had been chasing had gone through the wall.

"He is in another world," Grijpstra said to de Gier when the youth went into another long monologue.

"Yes," said de Gier, "but we have to find out what we have to find out," and patiently they continued their questions and slowly some understandable answers were produced. They learned his name and profession. A student.

"What do you study?"

"I study life."

"Psychology?" de Gier asked. "Philosophy?"

"Sociology."

Grijpstra looked through the boat. There wasn't a scrap of a paper to be found, no ballpoint, no books.

"Did you ever pass any examinations?"

"Yes, a long time ago now. I am a candidate."

"You stopped?"

The boy began to ramble again. He hadn't stopped, but he hadn't gone to lectures anymore.

"The needle?" de Gier asked.

The boy sneezed a few times.

"He needs the needle now," Grijpstra said.


They turned to the crime. There was no crime, the youth said, he had met the girl in the Dam square. He had asked her to come to his boat with him. They had slept together, she had died. De Gier admitted to himself that there had been no crime. The girl must have been over nineteen years old, and crime stops at the last day of a minor's fifteenth year, unless, of course, in case of rape. They couldn't even prove that he had seduced the girl. She must have come of her own free will, nobody had dragged her to the boat. And he had reported her condition as soon as he had become aware of it. No, no crime. So there would be no arrest.

Grijpstra looked through the girl's handbag. It contained a pack of cigarettes, a dirty handkerchief and a purse with less than twenty guilders. And a needle, and some heroin in a small plastic bag.

"Can I have that?" the boy asked.

"Is it yours?"

"No."

"You couldn't have it even if it was yours, we'll need it as evidence."

"Of what?" the boy asked.

"Death," Grijpstra said.

"So you have no idea who she is?" de Gier asked again.

The youth shook his head. He knew her first name, and that was all.

"Well," de Gier said, "we'll find out who she was, in due course. Goodbye for now, don't leave town for the time being. Here is my card, if there is anything else you think of, let me know."

"Do you think he cared?" Grijpstra asked in the car.

"No," de Gier said. "He may have been afraid for his own sake, frightened of arrest, I mean, but he didn't care about the girl. Life and death don't matter much where he is."

"Where do you think he is?"

"No idea," de Gier said, "and the only way to find out is to take opium."

"Shit," Grijpstra said.

De Gier agreed. He drove slowly and carefully.

"Do you care?" Grijpstra asked suddenly and de Gier was surprised. In all the years he had worked with Grijpstra the question had never come up. He looked at his chief but Grijpstra's expression was the same as ever, quiet, patient, noncommittal.

De Gier found himself talking at length.

"Yes," he was saying, "I care. I do care. I didn't like the way that girl died. We are supposed to maintain order so that society can live peacefully and rightfully and is protected against disturbing forces. Drugs disturb. That girl shouldn't have suffered, she should have had some job or other, a boyfriend or a husband, a child perhaps. She shouldn't be wandering around the city, thin as a knitting needle and full of little pricks and scars, and full of poison. But what can I do? The opium law is a joke, and whoever contravenes it is released as soon as he is caught."

"Now, now," Grijpstra said.

"O.K. Some of them go to jail. For how long?"

"For a little while," Grijpstra said.

"In Persia they are shot," de Gier said.

"Would you like to live in Persia?" Grijpstra asked.

"Let's do some work," Grijpstra said.

"No patrol duty," de Gier said. "I don't want to see another dead girl."

"No, we still have our case. We'll go and see what happened to those nice young people of the Hindist Society."

They found the boat the nice young people were living in but nobody was home and a card on the door said that they would be back at five thirty.

They tried again at five thirty.

Eduard opened the door and smiled. "Look who we have here."

"The police," Grijpstra said. "May we come in?"

"Sure. You can have some coffee. We are here, all of us."

The detectives said good evening, to Eduard, to Johan, to the fat girl Annetje and to the beautiful girl Thérèse.

"I thought you were with your mother in Rotterdam?" de Gier asked.

"I was, but I came back. I prefer Amsterdam and I can live on this boat."

"We found work," Annetje said proudly, "real work for real pay. We assemble art-needlecraft kits in a factory and we make as much in a day as we used to make in a week, and we only work seven hours."

"Not bad," de Gier said, "where do you work?"

He wrote down the address.

"You going to check?" Johan asked. "Don't do that. We are still on trial and they'll fire us for sure if they know the police are interested in what we do."

"We'll be discreet," Grijpstra said and sipped his coffee.

"Why do you want to check?" Johan asked.

"I won't have to check if you are honest with us," de Gier said. "Will you be honest?"

"Why not?" Johan said. "We have nothing to hide."

"I hope not," de Gier said, "but we may have reason to suspect you of this and that. A tin of hash disappeared from the Hindist Society, a large tin full of hash. Where is it?"

Grijpstra noticed that Annetje had become very red in the face.

"Show me where it is," he said to the fat girl.

Annetje looked at Johan.

"All right, show him."

Annetje went out of the room and came back carrying a tin. Grijpstra opened it. It wasn't a large tin and it was half full of loose marihuana.

"We didn't steal it," Johan said. "It belonged to the Society and we were all part of the Society, or supposed to be anyway."

"What did you intend to do with the tin?" de Gier asked.

"Smoke the marihuana sometime," Johan said. "You know, a little in the evening, every now and then. None of us are habitual smokers but it is nice to have it at times, on a quiet night when there is nothing special to do."

Grijpstra put the tin on the floor.

"Some money is missing," de Gier said.

"You mean the money that I took up to Piet and that he put in his cash box?" Johan asked.

"Yes."

"We didn't take it. There was a burglary that night, the thieves must have taken it."

"We could have taken it," Annetje said. "The Society owed us some pay. We might have taken it too, but we didn't."

"All right," Grijpstra said.

"Are you going to take the tin and charge us with being in possession of drugs?" Eduard asked.

"No," Grijpstra said.

"So what are you going to do?"

De Gier lit a cigarette after having offered his pack around.

"Ask some more questions," he said. "We suspect Piet of having dealt in drugs in a big way. Do you know anything? If you tell us, it'll help us and we won't give in until we know anyway. You'll save a lot of time if you help us."

"Why shouldn't we tell you?" Eduard said. "We don't hold with dealing in drugs. The drug dealers are all capitalists and criminals, selling rubbish at high prices. Marihuana and hash should be legalized and the rest should be prohibited."

"Are you a communist?" Grijpstra asked mildly.

"No. Are you?"

"No," Grijpstra said, "but I sympathize with some of the ideas of communism. Most people do, I suppose."

Eduard smiled. "A communist policeman."

"I didn't say I was a communist," Grijpstra said. "Now what do you know about Piet's drug dealing?"

"Nothing concrete," Eduard said, "but mizo soup, do you know what that is?"

"Yes," Grijpstra said.

"Mizo soup, the way it comes as a paste, without being actual soup yet, looks very much like hash. Piet imported a lot of mizo, twenty little casks every six weeks or so. It came from the Far East. We never used that much. We used a quarter of a cask a week. The rest was sold. I think it was hash. Maybe one cask in twenty was mizo, the rest must have been hash."

"The stuff in the tin isn't hash," de Gier said. "It's loose marihuana, not hash."

"Same thing, really," Eduard said. "Hash is a paste made from marihuana. But the marihuana was bought by Piet from a fellow who grows it in Holland. We hardly ever used the paste. I think he sold the paste, it's more potent than the loose stuff."

"Who did he sell it to?" de Gier asked. "Do you know?"

"I don't know anything," Eduard said, "but I think he sold it to two types who used to come to the bar. In fact they were there on the evening of the murder. Your detectives took their names and addresses."

"Why didn't you tell us?" de Gier asked.

Eduard shrugged. "Why should I have told you? There was enough trouble as it was, and drug dealers are dangerous. I only wanted to get away from the place."

"So why are you telling us now?" Grijpstra asked.

Eduard shrugged again. "You are all right," he said. "You have treated us politely ever since you came into contact with us. Maybe you are real policemen, servants of society. Maybe you really want to help."

"Thanks," de Gier said.

"What do you know about the two types who used to come to the bar?" de Gier asked.

"Not much," Eduard said. "Their names. And the fact that they drive a Mercedes bus, very expensive. They have a tape player in it with double loudspeakers. I noticed it one day when they parked the car on the sidewalk. And I didn't like them, they were obviously making fun of us."

"Hmm," de Gier said, and threw his cigarette stub through the open window into the canal.

"Don't do that," Annetje said. "It's a dirty habit. The nicotine will kill the fish, if there are any fish left."

"Right," Grijpstra said. "My house faces the water, and I can't stand people throwing rubbish into the canal."

"Hell," de Gier said and looked hurt. "I'm sorry. I'll never do it again. I'll fish it out if you like," and he got up to look out of the window.

Thérèse laughed. "It's all right, sergeant."

De Gier felt comforted and smiled at the girl.

"Are you all right now?" he asked.

"No," Thérèse said, and began to cry, "I am still pregnant."

"For God's sake," de Gier said. "I do everything wrong today. I am sorry. I didn't mean to make her cry."

"All right sergeant," everybody said in choir.

They left. Annetje saw them to the door and waved.

"Cheer up," said Grijpstra, in the car.

"Isn't this where Claassen died?" de Gier asked a little later as they were driving past a site that belongs to the Public Works Department.

"Yes," Grijpstra said, "and you know it is."

De Gier knew. He had known Claassen well, they were in the same group at school.

Claassen had shot himself on the vacant site, early one morning. The body had been found by a patrol car. Claassen had used his service pistol. Grijpstra had been ill at the time and another adjutant had investigated the death, together with de Gier. Suicide. No apparent reason. No family trouble for Claassen had no family. No girlfriend. No boyfriend. No money troubles.

Depression.

"What causes depression?" de Gier thought.

What makes a man shoot himself, on a vacant lot in winter, between two rusty cranes of the Public Works Department, at two o'clock in the morning?

"Claassen was a good policeman," de Gier said. "Serious. Intelligent."

"Yes," Grijpstra said.

# CHAPTER 10

"A proper raid," de Gier said contentedly. "We haven't done that in a long time. And at the chief inspector's orders."

"I thought we only had to question them," Grijpstra said. "To raid them is overdoing it a bit. But perhaps we can arrest them."

De Gier had managed to overcome the trials of the day and looked agreeable.

"Yes. So far they are the only suspects that we *know* are no good."

"We'll need another car," Grijpstra said. "You can stop at that café over there and I'll phone the garage."

They went into the café and de Gier ordered two coffees; the waiter wasn't enthusiastic. It was a very hot day. It was stuffy in the bar and half a dozen large bluebottle flies buzzed about at top speed and crashed into the windows, surviving their accidents and trying again.

"Get some good help," de Gier said when Grijpstra

walked to the call box at the rear of the room. "At least two."

Grijpstra came back and sat down. The owner of the café came to talk to them and offered cigars.

"How are you doing?" Grijpstra asked.

"All right," said the owner, a sad old man with a drooping mustache. "Did you hear about the fight we had here last night?"

"No," Grijpstra said.

"Then I won't tell you about it," the owner said and shuffled back to his living quarters. "Nothing to do with us," he whispered to the waiter as he came past him.

"So where do we go?" Grijpstra asked.

"I have two addresses," de Gier said, finding the right page in his notebook, "one in the Vossiusstraat and one on the Leliegracht."

"Complications again," Grijpstra said.

De Gier agreed. "They may be at neither address, they may even be on holiday, sunning themselves on a Spanish beach. But we better try both addresses."

They paid, in spite of the waiter's protests, and returned to Headquarters. While Grijpstra went to find the two detectives scheduled to help that night de Gier checked the contents of their own gray VW; the car had been used by others and he wanted to make sure that everything was still there, and in its proper place.

When Grijpstra returned with his two assistants he found de Gier with a carbine in his hands.

"What do you want to do with that?" Grijpstra asked. "The war is over."

"I know," de Gier said, "I saw too many movies. And a carbine is a beautiful weapon, it has to be handled every now and then. When it lies under the back seat it dies."

"A point fifty machine gun is a beautiful weapon too," one of the detectives said. "I used to have one in Indonesia. Ah, the sound of it. Rattattat it would go. And afterward we would eat real fried rice, with shrimps on the side, and some good fried vegetables. A good life. And to think that all I do now is walking about the street markets, sniffing about for stolen goods."

"A warrior," de Gier said.

"Well," the detective said, as if he were apologizing, "my friends were killed over there and I have been in a hospital for a while, with a splinter of a shell in my leg, a splinter of a Dutch shell, of course. But it was another sort of life. Not monotonous at all."

"This may be very exciting," de Gier said. "Perhaps you'll be climbing about on the roof of a house in the Vossiusstraat tonight."

"That'll be fun," the detective said, "providing a spectacle for the hippies in the Vondelpark. It may stop them from picking their noses, for a while anyway."

But they found no one at the Vossiusstraat. They showed photographs to the neighbors. The neighbors recognized one of the photographs.

"Moved out a long time ago," they said.

"Without registering their new address," one of the detectives said. "That's one offense we can prove."

Grijpstra chuckled and patted the eager young man on the shoulder. "We can't arrest him for an offense, and the fine is ten guilders."

De Gier parked the car close to the Leliegracht and went off on his own to have a look at the house. A lovely gable house, recently restored by the city's architects and resplendent in its seventeenth-century luster.

He returned to the car and reported.

"Those houses have small gardens in the rear," Grijpstra said. "Two of us will have to watch from there." He looked at the detectives on the back seat.

"All right," said the smaller of the two, "we'll ask the neighbors for permission. Don't forget to let us know when it's all over, or we'll be sitting there until tomorrow morning. It has happened before."

*     *     *

De Gier rang the bell and the door opened at once. He saw a wide-shouldered young man at the top of the stairs. A long-haired young man, a luxurious growth of shining golden hair hanging down to his shoulders.

"Yes?"

"Police. Can we come in a minute?"

"Do you have a warrant?" the young man asked.

"No," said de Gier, "but we can fetch one in a minute. My colleague will wait here for me to come back with it."

The young man thought for a few seconds.

"No," he said. "I don't want to inconvenience your colleague. Please come in."

Grijpstra looked about him in the living room and admired what he saw. The city's architects were top notch, no doubt about it. Thick oak beams, elaborate wood-sculpture on the windows and windowsills. The aristocratic style of the past had come to life again.

He introduced himself to the young man and his friend, who had been watching TV, but had switched the set off and got up to greet the guests.

"Beuzekom," the young man with the golden hair said, "but I can safely assume that you are already aware of my name. And this is my friend, Ringma."

"Please sit down," Ringma said, and pointed at a low couch with an inviting smile. Ringma was a little fellow with a rat's face; he was going bald but he had allowed the fringe on his head to grow and the spare hairs partly covered his small ears.

Grijpstra sat down and looked longingly at the bar that occupied a corner of the room. Beuzekom stood behind the bar.

"What can I offer you?"

"Something nonalcoholic," Grijpstra said.

"Lemonade? Tonic? Limejuice ice and water?"

"Lemonade," Grijpstra said.

Beuzekom cut two lemons and squeezed them with a

practiced gesture using a small strainer. Ice cubes tinkled. A silver stirring ladle appeared as if by magic. The glass was served on a small antique tray, solid silver.

"Have you ever been a barman?" asked de Gier, who had been watching the performance with interest.

Beuzekom smiled. "Can you see it? You are right. As a student I used to make some money during the holidays. I started as a lavatory scraper on a cruise ship, I was promoted to cabin steward on the second trip and became barman on the third. Nice work, and it brought in a little pocket money as well. Would you like a lemonade, too?"

"Yes, please," de Gier said.

"I hope you don't mind if we drink something a little stronger?"

Beuzekom poured two glasses from a bottle of an expensive brand of whisky.

"Neat?" he asked Ringma.

"On the rocks," Ringma said.

"And what can we do for you two gentlemen?" Beuzekom asked. He had sat down, in a highbacked velvet-covered chair and smiled down on his guests.

"The fellow has charm," de Gier thought. "It pours out of him. It requires an effort of will to dislike him."

De Gier made an effort of will.

"You have been convicted of drug dealing," Grijpstra said, put his glass down, pursed his lips and paused.

"That's correct," Beuzekom said, after a while. "The police are well informed. Three months in jail, one suspended. Ringma was acquitted for lack of proof. He did the housekeeping while I was away. But that's a year ago now, I had almost forgotten."

"And now there is some indication," Grijpstra said, "that you are back in the business. You may have been buying hash, packed in small casks. Hash that looks like mizo-soup paste. According to the information we received you picked up the merchandise yourself, in a house at the Haarlemmer

Houttuinen, property of Piet Verboom, now deceased."

Beuzekom nodded, gulped his drink down, and shivered. "First drink today," he said. "Always gives me the shivers."

The room gradually filled itself with a nervous silence. Its occupants merely looked at each other.

Beuzekom poured himself another drink. "Your information is correct, up to a point. I did buy some mizo-soup paste from Verboom for he was overstocked. I thought I might be able to sell it to other restaurants. But so far I haven't had any luck, not yet anyway. There are some restaurants in The Hague I have to try. I bought five casks and I still have five casks. They are here, in the house. Would you like to see them?"

"Damn," thought de Gier, who had been studying Ringma's face meanwhile. Ringma's eyes had twinkled.

"I'd like to see them," Grijpstra said.

"Give us a hand, Ringma," Beuzekom said and together they rolled five little casks into the room. They hadn't been opened and had been wound with thick rope.

"Shall we open them up?"

Grijpstra nodded.

"Don't," Ringma said. "Once we have opened them we can't sell them anymore. They are nicely closed and that rope looks very decorative. I'll never be able to make them look the way they look now. I am no Japanese."

"Don't be a bore," Beuzekom said. "Open them up yourself and be careful about it. Maybe you can get them back into their original state afterwards. If the police think that they contain hash they'll keep on thinking it unless they have been proved wrong. You know there is no hash in the casks, and I know there is no hash in the casks, but what matters now is that the police will know there is no hash in the casks."

"All right," Ringma said, and began to loosen the knots as carefully as he could. It took him a few minutes to open the first cask.

De Gier dug into its contents with a spoon and tasted it. It was no hash. He dug a hole into the paste and Beuzekom produced a long meatfork so that de Gier could get right to the bottom.

Meanwhile Ringma opened the other four casks.

"Convinced?" Beuzekom asked in the end.

"Can we search the house?" Grijpstra asked.

"But of course," Ringma said. "We have nothing to hide. But don't make a mess, please. I'll have to tidy it all up again if you do."

"You are the woman about the house?" de Gier asked.

Ringma giggled. "Yes."

They didn't find anything except cupboards full of expensive clothes, antique furniture, luxurious wall-to-wall carpets, and a few paintings of the lesser old masters.

"Let's give in," Grijpstra said. "Can you explain that mizo-soup business?"

"No," de Gier said.

"It's illogical," Grijpstra said. "What would these men do with the mizo-soup paste? And what happened to the rest of it? Didn't those Hindist Society people tell us that Piet sold them various lots of twenty casks each? Perhaps we can prove the sale, there should be purchase invoices in Piet's bookkeeping files. We might get some statements signed by those boys in the houseboat. If Johan and Eduard declare that Piet Verboom didn't use more than one cask a month in his restaurant and that he sold his surplus and that these men here were the buyers . . ."

De Gier wasn't impressed.

"It will never hold in court if the public prosecutor would allow it to get into court. All right, so these men bought mizo soup from Piet. Well, they still have it don't they? And who cares about mizo soup anyway? If we want to make it stick we have to produce evidence of dealing in drugs."

"Yes," Grijpstra said thoughtfully. "Hash is only a soft drug but sixty casks of it is a lot of soft drug. The prosecutor would be very interested. But where are the sixty casks? These five we found were planted here, in case we would ever discover the link between these dealers and Piet's Society. Mizo soup? Sure, here is mizo soup. The real stuff must have been sold as fast as it got here, maybe it never got here. Maybe they have another address, the inner city is full of little cellars."

"Well," Beuzekom asked when the detectives had returned to the living room, "did you find anything?"

"No," Grijpstra said.

"So you must be satisfied that we are in the clear. Another lemonade?"

"Not for me," Grijpstra said.

"I'll have a drink," de Gier said. "You go home, Grijpstra. I think I'll have another little chat with Mr. Beuzekom and his friend."

He winked at Grijpstra behind Beuzekom's back.

"All right," Grijpstra said. "I'll see you in the morning. Try and be on time. It can be done, you know, you mustn't give up. It's all a matter of habit."

Beuzekom had relaxed in his velvet chair and Ringma was stretched out on the settee. Grijpstra had been gone for more than two hours. Of the two bottles on the bar one was empty and one half full.

"Are you allowed to drink when you are on duty?" Beuzekom asked. He spoke with some difficulty but his grammar was still impeccable.

"I am not on duty now," de Gier said. "I only work eight hours a day, just like everybody else. I am visiting, visiting good friends."

"Ha," Ringma said, "filthy fuzz!"

"Now, now," Beuzekom said, "be nice to the guests, little mate. Maybe this gentleman is filthy fuzz but now he is here at our invitation. You can call him names when you meet him in the street. 'Fascist,' or 'SS man,' that sort of thing, and then run for it."

Ringma began to cackle.

"Mizo soup hahaha," Ringma cackled, "and they are looking for hash. They are suckers, aren't they Beuz?"

"Shut up, little mate," Beuzekom said. "We don't even know what the gentlemen are looking for. And you must respect another fellow's job. If you hadn't been so lazy at school you might have joined the police yourself."

"Come off it," Ringma cackled and fell off the settee.

De Gier waited until Ringma's cramps had subsided.

"What you told me is very interesting," de Gier said, "the story of your life I mean. So you graduated in psychology, did you?"

"Yes," Beuzekom said, "and I graduated in the shortest possible number of years. I was, the professors said, a remarkably intelligent student. But I never got a job. Well, I did get a sort of job, assistant to somebody's assistant, at about the same pay a bus driver gets. So I got myself fired. I hadn't studied to become a clerk."

"So you aren't working now," de Gier said.

"No," Beuzekom said, "I don't work. I get unemployment pay, eighty percent of my last wage."

"Nonsense," de Gier said, "this is an expensive house and you are living in style."

"Part of a house," Beuzekom corrected.

"An expensive part of a house," de Gier repeated. "Sorry. But it is expensive. High rent. And you must have things in it worth at least fifty thousand."

"Where?" Ringma asked. He jumped off his settee and began to run around the room. "Where? Where? Fifty red backs. You see fifty red backs anywhere Beuz?"

"Easy now," Beuzekom said. "We don't have fifty thousand worth of things in the house. Our guest is dreaming aloud."

"Balls," de Gier said. "Color TV, three thousand at least, antique furniture, restored, worth twenty thousand, carpets worth eight, old paintings worth fifteen. Clothes, at least five. I am over fifty thousand already, do you want me to go on?"

"You can go on forever," Beuzekom said, "but you talk rubbish. Ten thousand would just about cover the lot. The TV was bought new but I got a nice discount. The other stuff was all bought at auctions, or at factory prices, or in some other intelligent way. You don't think I am the type who allows himself to be robbed by shopkeepers do you? You can save about seventy percent markup if you know how to go about it."

"Maybe you can save thirty percent," de Gier said, "and then I can still count up to fifty thousand in this house."

"I inherited some money from my father," Beuzekom said.

"Are you working, Ringma?" de Gier asked.

Beuzekom had gone to the bar to fill his glass again and turned around halfway.

"I am a pimp, sir," he said, "but don't tell anyone. My little mate earns a lot of money. But not illegally, he even declares his income. We occasionally have a sugar uncle who visits our little mate. How much did you write in your taxform last year, Ringma?"

"Twenty," Ringma said.

"So you see?" Beuzekom asked. "My nice little self-employed charmer. Twenty red backs he earned, all with his little bottom. And some of it we spent on furniture and what have you, and it's all around you. We don't deal in drugs. Drugs are dangerous. You people caught me once. I don't like being caught. I am still a dealer, but not in drugs."

"Aren't you driving around in a little Mercedes bus?" de Gier asked. "Those buses aren't cheap, you know."

"Don't be an utter bore," Beuzekom said. "Your lot never know where to stop. On and on and on and on. That

Mercedes camper is in my brother's name. My brother is a surgeon earning two hundred thousand a year. He bought the bus for his holidays but his garage is full, you can't put three cars into one garage. So I have the bus when he doesn't need her for his holidays. I have a garage and I look after the car. I am his only brother and he likes me. Do you want to see the car's registration?"

"Please," de Gier said.

Beuzekom lost his temper.

"All right, I'll show it to you. But after that you can clear out. I haven't done anything, I won't do anything and I'll never do anything that would land me in jail again. I didn't get my brains for nothing. I deal in antique furniture, in Persian rugs, in odd lots, in anything that'll give me a good profit. Within a year I'll register my business. I have been at it for more than a year now and I am a hardworking and patient man. The turnover is growing. I thought you were a pleasant fellow when you came in and you have your job to do but you shouldn't make an ass of yourself."

"You can give me another drink," de Gier said and held up his glass.

"I'd like to shuffle around for a bit," Ringma said. "You like music, filthy fuzz?"

"Yes," de Gier said.

"Well, if you do, you can select your own tune," Ringma said and pointed at the lowest shelf of the bookcase that contained several feet of stacked records.

De Gier took his glass to the bookcase, sat down, and looked through the records. He took his time and Beuzekom filled his glass again. De Gier selected a Japanese record, showing a picture of a fluteplayer on its cover.

The flute was a bamboo flute and the music very delicate. It seemed as if its notes were altogether different from the notes de Gier could abstract from his own metal flute. De Gier remembered that he had read about bamboo flutes. Their insides cannot be calculated and each flute has its individual sound, depending on the uneven parts inside the naturally formed bamboo, even depending on the thin hairs and splinters waving about with each breath of air.

De Gier stretched out on the thick carpet and listened to the flute. He was drunk. He hadn't had much to eat that day, sandwiches at the police canteen and a bowl of hot noodles at a Chinese restaurant. The seven glasses of whisky had changed his perception. The flute made him tremble a little. He saw a temple and a wisp of a girl, dancing on a balcony, the night was very black behind her but some mysterious light showed up her movements. And the flute went on. The vision became so real that he surrendered completely to it, leaving the world of crime and misery in which he had plodded all day, all year, all his life it seemed. His thoughts were very quick it seemed, clicking through his brain. He switched off his thoughts and returned to the vision. A temple, a dancing girl on its balcony and he, the observer. He had to bundle what little force he could muster to return to the room of the house in Amsterdam. He was a detective again, investigating a crime, questioning two suspects in their own surroundings, only interested in information and prepared to perform a little act to get close to the source of the required information. He opened his eyes and sat up.

He saw Ringma dance. Beuzekom had switched off the lights of the room and only the light of the streetlamps filtering through the curtains lit the frail little body. Of Ringma's ratface and balding head nothing could be seen. Ringma danced, using small steps, hardly lifting his feet. Suddenly he crouched, making himself very small, and jumped. He jumped high, nearly touching the ceiling and landed elastically. He stood still and started a movement of his arms and hands, silhouetting against the white curtains. Ringma was a doll, a bewitched doll moving mechanically, drawing life from someone else. De Gier looked around and saw Beuzekom, still standing behind the bar, staring fixedly at his little friend.

The flute broke halfway through a note, there was the metal sound of a gong suddenly struck, the record stopped and Ringma collapsed.

Beuzekom walked over to his friend and patted him softly on the head. "My little mate used to be a ballet dancer once," he said to de Gier.

"Let's have a drink," Ringma said hoarsely, "a tiny little drink, Beuz."

Beuzekom poured him a small whisky.

"That was very good," de Gier said.

After a few minutes the conversation started again.

Beuzekom had lit a thick church candle and was observing his visitor.

"How much do you make in the police?" he asked.

"Not much," de Gier answered.

"What's your rank?"

"Sergeant," de Gier said.

"So you'll be earning about fifteen hundred or two thousand a month, I expect."

"That's about right."

"You could get that anywhere," Beuzekom said. "I think an inspector of the city's cleaners gets more."

"And what do you earn?" de Gier asked.

"A lot," Beuzekom said. "More than you'll ever earn if you stay with the same boss. Why don't you work for me? I do all right but there are a lot of things I could do if I had someone working with me, someone like you. I wouldn't pay you a wage but a percentage. You could make more on one deal, a deal taking a few weeks, than you are now making in a year. Do you speak any languages?"

"English," de Gier said.

"Fluently?"

"No, but I know a lot of words. I read it well and I have taken a course. My grammar is all right."

"How long have you been with the C.I.D.?"

"Six years."

"And before that?"

"Five years on the street as a constable."

"You should have enough experience. I am quite serious, you know. I can really use you."

"And what can you use me for?" de Gier asked.

"Not drugs," Beuzekom said, "antique furniture. Paintings. Good stuff that we can sell to the American dealers. And some black-market buying and selling. Odd lots that are sold for cash to the street markets and the shops. I'll have a proper office soon, complete with a beautiful secretary."

"What do we want a beautiful secretary for?" Ringma asked petulantly. "She would be frustrated, poor thing."

"Think of others," Beuzekom said. "Our friend may like her, and our clients may like her."

De Gier got up, swaying slightly. He walked over to the window and looked at the quiet water of the canal where some ducks were floating about, fast asleep.

"The real money is in drugs," he said. "There may be money in the sort of trade you mentioned but there won't be a fortune in it."

"That's true," Beuzekom said.

"And drugs mean the end of everything," de Gier continued. "It was the end of China before the communists solved the problem. Drugs mean dry earth, dust storms, famine, slaves, bandit wars."

"Yes," Beuzekom said, "that'll be the future."

"And you want to be part of it?" de Gier asked.

"Don't be ridiculous," Beuzekom said. "You know what's coming. You can read statistics, just like I can. We can waste our time being idealists, or refuse to stare facts in the face, but it's coming all the same. It's probably a cosmic apparition, part of the destruction of this planet. But meanwhile we can make a profit out of it and live well, if we live *with* our circumstances, not against them. If you want to fight the general trend I would suggest that you buy an antique helmet, find yourself an old horse, and attack the windmills with a lance. There are enough windmills around, you'll be busy for the rest of your life.''

"I saw the dead body of a girl today," de Gier said, "some nineteen or twenty years old perhaps. She had sticks instead of arms and legs and her face was a skull."

"Heroin?" Beuzekom asked.

De Gier didn't answer.

"O.K." Beuzekom said, "heroin. Heroin is bad for the health. So is quicksilver poisoning. Atom bombs are even worse. And machine guns, and tanks, and guided rockets. Very unhealthy. So do you want me to cry? The world is the way it is. And we are on it. We can fly to the moon but we can't stay there."

"I hope your business is profitable," de Gier said, and closed the door behind him.

# CHAPTER 11

Grijpstra left the house of the drug dealers thoughtfully. On the gracht he paused and blew his whistle. The sound wasn't very loud, but loud enough for the two detectives to hear, and they joined him within a few minutes.

"Nothing doing, hey?" one of them asked.

"No," Grijpstra said, "but de Gier is still there and maybe he'll learn something, although I doubt it. Our friends in there aren't silly."

"That's the trouble," the detective sighed. "Criminals are cleverer than we are. They also have better equipment. Nice fast cars, for instance."

He kicked one of the tires of the small VW as he said it. Grijpstra sighed as well and got into the driver's seat. De Gier had given him the keys. He drove off, dropped the detectives at their homes, and telephoned from a public call box.

"I know it's late," he said to Constanze's mother, "but I would like to drop by for a few minutes and see your daughter. She hasn't gone to bed yet, I hope?"

"It isn't ten o'clock yet," Constanze's mother said, "and my daughter is still up and about. We'll be waiting for you."

Grijpstra left the car in the courtyard of Headquarters and set out on foot. The long narrow Jacob van Lennepstraat didn't improve his mood. Its sidewalks were blocked by parked cars and he had to walk in the middle of the street, jumping aside every minute or so for gleaming motorized bicycles ridden by young mobsters taking fierce pleasure in revving their engines and missing the pedestrians by a hair-breadth.

Grijpstra gave in and walked in the one-foot-wide corridor left on the sidewalk by the parked cars. He could follow a TV program by glancing into the windows he passed. He was watching a police thriller and he saw fast cars taking hairpin corners with squeaking tires, handsome men firing pistols and shortbarreled machine pistols and one window gave him a view of a beautiful woman whose blouse was being ripped off by a bad man with a squint.

He rang the bell, the door opened immediately and Constanze's father welcomed him on the stairs.

"You are alone?" the father asked disappointedly. "Your young colleague didn't come with you?"

"No sir," Grijpstra said. "He is very busy tonight. Is your daughter at home?"

"Yes," the father said, "second door on the right. She is doing some sewing in the bedroom, she has been busy for hours. I am sure she'll welcome a break."

Grijpstra knocked, there was no answer and he opened the door.

"No," Constanze's voice yelled. "NO, please. Close that door." All Grijpstra saw was a white fluffy cloud. He couldn't understand what it was. He closed the door quickly but the movement caused a fresh draft and the cloud became even more opaque.

"What the hell," Grijpstra thought. He felt frightened. The reaction-program that his training had imprinted on his brain began to work. He was investigating a crime, dealing with suspected criminals, capable of causing violent death. His response to the sudden incomprehensible situation was automatic. The pistol was in his hand, he had loaded it as it came out of its holster.

"Oh NO," Constanze yelled again.

The cloud became transparent and he quickly holstered the pistol.

There were feathers all over the room, small white feathers. Constanze chuckled and then began to laugh.

"You do look a sight," she said, and came close and began to pluck the little feathers off his suit. "You even have some in your mustache," she said. "Here, let me take them out. You look like a white rooster."

She laughed as she worked and Grijpstra stood very still.

"I was trying to fix mother's eiderdown but the cover was too worn so I was taking all the feathers out and I was just putting them into a bag as you opened the door. What a mess. Mother won't be pleased."

"I am sorry," Grijpstra said.

"It's all right. We better get out of here, I'll clean the room later."

The story was told in the living room and Constanze's parents laughed.

"You better not tell my partner," Grijpstra said. "He'll tell everybody at Headquarters and it'll be the story of the day."

"Don't worry," Constanze said. "I won't tell anyone. Why didn't he come with you tonight?"

"He is very busy," Grijpstra said. Constanze smiled and opened a can of beer.

"Did you want to ask me something?"

"Yes," Grijpstra said gratefully. "We were told by the police in Paris who spoke to your employer, your uncle I believe, that you didn't come to work on the day your husband died."

The question caused some disturbance in the room. Constanze's father lowered his newspaper and her mother dropped her embroidery.

The sweet expression on Constanze's face didn't change. "That's right. I wasn't feeling well that day. I took my daughter to the crèche and wanted to go to work but I went home instead and spent the day by myself, in bed, until it was time to collect Yvette again. I wasn't really ill, but very tired. I was playing truant really. It means I have no alibi, doesn't it?"

"But you were in Paris weren't you?" her father asked. "You can't be in Paris and in Amsterdam at the same time."

"There are airplanes," Grijpstra said.

"Yes," Constanze said, "but I wasn't in a plane, I was home, in bed, in Paris."

"Why didn't you tell us?" Grijpstra asked.

"You didn't ask me," Constanze said, "and I thought that perhaps you would never ask me."

The mother poured the rest of the beer can's contents into his glass. Her hand shook.

"Will you arrest me now?" Constanze asked.

"Should I?" Grijpstra asked.

"I didn't kill Piet," Constanze said.

Grijpstra sipped his beer, put it down, and plucked another feather off his trousers.

Constanze began to laugh again.

"You really looked very funny just now. What did you have in your hand? A gun?"

Grijpstra shook his head and looked at her as if he expected her to say something important.

"I really didn't kill him you know," Constanze said. "I admit I have thought about it at times. He did annoy me, what with all the girls he tried to make and the way he treated me."

"But you didn't kill him," Grijpstra said.

"No. I thought the best punishment would be to let him live. He suffered, in spite of all his so-called pleasures. He was a nasty depressive little man and he was attracting a lot of trouble. To allow him to go through all that trouble was my best revenge. And I can't kill anyway, I couldn't even kill a mosquito."

"That's true," the father said. "When we have bugs here she would rather try to flap them out of the window using a newspaper. She is very soft-hearted."

"Soft-hearted," Grijpstra repeated, tasting the word.

"But you are a policeman," the father continued. "You know what people are like."

"I don't know anything at all," Grijpstra said, "and it's time to go home. Thank you for the beer."

"What about me?" Constanze asked. "You want me to go with you?"

"No. You get that eiderdown fixed," Grijpstra said. "But I would like you to stay in Amsterdam until we know a little more. If you have to leave let us know first, please."

Grijpstra walked home. In another part of the city de Gier was walking home as well. He walked carefully, worried that the alcohol in his blood might make him stagger. Gradually his condition improved.

That night he dreamt again. The little men in the bowler hats danced around him producing weird music by blowing into the barrels of their machine pistols. The gable houses of the inner city were leaning on each other, desperately trying to remain upright. Naked female nineteen-year-old bags of bones danced with the bowler-hatted little men and stopped every now and then to inject themselves. The canals were filled with mizo soup. Old Mrs. Verboom had joined the party as well, and she wasn't dressed, her breasts were shrunken empty bags of skin, she had stuck a rhododendron flower behind one ear. When Grijpstra waltzed past, in the arms of the directress of the mental home, de Gier woke up, squeaking with fear and disgust. He was wet through, fighting with his blankets, and Oliver, suddenly frightened and in a bad mood already because de Gier hadn't given him his evening meal, growled and attacked the feet that were kicking him. The wound bled and de Gier got up to bandage it. Oliver was clearly sorry, rolling over on his back and making endearing little sounds as if he were begging for forgiveness. De Gier tickled the animal's belly.

"Go back to sleep," he said and squeezed the cat suddenly so that Oliver grunted deeply, the air from his lungs being pushed past his vocal chords.

The next morning the two detectives were facing their officers. Neither of them felt well, and their eyes were hollow. The points of de Gier's usually so merry mustache drooped down and Grijpstra looked as if his clothes were too large for him.

The chief inspector studied his assistants one by one, pointing at each of them in turn with the small cigar he held between his lips. The commissaris was in the room as well, a small unsightly man with a wrinkled gray face.

"So what are we going to do about all this?" the commissaris suddenly said in an unexpected, deep voice.

"Go on," Grijpstra said, "what else?"

"How?" the commissaris asked.

Grijpstra didn't answer.

"What do you think of it?" the commissaris asked and looked at the chief inspector.

"Grijpstra is right, I think," the chief inspector said. "We'll shadow Beuzekom and his friend for a while and call them in for questioning from time to time. And we'll be watching the other suspects as well. Perhaps something will happen, someone is bound to become nervous. Perhaps we'll receive an anonymous tip. Perhaps the psychiatrist of the mental home will come up with something."

"Perhaps," the commissaris said. "Perhaps you need more men. We have more men. This seems to be a murder and murders have to be solved."

The chief inspector lit his small cigar again.

"I have a plan," he said and looked at Grijpstra. "You want to hear about my plan?"

"Yes sir," Grijpstra said.

"We'll start at the other side and we'll stir the pot till the broth froths," the chief inspector said.

There were question marks on the faces of the commissaris and the two detectives.

"I'll explain," the chief inspector said. "Piet Verboom dealt in hash. We can be quite sure about that now. He imported it in casks and pretended they came from Japan. We found the invoices but the mizo paste didn't come from Japan, it came from Pakistan. There is no mizo paste in Pakistan, mizo is a Japanese dish."

De Gier came to life.

"But sir, we found mizo paste in the casks. There was no hash in them at all, I am quite sure of it."

The chief inspector nodded.

"You found mizo. The casks you discovered had been bought by Piet from a wholesaler who imports from Japan. The casks you found in Piet's cellar also came from the same wholesaler. But the stuff Piet imported came from Pakistan and was hash. The customs must have slipped up, for anything coming from Pakistan is suspect. Perhaps the customs were busy and didn't check properly."

"Right," Grijpstra said. "The real hash came from Pakistan, was imported by Piet and sold to Beuzekom and Company. But why? Surely Beuzekom and Company could have imported the stuff themselves."

"They could not," the chief inspector said, "for they didn't have a connection. We found Piet's passport and he has been to Pakistan. We also checked with the passport people and they produced his old passports from their files. He has been to Pakistan at least twice in the last ten years. He probably showed his supplier a Japanese mizo-paste cask and the packing was copied in Pakistan."

"How much did he import?" Grijpstra asked.

"Quite a lot. Perhaps over a hundred casks in all."

"Yes," Grijpstra said, "I suspected that the five casks we found in Beuzekom's house had been planted there, in case we got wise to them.

"But what happened to the seventy-five thousand guilders that are missing?" de Gier asked.

The chief inspector looked careful.

"So far we have gone on facts, now we'll have to begin to surmise. This Pakistan business is clear enough. We have found little wooden elephants full of hash, and fruitcases full of hash, all coming from Pakistan, so why not mizo-paste casks full of hash? But hash is bulky and fairly cheap. If dealers want to make real money they have to sell the hard stuff. Hash costs from twenty-five guilders to thirty guilders a stick now but the consumer gladly pays from one hundred twenty-five to one hundred fifty for a teaspoonful of heroin. The dealer who can sell hash can sell heroin as well, the channels are the same. But heroin doesn't come from Pakistan. Piet must have wanted to switch to new and bigger profits. If he had enough initiative to locate a supplier in Pakistan he must have thought that he could also find a heroin supplier. Heroin can be found in France, there are some refineries on the south coast where rough opium is transformed into powdered heroin, which can be packed into handy little sealed plastic bags."

"Did Piet go to France?" Grijpstra asked.

"Perhaps," the chief inspector said. "The French immigration doesn't stamp a Dutchman's passport anymore so we can't prove anything. But he traveled from time to time and was away from his house at the Haarlemmer Houttuinen for weeks at the time. He may have been in France."

"Yes," de Gier said, "so perhaps he found a supplier and needed money to buy a large supply, so he scraped together all the money he could find."

"That's what I think," the chief inspector said, "and when he did have the money he was killed. Perhaps by someone who knew that the money was in the house. Perhaps by the heroin supplier. Perhaps by the customer. For Piet would have sold it to a wholesaler, he didn't sell directly to the public.''

"Beuzekom and Company," Grijpstra said, "but why should they kill him? They didn't need the money that badly, they needed the business. Why hang a man who can sell you regular lots of goods you need for resale?''

"Yes, yes," the chief inspector said. "Beuzekom has a lot of money. He is spending a hundred guilders an hour in some of the expensive bars of Amsterdam. He needs a continuous supply of heroin, not just one catch of seventy-five thousand guilders. I think you are right there. In fact, you can arrest Beuzekom if you like. I have spoken to the public prosecutor and he'll give his permission if we apply for it. We could keep both Beuzekom and Ringma for a few weeks.''

"Interrogate them separately," de Gier said.

"You think it would be a good idea?" the chief inspector asked and lit a fresh little cigar.

"No," de Gier said, after some reflection.

"Why not?''

De Gier scratched his leg. "Beuzekom studied psychology, he is both clever and disciplined. We won't break him, not even by keeping him in a wet cell on the ground floor and refusing to let him smoke. Perhaps we might break that little boyfriend of his but I doubt it. They have too much to lose. They live in splendor now and they know we have no real proof. They would prefer a few weeks of misery in a cell to losing their golden future.''

The chief inspector looked at his cactus.

"All right then, we'll stir the pot. We'll give the underworld a thorough shake-up. The goal will be to get at the drug dealers, the real big fellows, who can sell or buy drugs in quantities. I have a list here of all likely addresses. It's a recent list compiled by the Investigations Bureau. Some of the addresses are of cafés and bars but there are also benches in public parks, tram shelters, public lavatories, student hostels, sleep-ins, houseboats and houses that have been empty for some time. I'll coordinate the raids from Headquarters and we'll have every detective out on the job. The uniformed police will be helping as much as they can, I'll be working with their chief. The action will start tomorrow night but you can begin earlier if you like. I would suggest that you put some pressure on that nasty young fellow who gave you the dead girl yesterday. He is a user and he will be buying his drugs somewhere. Find out where and go from there, and keep on going until you get a nicely sized fish on the hook."

"Yes sir."

"You can go and have some coffee now," the chief inspector said. "You need it, I think."

The detectives saluted and left the room.

"Good hunting, gentlemen," the commissaris said.

# CHAPTER 12

"Oliver," de Gier said as the cat strolled past the bed, "we'll tie your paws behind your back, march you to the park opposite, set you up against a stake, and shoot you, and it will be done at the crack of dawn."

Oliver looked over his shoulder and purred.

"No, no," Constanze's soft voice said and she nibbled de Gier's ear. "I don't mean that he has to be destroyed. He is a beautiful cat and I know some people who live on a farm and who would love to have a Siamese cat. And Oliver would be happier too, he could play on the farm and climb trees and chase mice. It would be a much more natural life for a cat."

"Yes," de Gier said and reached down to the floor, found his pack of cigarettes, took one out and lit it, using one hand, for his other was caressing Constanze.

"And you can get a bigger flat and I'll be working as well so the rent won't be any problem."

"Yes," de Gier said.

168

"And Yvette can go to school close by and she would spend a lot of time with my parents."

"Mmm," de Gier said.

"You don't want to, do you?" Constanze asked and put a leg over his.

De Gier twisted out of her embrace and got out of the bed.

"It's time to have breakfast," he said.

"You haven't answered me," Constanze said.

"I don't know," de Gier said. "I'll have to think about it."

He shaved while Constanze prepared breakfast. Early morning wasn't the best time of the day for de Gier, not if he had to go to work, and he groaned while he scraped his face with a blunt blade.

"In fact, we could probably *buy* a nice flat." Constanze's voice came from the small kitchen.

"Flats are expensive," de Gier said, taking the toothbrush out of his mouth.

"I have fifty thousand," Constanze said. "The house at Haarlemmer Houttuinen was sold, you know, and the other little house that Piet owned in the South was sold as well. Together they netted over a hundred thousand and with the mortgage and the solicitor's costs deducted I still have fifty thousand. Surely that would be enough for a deposit. We might even get a small house."

"I didn't know you were selling the property," de Gier said as he came out of the bathroom. "Who is the buyer?"

"Joachim de Kater," Constanze said, "our accountant. He was very helptul. It only took him a few days. We will sign the contracts at the solicitor's office at the end of this week, and then I'll have to make up my mind what to do. Return to Paris and buy an apartment for Yvette and myself or stay here."

"With me?" de Gier asked.

"With you," Constanze said softly, putting a dish of fried

eggs and bacon on the table and switching the toaster on, "if you want me to stay with you."

"Joachim de Kater," the chief inspector said and stirred his coffee. "I remember the name. Didn't you write a report on a visit to an accountant of that name, Grijpstra?"

"Yes sir," Grijpstra said.

"But how do you know all this, de Gier?" the chief inspector asked. "You weren't supposed to question her. Grijpstra did, the night before last night I believe. How come you know who she sold her property to?"

De Gier didn't answer.

"I see," the chief inspector said. "But personal relationships with suspects . . ."

The commissaris shifted in his chair. "I think the sergeant is aware of what you are hinting at," he said.

"All right," the chief inspector said.

"It's really my fault, sir," Grijpstra said. "I suggested that de Gier should date her last Saturday. I thought she might talk a little more easily if he did."

"It's all right, adjutant," the chief inspector said. "We won't mention the matter again, or rather, I hope we won't have to mention the matter again. I believe you asked young Mrs. Verboom to stay in Amsterdam while the investigation lasts. Perhaps you can contact her and tell her that she can go now. Mr. de Gier will be able to concentrate a bit better when she is out of the way and we don't really suspect her anymore, do we?"

"No sir," de Gier said relieved, "we don't."

"Do you want her out of the way?" asked the chief inspector, surprised.

"She wants me to get rid of my cat," de Gier said in a small voice.

Grijpstra suddenly roared with laughter and the chief inspector and the commissaris joined him. De Gier shuffled his

"Haha," the commissaris said, wiping his eyes, "you like your cat, huh? You don't have to feel silly about that. I like my cat too. It always snuggles up to me when I have rheumatism in my leg."

"I prefer dogs," the chief inspector said, "but we'd better get off the subject, we don't want to embarrass the sergeant. You say she sold the lot to her husband's accountant. That's strange. It looks as if he made use of an awkward situation. A widow needing money. Perhaps a hundred thousand is a low price for that large house on the Haarlemmer Houttuinen and another little house in the country thrown in. It doesn't sound much to me but I am no property expert. As an accountant he should protect his client's interests, not make use of them. Perhaps we should investigate this de Kater."

"We won't have a file on him," the commissaris said. "Accountants are pillars supporting society. If an accountant, a chartered accountant like this Mr. de Kater, ever comes into contact with the police, he loses his ticket, and that'll be the end of his career."

"Yes," the chief inspector said, "but we can ask around. Somebody will know something about him. I can ask some of the state accountants working for the Tax Department, and one of my friends is an accountant. They all belong to some society or other. I should have a report ready by tomorrow and I'll give it to you.

"Well, that's it," the chief inspector said, looking at the detectives. "If you have anything to report you can phone me at home tonight, but keep it short, I'll be watching football."

"An owl in a tree," de Gier said as they walked toward their car, "that's what he reminds me of. Sitting comfortably while he watches it all and meanwhile we develop flat feet."

"You ought to be grateful," Grijpstra said. "I am going to telephone Constanze today and you'll be free again to live with your cat, happily and peacefully."

"True," de Gier said.

*        *        *

The young man didn't open up when they knocked on the door of the shabby houseboat and Grijpstra put his shoulder against the door and pushed it through its lock.

"Hey," the boy shouted, "who told you you could come in?"

"Police," Grijpstra said, "do you remember us?"

"You shouldn't force my door. This is my house. What you are doing is breaking and entering."

"Sorry," de Gier said, "my colleague stumbled, fell against your door and here we are. Your lock broke. Do you mind if we come in a minute?"

"I mind," the young man said. "Get out."

The detectives looked at him.

"Well, all right. I lose anyway. Nobody would listen to me if I lodged a complaint. You all cover each other. What do you want of me?"

It was eleven o'clock in the morning but he was still under his blankets on the floor. The room smelled of unwashed bodies and rotten food.

"Do you mind?" Grijpstra asked and opened two windows. Some fresh air came in, but there was little wind and it was hot outside. The heat wave hadn't broken yet and the detectives were sweating.

"What's your name again?" de Gier asked.

"Koopman."

He got up and put on his jeans and the same buttonless shirt he had worn when the detectives met him for the first time.

"Did you find out who that girl was?" Koopman asked.

"No," Grijpstra said, "did you?"

The young man shook his head and combed his hair back with his fingers.

"No. How could I? I had never met her before. Picked her up in the street, or maybe she picked me up. She didn't talk much when I was with her. I told you before, didn't I?"

"Sure," de Gier said. "How do you feel about it now?"

"Rotten," Koopman said. "How do you expect me to feel? Nobody likes the girl he is making love to to die. I am not an animal."

"She is dead," de Gier said. "Do you believe in the hereafter?"

"I believe in the here and now," Koopman said, "and believe me, I know what I am talking about. The needle has taught me many things you wouldn't know about. You *couldn't* know about it. Maybe you think you know something when you have a few drinks but to be drunk is different. Alcohol makes you talk and relax and you lose your fears and inhibitions but the drug is different. It teaches."

"Look at the mess you are in," de Gier said. "Aren't you sorry you became a pupil of the drug?"

"Perhaps," Koopman said, "perhaps. Perhaps not. Heroin gives a lot but it takes a lot in return. I used to have a comfortable student's flat and I lived what you chaps call a decent life. The drug has changed it all. Perhaps I am sorry, but it doesn't matter now. The drug's got me, there's nothing I can do about it."

"You feel better now than you did last time," Grijpstra said. "Did you have your fix today?"

"Of course," Koopman said, and walked past the detectives to wash his face in the sink. He dried himself with a drity rag.

"Where do you get your heroin?" de Gier asked.

"At the institute," Koopman said, "free and for nothing. I was picked up in the street some time ago and the health service took me to the institute. They treated me for a while and now I am an out-patient. I get a free supply every day but they are decreasing the dose and it isn't enough anymore so I have to make up the difference."

"So where do you get the difference?" Grijpstra asked.

Koopman looked up as if he didn't believe what he heard. "You aren't serious," he said. "You want me to tell you where I get my fix?"

"Sure," Grijpstra said.

"You want me to end up in the canal? Like that boy they fished up last month? They had throttled him."

"Who are they?" Grijpstra asked.

"Ha," Koopman said.

"Look here," de Gier said. "We want to know. And you will tell us. If you don't we'll pick you up. Have you forgotten the dead girl? Maybe we aren't satisfied with your explanation. You were here, and we can take you with us for questioning. We can keep you twice twenty-four hours and the public prosecutor is sure to give us permission to keep you for a week, maybe longer. You'll be in a bare cell."

"No drugs in a bare cell," the youth said to himself.

"Exactly," de Gier said.

The boy thought for a while.

"We had a fellow in a cell some time ago," Grijpstra said pleasantly. "He was scratching the walls. He got his three meals a day and his tea and his coffee but that wasn't enough for him. So he was scratching the walls all the time."

Koopman looked at him.

"What are you?" he asked "Gestapo?"

"The Gestapo wasn't interested in drugs," de Gier said, "but we are. Now make up your mind. Are you going to tell us or do you prefer to spend a couple of weeks in a cell, sitting on a chair that is screwed to the floor. You know that you can't lie down during the day, do you? The bed is fastened against the wall. There's just the chair and the four walls. And a day lasts twenty-four hours in jail. That's a long time."

"All right," Koopman said, "you win. I buy it from a little shop in the Merelsteeg. They sell Indian clothes and cheap stuff from the Far East."

"Take us there," Grijpstra said. "Go into the shop and buy. Then we come in and arrest the shopkeeper. We'll arrest you as well but we'll let you go in the street."

"No," Koopman said.

The detectives lit cigarettes. The conversation went on for another few minutes. At one stage Grijpstra had Koopman by the shoulders and was hissing at him. Koopman trembled.

"All right?" de Gier asked.

Koopman nodded.

"They'll kill me," he said. "I'll be in the canal. Drug dealers never stay in jail long. They carry knives. You carry guns."

"We haven't pulled a gun on you have we?" Grijpstra asked.

"Let's go," Koopman said.

The Merelsteeg is a narrow lightless street dating back three hundred years. Its houses are on the verge of collapsing and are supported temporarily by thick beams jutting out into the street and put up by the Public Works Department. A few houses are being restored and the alley's inhabitants are encouraged to paint their woodwork. There are a few small trees and some creepers grow up the gables. The alley almost died and it's still sickly. Koopman went into the little shop, the detectives counted to five and rushed the door. The small plastic bag was halfway across the counter.

"Police," Grijpstra said. The tall thin man behind the counter looked resigned. A small child came from the back of the shop and looked at the policemen.

"Hello," de Gier said but the child didn't reply. A woman came down the stairs.

"I told you it would happen," the woman said. "It had to happen one day."

"Shut up," the man said. There was no anger in his voice.

"You," de Gier said to Koopman, "come with me."

"Can I go?" Koopman asked when they were back in the alley.

"Sure. Here is my card. Don't change your address without letting us know."

"This isn't my day," Koopman said. "Some people came

to tell me last night that I have to shift my boat to another canal. If I don't it will sink within three days. They didn't like that business with the dead girl. And now this."

"Too bad," de Gier said and walked back to the shop.

"Why do you sell drugs?" Grijpstra asked.

"Why?" the man asked. "Why do you think? I'll give you three guesses. Because I like it? Wrong. Because I want to be arrested by the police? Wrong again. Because I want to make a little money to keep my family? Right."

"Can't you work?" Grijpstra asked.

"No," the woman answered, "he's been in a mental home. He can't get a job."

"Doesn't the state pay?"

"Sure," the woman said, "and I wanted to go out and do some work as well but he wants me to be here."

"Grovel about on your knees and mop floors," the man said.

"What's wrong with being a charwoman?" the woman asked. "I'd rather mop floors than have you in jail."

"We'll have to search the place," Grijpstra said. "You better give me what you have."

The man gave him a little tin containing a dozen little plastic bags filled with white powder.

"Any more?"

"No."

"Where did you get it?"

The man shook his head.

"Tell him," the woman said. "I am not afraid."

But the man was and they had to spend a little time on him. The woman helped. Finally the man gave in. He bought his supplies in a little bar in the red-light district.

"We'll have to take your husband with us," de Gier said to the woman.

"Be easy with him," the woman said. "His mind isn't right."

"We'll see what we can do," Grijpstra said.

That evening the bar was raided. It was raided very professionally and some drugs were found but there were no arrests. The drugs were in a dustbin in a small courtyard but nobody knew how they got there.

All week the police force worked. Detectives looking like hippies raided the sleep-ins and parks. The bars were combed. People were arrested in tram shelters and under bridges. The stations were full of suspects and the city's detectives worked overtime night after night. The uniformed police helped and the state police helped, even the military police followed up tracks and caught a few dealers in the armed forces. The net was dragged through several provinces and some echoes were heard in Germany and Belgium. Suspects were charged and taken into custody but no connection with either Beuzekom and Company or the Hindist Society was found.

"I've had it," de Gier said and climbed on a barstool in a small café. Grijpstra had been waiting for him.

"A beer, sergeant?" the barman asked in a loud voice.

"Please," de Gier said, "and keep your voice down. You've been working here long?"

"All right," the barman said, "calm down. I didn't mean any harm."

"Go and serve the other customers, mate," Grijpstra said. "Any luck?"

"Nothing," de Gier said. "Sure, I caught someone, very small fry. The charge will stick, I imagine. But not what we are looking for."

"We won't find what we are looking for," Grijpstra said, "not this way."

De Gier looked at Grijpstra over the rim of his glass.

"No? Why not?"

"The man we are looking for isn't known. He is probably new to the game, to this game I mean. He'll be a criminal but he won't have a record. He is a big fellow, quite detached from the known contacts. He has offered or sold a bulk lot of drugs. My guess is that Piet Verboom was the only man who knew who our man was."

"So why didn't you tell the chief inspector?" de Gier asked.

Grijpstra smiled.

"Why should I? I would have spoiled his game. He was looking for an excuse to shake up the underworld. And he certainly has. The action hasn't been a flop you know, a lot of people have been caught, people we were looking for."

"We, the police, you mean," de Gier said, "not you and me."

"Not you and me," Grijpstra said, "but who are we?"

De Gier drank his beer and smacked his lips, holding up the glass. The barman filled it for him.

"You are very quiet all of a sudden," de Gier said.

"Lost my tongue," the barman said and smiled. De Gier smiled back.

"Pity Verboom was such a secretive little bastard," Grijpstra said. "He never told anyone anything. His own wife didn't really know what he was up to. His girlfriend didn't. The boys working in the Society didn't."

"And we don't either," said de Gier.

"It's all over," said the chief inspector.

"Yes sir," Grijpstra said.

"Well, it can't be helped. Your case is still stuck. You can go back on normal duty for the time being. I'll keep on working on the case from here and I'll let you know if something happens."

"Yes sir," de Gier said. "Did you learn anything about Joachim de Kater, the accountant?"

"Yes," the chief inspector said, "quite a bit. I'll tell you."

The detectives relaxed and the chief inspector began to pace the floor, hesitating every time he passed his cactus.

"De Kater was a brilliant student," he said, "finished his studies just before the war. He couldn't get a job during the war but he went into business for himself, manufacturing talcum powder for the German army and mixing a little grit with it so that the soldiers would have bleeding feet. A true patriot. He was arrested but released again, probably bribed the German police. He worked for several well-known firms after the war but left them and went into partnership with an old colleague who died. So far everything is fine. But we investigated his present business a little and he doesn't seem to be working much. He has a few clients who pay him some fifty thousand a year, all added. That isn't much for a regis- tered accountant. Usually they get at least four times as much. And he has an expensive office and lives in style, paying a fat alimony to his former wife. He doesn't have a girlfriend but he visits elegant sexclubs. We tried to work out what he spends and it's at least twice as much as he should be spending."

"May not be declaring his full income," Grijpstra said.

"Of course," the chief inspector said, "nobody does declare his true income anymore, except us officials and the poor blokes who work for others. It has gone out of fashion."

"So I expect you informed the tax inspector," de Gier said smiling.

"I did," the chief inspector said, "but they were already aware of his existence. They can't prove anything, however. They are watching him, that's all."

"Where did he get the money to pay for the two houses of Piet Verboom?" Grijpstra asked.

"Yes," the chief inspector asked, "that's exactly what I asked him when I invited him to come and see me. He says it was given to him and he won't tell me who gave it. A professional secret he said. Some investment company wanting to buy a lot of houses in the Harlemmer Houttuinen. To build a hotel, I imagine."

The detectives looked at the chief inspector.

"It could be," the chief inspector said.

"Perhaps you would like to look into this," the chief inspector said.

Within an hour the detectives were on the road again, on their way to visit a wholesale company dealing in electrical goods. Its owner suspected one of his directors of embezzlement.

# CHAPTER 13

Three weeks had passed since the detectives had found the neat corpse of Piet Verboom dangling from a hook screwed into a beam. The summer was approaching its end and another heat wave had started, laming the city's life. It was Saturday afternoon. The four policemen professionally interested in the Verboom case were off-duty. But they were still interested in the open file.

The commissaris had immersed his body into a very hot bath. Pain soared through his old thin legs, the hot water eased the mean slicing rays cutting through his nerves. He sweated and thought. He had served his community for a very long time now, too long to be frustrated. His mind was calm and orderly. He regathered the facts that the case had provided and sorted them out, fitting them into several patterns. Then he checked his suspicions with the clustered facts. He promised himself that he would go and see the chief inspector again.

*     *     *

The chief inspector ran, dressed in a sky blue training suit, through the Amsterdam forest, the city's largest park. The chief inspector was sweating as well. He was sorely tempted to sit down somewhere and light a cigarette. The temptation made him give in, almost. He argued with himself. He would run around the pond again, just once more, and *then* he would sit down and light that cigarette. He would think about the Verboom case while he ran around the pond. It would be easy to think about the case for it had begun to obsess him.

Grijpstra was fishing, leant over a railing, standing on the bridge of the Looiersgracht, close to his house on the Lijnbaansgracht opposite Police Headquarters. His float bobbed up and down but he didn't notice it. His mind was on the case. It was lasting too long. He was quite convinced that he had all the facts, that he had gathered enough material enabling him to make the correct arrest. But he could not, by his own fault. He blamed himself easily for he knew his own shortcomings. He had been very slow at school and his years at the police school had been a continuous brainbreaking effort. He had studied every night to pass its examinations. But he had passed and he knew that he had learned a lot, at school and afterward, during the thousands and thousands of miles of walking the city's streets and canals. He also knew that he had a good memory and the gift to concentrate his mind. And, for the umpteenth time, he forced his mind to return to the door of Haarlemmer Houttuinen number 5 where he had waited for de Gier to ring the bell

De Gier stood on his balcony, with Oliver cradled in his arms, and studied the geranium plants in his flower box. He debated with himself whether or not he should pull out the small weed growing in an open space in the middle of the box. He bent down to get a good look at the weed and Oliver, frightened that de Gier would drop him, protested with a yowl, and extended twenty recently sharpened claws.

De Gier dropped the cat, who landed with a thump on the balcony's tiled floor and stalked into the small living room, muttering to itself.

"No," de Gier thought, "I won't pull it out." He had discovered a dark green stripe on its stem. "Perhaps it will be a nice weed," he thought. "It may grow into a bush, that's what I need, a bush on the balcony." But the weed had only temporarily distracted his line of thought. He had forgotten it now and stared at the small park behind his block of flats.

The weed had been a new fact in his life, a small fact that would cause his life to alter somewhat. He might have a new view because of the weed, its leaves bristling in the breeze.

The words "new fact," which had popped up in his mind, had taken him back to the Verboom case. They needed a new fact, to inspire them again, to make the case alive once more. A new fact might untie the hopelessly twisted knot of facts, theories, suspicions, and tracks leading nowhere.

He protested. He had wanted a quiet weekend. He had planned to visit the new maritime museum and make a trip on the IJ River in the recently restored steam tug that the municipality was exploiting at a loss, to make its citizens recapture the atmosphere of days long past, when there were still thick plumes of fat smoke on the river and life was slower and transport was powered by machines whose well-greased parts moved at a speed that could be followed and admired by the eye.

He swore, and lifted the telephone.

"He is out, Mr. de Gier," Mrs. Grijpstra said. "He has gone fishing but he can't be far for he didn't take his bicycle. Shall I find him for you?"

"No, thank you, Mrs. Grijpstra, I'll find him myself."

"Go away," Grijpstra said. But the silent shape of de

Gier's body didn't move. It had been standing next to him for at least two minutes.

"What do you want of me?" Grijpstra said.

"Nothing," de Gier said. "I am watching the ducks on the canal, and the seagulls and that fat coot over there. Can't I watch the birds? Is nothing allowed in this city anymore? I am a free citizen you know, I can stand where I like. This is a public thoroughfare. You have no right to tell me to go away. There's nothing in the law that says that you can order me to move. What's your name? I am going to lodge a complaint against you. It's about time. . ."

"All right," Grijpstra said, "you need me for something?"

De Gier didn't say anything.

"You must be needing me or you wouldn't be here. Did anyone send you?"

"No," de Gier said.

Grijpstra watched his float.

A minute passed.

"O.K.," Grijpstra said, "the last fish must have died of suffocation a long time ago. This water is dead. And I don't want to fish anyway."

He unscrewed his fishing rod and put the parts back into its plastic cover.

"Tell me, why are you here?"

"I am restless," de Gier said.

Grijpstra began to laugh, a deep friendly laugh coming from his wide chest.

"Your nerves are bothering you, aren't they? You are too highstrung, you know. Well, you know the recipe. Go and see the city's psychiatrist and get some pills. If you give him the right answers he may give you a month's rest and you can wither in the Spanish sun. There must be a beach full of policemen from Amsterdam at Torremolinos."

They were walking toward Grijpstra's house and de Gier carried the fishing rod.

"Would you like to come in a minute?" Grijpstra asked.

"You can have some coffee. It'll be cold and there'll be a nice thick skin on it."

"Yagh."

"Why are you restless?" Grijpstra said as he put his fishing rod in the corridor and closed the door again behind him.

"I just want to know who hung Piet Verboom. Is that too much to ask?"

"You should know by now," Grijpstra said.

"So should you."

"So should I, but I don't know. And yet the indication must have been staring us in the face somewhere along the line. We can't have been very attentive. It blew right past us."

"Where are we going?" Grijpstra asked.

"For a walk," de Gier said. "We could have another look at Haarlemmer Houttuinen number five; the house may give us an inspiration."

They walked along the Prinsengracht, against the traffic, giving themselves a reasonable chance to stay alive. A woman was cycling against the traffic as well, a clear offense. The lady's lawlessness irritated de Gier. He could remember the time that policemen would write tickets for simple traffic offenses. He remembered how he, himself, some twelve years ago, on his first day on the street, neatly uniformed and complete with the police brooch on the left side of his tunic, had raised his hand to stop a lady cyclist who was ignoring a one-way traffic sign.

The lady had stopped. De Gier had been almost speechless with surprise. The lady had stopped because he, de Gier, a mere youth fresh from police school, had raised his hand. She had been a rather beautiful lady. He had given her a ticket and ordered her to walk back, and push the bicycle. "Yes, officer," she had said and she had walked back, pushing the bike. What exquisite power!

De Gier didn't feel so powerful now. He was walking with

some difficulty. The heat had made his feet swell and he hadn't been able to wear proper shoes for some days. He was wearing heavy leather slippers instead and he had to watch where he was walking. The slippers tended to stick on the heavy cobblestones.

Grijpstra, on the other hand, was enjoying himself. Anything rather than being home, he was thinking. He liked the architecture of the Prinsengracht and he chuckled to himself when he saw some little boys playing in the canal on a homemade raft. But then his face clouded. He had remembered his own son, who used to play in the canals as well. His son was growing up now and he wasn't doing well at school. He also seemed to be spending more money than he should. Grijpstra was suspecting him of stealing motorized bicycles and selling their parts. He had warned the boy.

"Isn't that the house where we discovered a stock of stolen motorbike parts?" de Gier asked, pointing at an expensive corner house, an elegant structure belonging to one of the richest men in town.

"Yes," Grijpstra said grumpily.

"Why would that boy have gone to all that trouble?" de Gier asked. "Surely the father must have given him a lot of pocket money. Adventure, I suppose. Got bored, and saw a good film with plenty of action in it and thought he was missing something."

Grijpstra didn't answer.

"He won't have much action now," de Gier said. "The judge gave him a good stretch in the reform school."

"Yes," Grijpstra said grumpily.

"Hey," de Gier said.

Grijpstra looked.

The woman who had been cycling ahead of them wasn't overdressed. A pair of very short pants and a sort of scarf wound tightly around large springy breasts. Two men, work-

ing overtime, and offloading a truck, had noticed the
wheeled goddess approaching and had staged a mock attack,
rushing at the bicycle with outstretched hungry hands. The
woman, suddenly startled, lost her balance when her front
wheel struck a bad patch of cobblestones. The bicycle skid-
ded and the woman fell off. The scarf came off and the men,
overjoyed by their success, pretended to help her on her feet
using the opportunity to squeeze her breasts and pat her
bottom. The woman screamed. The ever present passers-by
circled the miniature stage and gave their comments. The
woman scrambled onto her feet, covered her breasts with her
hands, and began to cry.

A sporting gentleman understood what was expected of
him and hit one of the bad men. It was a good straight punch
and the bad man went down. The other bad man, irritated by
the smile on the sporting gentleman's face, revenged his
mate.

"Here we go again," Grijpstra said and ran toward a
public call box. An old lady had just opened the door of the
call box to go inside and Grijpstra's sudden action nearly
knocked her off her feet. She was a tough old lady and jabbed
at Grijpstra with her umbrella.

"Police," Grijpstra said.

"They all say that," the old lady said, and nipped into the
box. "You wait," she shouted and banged the door in his
face.

Grijpstra waited. The old lady's conversation took two
minutes. Meanwhile the fight spread. Two bad men against
two sporting gentlemen.

Grijpstra finally made his call.

"Fistfight. Corner Prinsengracht Runstraat. One black
eye so far and worse to come."

"Can't you manage by yourself?" a sharp voice
answered.

Grijpstra grinned, they had recognized his voice.

"I am a detective, mate," he answered. "This is a little job for the uniformed police. They should do something too, once in a while."

"We are on our way," the sharp voice said.

Grijpstra joined the crowd. De Gier was close to the inner ring, not meaning to interfere. He was waiting for a police siren, but the city was quiet, and the fight continued. One of the bad men caught a punch on the nose, grunted, and fell.

"Enough," de Gier shouted. "Police! Stop fighting."

He kicked off his slippers, moved close to one of the sporting gentlemen and put a hand on his shoulder.

"You want something?" the sporting gentleman shouted and kicked. Grijpstra jumped forward and grabbed the foot that had missed de Gier. He pulled it up and the sporting gentleman crashed into the street. De Gier had gone very pale, he supported himself on a parked car. His spine had touched a lamp post with some force and he felt paralyzed.

"Are you all right?" a voice asked and a helping arm circled de Gier's shoulders from behind. De Gier turned his head and looked into a heavily bearded face, framed by a crash helmet.

"You stop that and come with us," another voice said. A uniformed policeman was looking at the bearded face as well.

"No no, constable," de Gier said, "this fellow is all right, he wanted to help me. You want those two chaps over there, and the fellow who is going to make a dash for it, there he is. And you can pick up the other one who is sitting against the wall over there, with the black eye. And that pink lady was the cause of it all, you can pick her up as a witness and give her a lecture on clothes. If she had worn some this wouldn't have happened."

"Right, sergeant," the constable said. "That's five people in all. I'll radio for a bus. Are you coming to the station to make a report?"

"In half an hour's time," de Gier said, and rubbed his

back. Grijpstra had caught the sporting gentleman who had tired to get away and handed him over to the other constable.

"Are you all right?" he asked de Gier.

"Fine," de Gier said. "I broke my spine, that's all. There are too many lamp posts in Amsterdam."

"Did it rush you?" Grijpstra asked.

The bearded man in the crash helmet grinned. "Can I offer you a beer? I was just going to have one myself when I ran into all this."

"Sure," Grijpstra said.

They found a quiet pub and lined up at the bar.

"Three beers," the bearded man said and took off his crash helmet. "Excuse me a minute, will you? I put my motorcycle against a tree. I'd like to have her in a place where I can see her and put her on her standard."

They saw their newfound friend through the window, pushing a heavy motorcycle.

When he came into the pub again de Gier raised his beer.

"Your health! Nice motorbike you have there. That's a Harley, isn't it?"

"Yes," the bearded man said, " a beauty. I love her. But she is getting old, poor thing. She was built in 1943, you know, an old war machine. There are a lot of things wrong with her now and her sound is getting terrible. Bit I'll keep her, spend some money and time on her again. She'll be all right."

"Are you looking after her yourself?" de Gier asked.

"Yes," the man said.

"Another three beers," Grijpstra said, and sat down, smiling pleasantly.

"Must be heavy work," Grijpstra said.

"Yes," the man said. "First it's this and then it's that. I should really spend a thousand on her and do a good thorough job but I haven't been saving lately. You know how it goes, wife wants a new dress, children go to holiday camps. I am working overtime as it is, almost every night."

"What's she worth now you think," de Gier asked.

The man smacked his lips. "A lot of money. You wouldn't think so but that model is antique. Even a wreck would cost you close to a thousand and then you have to spend a few thousand to get the wreck onto the road. A clever man would buy himself one of these small motorized bicycles, you can buy very good ones for just over a thousand and they'll be twice as fast in the city traffic. These Harleys are slow on the uptake. You can do over a hundred kilometers on the highroad of course but they are slow in town."

"That's a lot of money," de Gier said, "but suppose you wanted an old machine like this in top condition, how much would you have to spend?"

"Six thousand at least," the man said. "It would be worth the money. I have often thought about it. The dealers still have all the parts. For about four thousand you could buy a complete set, and then you'd have to pay a man another two thousand to put them together. I could do it myself perhaps, but I couldn't do all of it. You need a real expert."

"Are there still any Harley experts around?" Grijpstra asked.

De Gier was glad Grijpstra asked the question for the blood was throbbing in his veins and he might have sounded too eager if he had asked the question himself.

"Not many," the man said.

"I have a friend," Grijpstra said, "who likes old motorcycles and he has some money as well. He was telling me he would like to have a Harley. I wonder where he should go."

"Seket," the man said. "He is the best man I know. And he is in Amsterdam. There's another fellow in Rotterdam and there's one in Gouda I believe but maybe this man is better. Lou Seket. His workshop is on the Bloemgracht, you can't miss it. It has a big sign on the door and he has a nice poster in his shopwindow, two naked girls sitting on a green Harley. I wouldn't know the street number but it is close to the end of the gracht, near the Marnixstraat."

"Thanks," Grijpstra said. "I'll remember it. We'll have to be on our way now."

He asked for the bill.

"No, no," the man said. "You police fellows can't make a guilder on the sly. Let me pay. I've just done a nice little job, built a kitchen for somebody I know. Couple of hundred tax free."

He winked and paid. The detectives thanked him.


"Doesn't declare his full income," de Gier said in the street.

"Who cares?" Grijpstra said. "Let's go and see this Seket. Right now."

"I have to go to the station first to write a report on the fight."

"Never mind that report. I'll phone. If they want a report they can have it tomorrow. They may not even need one. Come."

"This Seket fellow's probably spending the weekend in the country somewhere," de Gier said.

"Don't *fuss*," Grijpstra said. "He'll be somewhere and we'll find him. We only want to ask him one question. Just one."


It didn't take long to find the shop. De Gier admired the poster. Two attractive girls, both naked, faced each other. Their legs straddled the heavy frame of an old Harley. One girl was leaning back on the handlebars, the other leered lustfully at her inviting friend.

"Nice," de Gier said. "Two lesbians taking a sharp corner."

"They aren't lesbians," Grijpstra said, "they are just trying to do what the dirty photographer tells them to do. Stop ogling."

The shop was closed.

"You see," said de Gier, "he is spending the weekend in the country. On an island in the North I bet."

"If he is we'll go there."

"There's only one ferry a day."

"We'll get a helicopter from the air force," Grijpstra said.

"Ah here," de Gier said, "look. He is living above his shop. There's his name on the door."

He pressed the bell and the door opened.

A short fat man, in his early sixties, with a mane of white hair, was looking at them from the staircase.

"Mr. Seket?" Grijpstra asked.

"I am. But if you want anything done to a motorbike you'll have to come back on Monday. I have locked up for the day."

"Police," Grijpstra said. "Can we see you a minute?"

"I have nothing to do with the police," Seket said and came down the stairs. He stopped in front of the detectives and glared at them.

"Well, what is it? Not a stolen Harley-Davidson I am sure. Nobody steals a Harley."

"Why not?" de Gier asked.

"Too hard to start."

Grijpstra didn't understand.

"Too hard to start? But what if you know how to start a Harley, then you could steal one couldn't you?"

Seket smiled, showing broken dirty teeth, as dirty as his overalls.

"No mate, I see you don't know about Harleys. If you know how to start one you would be a member of the brotherhood. Harley owners stick together, they would never steal from each other."

"How nice," de Gier said.

"So what do you want to know, friend?" Seket asked and glared again.

"All I want to know," de Gier said, "is if you ever built a motorcycle for a man called van Meteren."

"I did," Seket said promptly, "the best I ever built. Brand new parts, new accessories, the lot. A riding advertisement. A beauty. About a year and a half ago. I still service the machine, there's nothing, absolutely nothing, wrong with her. But that van Meteren fellow knows how to look after her. Polishes her up like a baby."

"One more question," Grijpstra said. "How much did he pay?"

"A lot of money. A hell of a lot of money. Close to seven thousand it was, but she is worth it. I didn't overcharge him, in fact I undercharged him for I liked the man."

"Cash?" de Gier asked.

"With me everything is cash. I wouldn't even take a bank check."

"No bookkeeping, hey?" Grijpstra asked.

"You aren't from the Tax Department?" Seket asked and stepped back.

"No," Grijpstra said. "Don't worry."

"Shit," Seket said. "I shouldn't have told you nothing. Fuzz. Bah. Now van Meteren will be in trouble, I suppose. I was wondering where he got the money, but I didn't ask. I never ask."

"He is in trouble," Grijpstra said, "and so you will be if you warn him."

Seket closed the door in his face.

"Let's go," de Gier said.

"We need a car," Grijpstra said.

"What for?"

"We need a car," Grijpstra said stubbornly. "Headquarters is close. We'll get it and then we'll go and see him."

# CHAPTER 14

"What's van Meteren's new address?" Grijpstra asked as they were getting into their car in the courtyard of Headquarters.

"Don't know," de Gier said.

"What do you mean 'don't know'? You should know. It's in your notebook."

"Yes," de Gier said, "but my notebook is in my other jacket. It's Saturday today."

"What," Grijpstra asked, "has Saturday got to do with it?"

"On Saturday," de Gier explained, "I often wear another jacket. This jacket. My old corduroy jacket. And its pocket is too small for the notebook, so I leave the notebook behind, in my other jacket, at home."

"Ach no," Grijpstra said, "now what?"

"You look in *your* notebook," de Gier said, "simple."

Nothing happened for a while. They sat in the car. De Gier had started the engine. The engine turned over, quietly.

"Well?" de Gier asked.

"My notebook," Grijpstra said, "is at home. In my other jacket. I was fishing this morning. When I go fishing I put on this windbreaker. It hasn't got an inside pocket."

De Gier switched the engine off.

"I'll be right back," he said.

Constanze answered the phone herself.

"It's you!" she said. "I was hoping you would call."

"Yes," de Gier said nervously. "I mean no."

"What do you mean?" Constanze asked.

"I don't know what I mean," de Gier said nervously, "but do you have van Meteren's new address? He gave it to us by telephone some time ago and I wrote it down in my notebook but I left my notebook at home. I remember that it was Brouwersgracht but I can't remember the number. I thought maybe he had told you?"

"Why should he tell me?" Constanze asked, an icy note creeping into her voice. "Are you cross-questioning me again? I have told you that there is nothing between him and me."

"No, no," de Gier said. "I am not cross-questioning you. Sorry I bothered you."

"Just a minute," Constanze said quickly, "you aren't ringing off are you? Don't you want to see me tonight? Shall I come to your flat?"

"No," de Gier said, "no, not tonight. I am busy. Work, you know."

"You don't *have* to see me," Constanze said, her voice now definitely icy.

"No," de Gier said. "I mean yes. Later maybe. Next week. Yes?"

"Find out what you mean first," Constanze said and hung up.

"Please. . ." de Gier said but the telephone gave its two-toned note.

He slammed down the phone.

He ran back to the car.

"You know it?" Grijpstra asked.

"No. Let's go to your house."


"So now we know the address," Grijpstra said. "Anything else we need? You have your pistol?"

"Yes," de Gier said, "but we won't need it."

Grijpstra didn't agree but he didn't say so. He remembered the Papuans who had fought in his unit in Java. They would never have surrendered without a fight. He shook his head. He thought of the evening they had played their jungle song together. Perhaps the personal relationship between them. . . Perhaps not.

"Do you know how a Papuan thinks?" he asked de Gier.

"No," de Gier said, "do you know how Japanese think?"

The car had stopped. They were on the Keizersgracht and the road was blocked by a gigantic luxury bus that had stopped in front of a hotel. Japanese were pouring out of the bus. Very neat Japanese, the men dressed in blue blazers and gray slacks and strapped into their cameras and light meters, the women dressed in many-colored kimonos with wide belts made of cloth.

De Gier's face reddened.

"A hundred thousand Japanese. Did you ever see so many Japanese in Amsterdam? They couldn't all have been in that bus, there must be a machine near the door, manufacturing them. Look at it now. Another one, and another one, and another *two*."

Grijpstra looked.

"Switch the engine off," he said. "You'll stink up the canal with your exhaust. We'll be here for hours."

A very pretty girl came out of the bus. De Gier smiled at her, a nasty smile, little more than a display of teeth. The girl smiled back and bowed slightly.

"That's nice," Grijpstra said, "a nice polite girl. If they are like that I don't mind waiting."

"Yes, she is nice," de Gier said.

"A kind smile, wasn't it?" Grijpstra asked.

De Gier agreed. "There is no defense against kindness."

Another five minutes and the bus had left.

They crossed a bridge and waited at a traffic light. They crossed another bridge and waited at another traffic light.

Then they were stuck again. A taxi driver had run into the back of a delivery van.

Grijpstra got out and argued with the two drivers.

They wouldn't listen to him.

He showed his police card.

"Ah," the cab driver said, "then you can write a report. Write your report and we'll move."

Grijpstra wrote a report. It took six minutes.

De Gier had switched the engine off. He felt very calm. He lit a cigarette and watched the seagulls.

"Who was right?" de Gier asked when Grijpstra got back into the car.

"Don't know," Grijpstra said. "The van driver says the van cab smashed into him and the cab driver says the van backed into him. I wrote it all down."

"But what do *you* think?" de Gier asked.

"What's got into you?" Grijpstra asked. "Since when do the police think? The public prosecutor thinks and the judge thinks, all *we* ever do is report."

"All right," de Gier said, "but what are we going to report on van Meteren when we arrest him?"

"Depends on what he says, doesn't it?"

"He won't admit anything," said de Gier. "He has been with the police a long time. I don't think he'll say anything at all. He'll come with us and let himself be locked into a good cell, he knows we owe him a good cell at least, and that'll be the end of it."

"How is he going to explain the money he spent on the motorcycle?" Grijpstra said. "And the lie he told you about it? A few hundred guilders he had spent on it, didn't he say that? But he spent seven thousand. Where did he get it?"

"He found it," de Gier said.

"Yes. He found it in his pocket where Verboom had put it. They must have been dealing in drugs together."

"That's our suspicion, and that's all it is."

"Yes," Grijpstra said, "but the prosecutor will let us keep him in custody for a long time. And while van Meteren is in custody we'll go on searching. We are bound to find out that he has money somewhere, a lot of money."

"Seventy-five thousand?" de Gier asked.

"Brouwersgracht," Grijpstra said. "Number fifty-seven. Park the car."


They parked the car behind van Meteren's motorcycle, which gleamed quietly in the light of a street lamp.

Grijpstra looked up.

"It's a very high house," he said, "and our friend lives on the seventh floor. I remember he said so when he phoned. His light is on."

"Did you suspect him?" de Gier asked.

"I did, at first. But then I didn't know because there didn't seem to be any motive. And I liked him, I still like him. He must have been a good policeman. Very trustworthy, and efficient. I think the chief inspector suspected him as well. Did you?"

"Yes," de Gier said. "That girl Thérèse suggested that Verboom might have committed a Japanese style suicide but he was no Japanese Samurai, he was a Dutchman, with Dutch ideas. It wasn't suicide at all. He looked too neat. Combed hair, beautiful mustache. Clean. New shirt. A man who commits suicide has lost his routine. He stops shaving, doesn't look after himself. They live in a mess for a bit and then they kill themselves. The room was clean. Everything about Verboom was very neat."

"And you thought van Meteren had killed him?"

"You remember the noose?" de Gier asked.

"Yes, the noose," Grijpstra said thoughtfully. "That noose gave him away. A very professional knot, made by a soldier or a sailor. And he had told us how he had tied up his prisoners, in New Guinea. Remember?"

"Yes," de Gier said. "He told us that story because he thought we were with him. Three policemen. And in a way I *am* with him. I don't really want to arrest van Meteren."

"I wonder how many Indonesian soldiers he has killed in New Guinea," Grijpstra said.

"He was exercising his duty, lawfully exercising his duty."

"Yes," Grijpstra said, "we have some marvelous laws. Let's go."

They stood on the narrow Brouwersgracht and looked up at the house again.

"Pretty shaky house," de Gier said. "We better go easy on the stairs. It may come down any minute."

De Gier slid a cartridge into the barrel of his pistol and Grijpstra, after some hesitation, followed his example.

He was muttering to himself.

"You ring the bell," he said.

"Like that time at the Haarlemmer Houttuinen?" de Gier asked.

"Yes. I am getting superstitious."

De Gier rang the bell and read the nameplates screwed into the mouldered doorpost. There were six nameplates, only van Meteren's looked tidy, the others were handwritten or typed, some of them stuck behind little pieces of cracked plastic. "Student couples," de Gier thought, "and some old people, living on old-age pensions and waiting to go into homes. It'll be smelly in there."

It was. The door opened and they began to climb. Grijpstra rested on the fourth floor. They had attacked the fifth staircase when van Meteren met them.

"Ah, it's you two," he said pleasantly. "That's nice. You are in luck. I have plenty of cold beer. It's a hot evening for patrol duty."

"Evening," de Gier said. "Just thought we'd drop in a minute when we saw your light."

"Are you on duty?" van Meteren asked.

"Well," Grijpstra said, "no. Not really."

"Then I can offer you beer. Follow me, just two more flights."

Van Meteren pointed at a chair and Grijpstra sank into it immediately.

"Careful," van Meteren said, "that chair is old. It came with the place, it's comfortable all right. I prefer these rooms to the Haarlemmer Houttuinen really. I have a good view here, but seven floors is a lot of stairs."

"You ever forget anything?" de Gier asked. "Climb all the stairs, I mean, and then you find you have left something downstairs?"

Van Meteren smiled.

"Yes. This afternoon. I bought a pack of tobacco but I forgot to buy cigarette paper. I went all the way down, walked to the shop and bought some. And then, when I was here again, I found I had no matches."

They all laughed. Van Meteren looked very pleased. He wouldn't have too many visitors in his new quarters.

"Beer," he said. "Just a minute. I'll get it from the fridge. Should be nice and cold by now; I bought it this afternoon."

They looked around the large room which, like the room van Meteren occupied at Piet Verboom's house, had been whitewashed and hung with a number of strange objects. De Gier recognized the large animal skull, the map of the great inland lake, the strangely shaped stones. One of the walls featured a large slice of an old tree trunk. The grain of the wood stood out; it had been dabbed with red paint that contrasted with the white of the wall behind it. De Gier shuddered involuntarily. The wood looked natural enough but the red paint, sunk deeply into the grain, reminded him of blood, of a cannibal's feast, of the deep vibrations of van Meteren's wooden jungle drum. The drum stood in the corner.

"I must ask him if he still has his rifle," de Gier asked, and remembered that he hadn't checked with the armory. Van Meteren should have had the barrel filled with aluminum.

"He may still have the rifle," he said to Grijpstra.

"That's all right," Grijpstra said. "He can't use it here,"

"What if he comes back with the rifle instead of the beer?"

"He won't," Grijpstra said.

De Gier moved toward the front door of the apartment. They would arrest him in a little while, after the beer. The front door was the only way out. He had already looked into the small bedroom. It had one door only, he had also been able to get a look at the kitchen as van Meteren went into it. The kitchen didn't have another door either.

"Can I help you?" Grijpstra asked and went into the kitchen where he found their host cutting slices of cheese.

"You take the tray," van Meteren said.


"Your health."

They raised their glasses.

Grijpstra put his glass down first. Van Meteren filled the glasses again. He had brought his glass to his lips when Grijpstra spoke.

"I am sorry, van Meteren," Grijpstra said. "Perhaps I should have refused the beer but I was very thirsty. We haven't come as friends, you see, we have come to arrest you."

De Gier had moved a little closer to the door and his hand was under his jacket, an inch from his pistol's butt.

"Arrest me?" van Meteren asked, still smiling pleasantly but with the corners of his mouth sagging as an immense sadness seemed to overcome him.

"Yes," Grijpstra said. "We suspect you of having committed a murder."

"Why?" van Meteren asked softly.

"Seket," de Gier said.

"Ah," van Meteren said.

De Gier jumped aside but it was too late. He couldn't see anymore, the beer from van Meteren's glass had hit him in the eyes.

At the same moment Grijpstra's chair collapsed, due to a kick in its weakest spot. Grijpstra's hand, which was on its way to his pistol, now had to support his suddenly falling body.

When de Gier had wiped the beer out of his eyes and could, vaguely, see again, he was alone in the room with Grijpstra.

Grijpstra was looking out of the window. "Come and see," Grijpstra shouted.

De Gier pushed him aside and looked down. Van Meteren was three stories down, holding on to a thick rope.

"Your knife," de Gier shouted.

"No use," Grijpstra said. "I can't reach the rope. It was attached to that hoist above us, out of reach. He must have planned it all carefully. A perfect escape."

De Gier looked down again and saw van Meteren veering off the gable, very close to the street now. "He is back in New Guinea," de Gier thought, "getting away from the Indonesian commandos."

But he was thinking it on the stairs. He was falling down the stairs, rather than running, and when he reached the street Grijpstra was still on the fifth floor.

De Gier reached the street in time to see the Harley ride off the sidewalk. Van Meteren didn't appear to be in a hurry.

De Gier didn't use his pistol. There were bicycles in the

street and several cars. Students were coming from the pub opposite and a boat full of tourists was moving into the canal, having successfully maneuvered itself from underneath a bridge. The chance that he would have hit van Meteren or the Harley was small, the chance that he would have hit something else much larger.

He ran to the car. The key stuck in the lock. When the door finally opened the Harley had turned a corner. He switched the radio on and heard Sientje's voice giving instructions to a patrol car. He had to wait for her to pause.

"One-three to Headquarters," de Gier said.

"One-three come in."

"A white Harley-Davidson, just turned off the Brouwersgracht toward the Haarlemmer Houttuinen. Going east by the sound of her, toward the new Singel bridge and Central Station. The rider is suspected of murder. Dangerous, probably armed. Small man, colored. Registration Victory Ferdinand seventeen-seventy-two. Over."

"Understood. Out." Sientje's voice was very calm, and still slightly hoarse.

"Lovely voice," de Gier thought.

He heard her pass the message to all cars, and called her again.

"One-three come in."

"How many cars do you have to help us?" de Gier asked.

"One right now," Sientje said, "on the Prins Hendrikkade. All the other cars are busy but we have called the station on the other side of the river and they should have two cars on standby. We are also calling the motorcycles, they should be able to send two men at least, but that's all we have, I think."

"Maybe you should let the State Police know in case he leaves the city."

"We are letting them know now," Sientje said reproachfully. "It's standard procedure. Out."

De Gier blushed.

Grijpstra had got into the car.

"Well?" Grijpstra asked.

"We are moving, aren't we?" de Gier snapped. "I think I heard him turn east. At least one car should be close to him and others are being alerted. But he may have turned back through the Haarlemmerstraat."

"No," Grijpstra said, "the Haarlemmerstraat is being taken apart by public works. New drains or something. He might be able to ride on the sidewalk. Is he in a panic?"

"Never," de Gier said. "He is a proper policeman. You should have seen him ride off, as if he was going to work."

"No panic," Grijpstra said to himself. "So he won't hit anything," he thought.

"Ha," he said aloud.

"What shall we do?" de Gier asked. "Go east or check the canals? He may be on a merry-go-round, trying to shake us off, or park the motorbike in a quiet place and have a beer."

"Go east," Grijpstra said. "He must leave the city. He knows everyone is watching for a white motorbike now. And he knows the country. He has been spending all his weekends riding around. If he leaves town he must either keep on going east or he must go through the tunnel. He'll take the tunnel, Amsterdam North isn't being patrolled as heavily as Amsterdam East."

De Gier shook his head.

"I wonder if they'll see him. He'll be riding slowly. I bet he is even stopping for orange traffic lights."

"No," Grijpstra said, "don't exaggerate. He knows how to handle himself under stress but he shouldn't be riding that motorbike. A white Harley is a white elephant, even in Amsterdam. Patrol cars aren't blind. They might have trouble spotting a white Volkswagen or a blue Fiat, but they are bound to spot a Harley."

Sientje's voice came through.

"Your motorcycle has just emerged at the other side of the

tunnel. A patrol car is after him and its siren is going."

"You see?" Grijpstra asked.

"Pity we have no siren," de Gier said and put his foot down. The VW went through a red light. Two cars honked at them and a man on a bicycle shouted something and tapped a finger on his forehead.

"No race," Grijpstra said, "I have a lot of children."

"I have a cat," de Gier said.

The VW dived into the tunnel and Grijpstra closed his eyes. De Gier was zigzagging through the tunnel's traffic. The radio had stopped crackling.

"You can open your eyes," de Gier said. "Sientje is calling us."

"One-three," Grijpstra croaked.

"Were you in the tunnel?" Sientje asked.

"Yes. Did they catch up with him?"

"No," Sientje said, "they've lost him."

"Where?"

"In that new housing development where all the streets have bird names," Sientje said. "They saw him last in the Hawkstreet and think he is riding about close by now. The patrol car is still looking for him, but I think they have run into a little trouble. They have dented a mudguard."

"We'll go there as well," Grijpstra said, and held on as de Gier made the little car scream through a corner.

"Ha," de Gier said. "Probably ran into something, got their mudguard right into a tire, had to stop, get out and pull the mudguard free, and meanwhile van Meteren smiled and got lost."

"He won't be lost," Grijpstra said. "This is the Goldfinchstreet."

De Gier stopped and switched the engine off.

"No use driving around in circles," he said. "Listen! Can you hear the Harley anywhere? It's quiet here and that motorbike has a very remarkable sound, a deep gurgle."

"No," Grijpstra said.

"The map," Grijpstra said suddenly, "that map in his room!"

"Map," de Gier repeated, "map in his room. The map of the IJssel-lake. You think he has a boat?"

"Yes," Grijpstra said.

"A boat," de Gier shouted, "of course! That map is a proper maritime map, indicating depths and so on. Only a sailor would have a map like that. A boat somewhere. But where is the boat?"

"Close by," Grijpstra said.

"So we hope." De Gier lit a cigarette, inhaled deeply and coughed.

"In Monnikendam," Grijpstra said, "closest IJssel-lake's port to Amsterdam."

De Gier shrugged. "Could be Hoorn as well, or Enkhuizen, or Medemblik."

"No," Grijpstra said, "too far. We have a lot of rain here and it must be damn uncomfortable on that motorcycle. He bought it because it satisfied some need, made him think of his New Guinea days. But this is a cold wet country. He had plenty of money, so he bought a boat and kept it in a harbor close to Amsterdam. He would ride out there, park the Harley, and get on his boat. A nice comfortable boat with a cabin and a little stove. Could make himself a hot cup of coffee and soup and stew, much nicer than going into a restaurant and being stared at. New Guinea is an island, he may have had a boat out there as well. I think the boat is in Monnikendam."

"We can ask Sientje," de Gier said. "She can phone the chief inspector's house. The chief inspector had van Meteren shadowed for a while."

"No use," Grijpstra said and shivered. "Let's get back into the car."

De Gier got into the car.

"No use perhaps. Van Meteren knew he was being followed, ever since Verboom died. So he wouldn't have gone near his boat. You are probably right. His boat was his escape, he wouldn't show us where he kept her. In any case, he couldn't let us know that he owned a boat. He wasn't supposed to have any money. If we could have proved that he had money we would have arrested him on suspicion of murder. He jumped out of the window when I mentioned the name of Seket.''

Grijpstra nodded thoughtfully.

''But where is that boat? He must be on her now and the IJssel-lake is big. If he had stuck to the Harley we would catch him easily enough. Every policeman in Holland will be watching for that Harley by tomorrow. He may stick to his boat now, he may have enough food on her to last him for months and we don't know what the boat looks like.''

De Gier called Sientje.

''Headquarters,'' Sientje said, ''come in, one-three.''

''We think he has a boat and may be on the IJssel-lake by now. We will be leaving the city soon in the direction of Monnikendam. Please alert the State Water Police.''

''I will,'' Sientje said. ''Have a pleasant time. Out.''

''And that,'' Grijpstra said, ''is the end of Sientje. Another few minutes and she won't be able to hear us.''

''Two little men in a biscuit tin,'' de Gier thought, ''and the biscuit tin is going nowhere.'' He started the car.

They found nothing in Monnikendam's little port. They left the small city and followed the dikes, keeping close to the lake. Half an hour passed. They met no one.

''*There's* somebody,'' Grijpstra said and pointed into the direction of the lake. A small yacht was moored to a jetty.

De Gier put his pistol back into its holster when he got close to the man. The man was tall and had very blond hair.

''Evening,'' the man said.

''We are policemen,'' said de Gier, ''and we are looking for a small colored man who rides a big white motorcycle. A Harley-Davidson. We thought you might have seen him.''

"I have," the man said. "The motorbike is over there, parked behind that hedge. And your man is on the lake, in his boat, a flat-bottom, a botter with brown sails. But he isn't sailing, he is using his diesel engine. He left about an hour ago."

"Beautiful," Grijpstra said.

"Did he know you were after him?" the man asked.

"He did," de Gier said.

The man shook his head.

"Strange. He seemed quite calm. He even talked to me for a minute. Said he couldn't sleep and was going to spend the night on the water."

"Do you know him at all?" Grijpstra asked.

"Not very well, but his boat has been here for about a year now, we share the jetty, it belongs to a retired fisherman. I have often talked to your man, he is a Papuan isn't he? I always thought he was a very likable fellow, I even asked him to come to dinner once but he refused and I didn't try again."

"Oh, he is a likable fellow all right," de Gier said, "but he is suspected of having committed a murder. We'll have to go after him. Can we use your boat?"

The man smiled.

"Why ask?" he said. "I couldn't refuse anyway. A civilian has to assist a policeman at the first request. That's the law, isn't it?"

Grijpstra smiled as well.

"That's the law. But a civilian can refuse if there is any risk to the safety of his person. So we are only asking for the boat. You don't have to come with us. Just explain to us how we should handle your yacht."

"That's all right," the man said, "I'll come with you. I may be of use. I can handle the boat and I used to be an officer in the commandos. My name is Runau."

They shook hands.

De Gier had gone back to the car, grinning to himself. He

brought out the carbine and its six spare magazines, the searchlight and a rope with a heavy metal hook attached to one end.

He had to make another trip to fetch the large tin marked with a Red Cross.

"I hope we won't have to use the tin," he thought.

"You didn't have to bring all that," Runau said when de Gier clambered aboard. "I've got everything on this boat. Everything except the carbine of course." He took the weapon from de Gier and handled it lovingly. "Long time since I've had one in my hands. Much nicer than a rifle but not as deadly. I used to be pretty good with a carbine."

"Give it here," de Gier said. "We shouldn't lead you into temptation."

Runau laughed. "You aren't tempting me. I wouldn't aim it at a man, not even at a bird. I may have been a commando but I respect life."

"So do we," Grijpstra said. "You wouldn't have any coffee aboard, would you?"

"Plenty of coffee," Runau said, and started the yacht's engine. De Gier untied the mooring rope and the slender vessel nosed its way toward the lake.

"Were you going to spend the night on the water as well?" Grijpstra asked.

"Yes," Runau said grimly. "My wife and I don't get on very well lately. I don't always go home after work. It's peaceful out here."

"I see," Grijpstra said.

They watched de Gier rummaging about on the yacht's deck. De Gier was still grinning to himself.

"Your colleague seems to be enjoying himself," Runau said.

"He does. He is an adventurer. This is different to patrolling the streets. He is still a little boy at heart and he reads too many books."

Runau moved the throttle and the yacht increased her

speed noticeably. "We all are little boys at heart," he said.

"Hmm," Grijpstra said. "Will you be divorcing your wife?"

Runau was looking straight ahead. He looked suddenly tired.

"I think so."

"Any children?"

"No," Runau said. "We haven't been married very long. She is very young, we were going to wait."

"I see," Grijpstra said.

"Nice night, isn't it?" de Gier asked, sticking his head into the cabin. He was rubbing his hands. "Show me where the coffee is and I'll make it."

De Gier busied himself with the small paraffin burner. When the coffee was ready Runau switched the engine off and they listened.

"Can't hear anything," Runau said. "He must have gone the other way. His engine is noisy and the sound carries far on the lake. We'll bear north for a while, he won't have gone south toward Amsterdam, not if he wants to get away. Has he really murdered somebody?"

"We think he has," de Gier said. "He may have been dealing in drugs and we think he has killed his partner. Hung him, making it look like suicide."

"Hung him?" Runau asked. "That's a nasty way to kill somebody. I thought a Papuan would prefer a knife, or a bow and arrows, or a blowpipe."

"He stunned him before he hung him," Grijpstra said.

"That botter he is sailing, is she fast?" de Gier asked.

Runau shook his head.

"Not very fast. This boat is much faster, but the botter is nicer. She has a lot of character, that boat. Must have cost him money too. A restored boat, some sixty or eighty years old, but the engine is brand new."

"This is a nice boat too," Grijpstra said.

"She is all right," Runau said, "but I would prefer the

botter. This is just a little thing for pleasure. I work for the municipality and I don't earn very much. I had to save for years to buy this one but I should have bought a bigger boat. I'd like to cross the ocean one day; this boat will never make it. The botter could make it, if her deck is sealed properly."

Grijpstra laughed. "Van Meteren may be on his way to New Guinea. We better warn the Water Police to watch the locks in the dike."

"He won't make the dike," Runau said. "We'll find him before he does. Pity I don't have a radio on board."

"That's all right," de Gier said. "The Water Police have been alerted. We'll catch him on the lake, unless, of course, he makes for another port and gets off his boat."

"He won't," Grijpstra said.

Runau had switched the engine off again and raised a finger. They listened.

"You hear?"

"Yes," they said. The heavy plof plof plof of the diesel engine was clearly audible.

"Bah," Grijpstra said, "we need a radio now. The Water Police are watching but they don't know *what* they are watching."

"There she is," Runau said.

The boat was no more than a black dot on the horizon. Runau got his binoculars and the dot became a little bigger.

"He has a rifle," de Gier said suddenly.

"A what?"

"A rifle," de Gier repeated, "a Lee Enfield rifle. He must be a crack shot with it and I am sure he has hundreds of cartridges."

"But how . . .?"

"Smuggled it from New Guinea," Grijpstra explained. "We knew he had it but he said it was a souvenir and we let him keep it. Never be kind to anyone. Now he'll kill us with his souvenir."

"We have the carbine," de Gier said.

"No match for a Lee Enfield," Grijpstra said. "Tell you what—let's just follow him, keeping out of range. It may take a long time but the Water Police will come eventually."

"You could go back to the coast," Runau said, "and make contact with the Water Police. They have some small planes as well."

"No," de Gier said, "I prefer to catch up with him and tell him to surrender. He is a reasonable man and he will have to give himself up. If he starts shooting we can always duck."

Runau laughed. "That's commando talk. I am with you."

They were both looking at Grijpstra.

"All right," Grijpstra said.

"More coffee," Runau said and filled their cups. "I am beginning to enjoy this. Better than filling in forms at the office."

The botter was visible now. They saw the thick line of its single mast and a thin short line at the rudder.

"That's him," de Gier said and lifted the carbine. "He must know that it's us."

He aimed the carbine's barrel at the moon and fired. "We are in range already," Grijpstra said. "If he knows how to handle his rifle he can have us with three bullets."

They heard the shot, van Meteren's bullet whined past them.

"That's a warning shot as well," Runau said. "Two meters off at least."

"We'll impress him," Grijpstra said.

De Gier gave Runau his pistol and together they fired a ragged salvo at the moon. The crack of the carbine swallowed the small explosions of the pistol cartridges.

They were close now, sixty meters at the most, going into the same direction.

"Careful," de Gier said and ducked.

Van Meteren fired three times, the bullets just missed.

"He is serious now," Runau said.

"Not really serious," Grijpstra answered. "He missed us didn't he?"

"Hello," van Meteren called.

"Yes?" Grijpstra's voice was very pleasant.

"You can stand up," van Meteren shouted. "I want to talk to you. I won't fire."

"That's all right, friend," Grijpstra shouted, he got up, de Gier and Runau following his example.

"I can hit you easily from here," van Meteren shouted. "I have enough ammunition on board to keep it up all day, far more than you have. But I don't want to kill you. Go away and let me go."

"We can't," Grijpstra said, his deep voice being carried by the still air above the water.

"You are suspected of having committed a murder, van Meteren. It's the most serious crime our law knows. You have to surrender or we'll be following you until the Water Police catch up with you. We would prefer you to surrender now. If you hit or wound us you'll be in worse trouble than you are now."

Van Meteren looked at him. He was holding the rifle. De Gier was holding the carbine.

"You are crazy," van Meteren shouted. "I am a better shot than any of you. This rifle is powerful, I can shoot holes in your boat."

"Surrender," de Gier shouted. "Put your rifle down."

"No. I want you to go into the cabin and sit on the table. I am going to approach from behind and sink your boat. Then I'll drop my rubber dinghy and sail away. I'll phone the Water Police and tell them where you are."

"You'll be caught anyway," de Gier shouted.

"Not necessarily," van Meteren said. "Please go into your cabin. Sit on the table. I'll aim as low as I can."

Grijpstra and Runau went into the cabin. De Gier pretended to follow but he turned at the last moment. Van Meteren had been expecting the shot. The bullet missed him by at least a foot.

De Gier wanted to fire again but Grijpstra pulled him into the cabin.

"Idiot," Grijpstra said.

De Gier breathed deeply and got onto the table. They heard the botter turn around and the Lee Enfield began to fire, slowly and methodically. Five holes appeared near the yacht's rudder, a few inches above the waterline.

Van Meteren wasn't satisfied.

The next five holes were lower.

"Good work," Runau said. "We'll sink for sure. I hope the dinghy isn't too small."

The botter's diesel accelerated. De Gier jumped off the table, aimed and emptied his carbine's clip. He had been so quick that Grijpstra's hand hit his shoulder when the last bullet had left the carbine's barrel.

"Fool," Grijpstra roared.

"I hit him," de Gier said. "The first shot got him. In the shoulder. I saw him go down."

"Not very nice," Runau said. "He was aiming at the boat. You aimed at his body."

De Gier didn't answer. His face was very pale, he was staring at the botter.

"Are you hurt, van Meteren?" Grijpstra shouted. There was no answer.

"Are you hurt?"

"I am," van Meteren's voice came back.

"We are coming," de Gier shouted. "Don't move."

"I'll swim to the botter," Runau said and stripped. Within five minutes they were all in the botter. Van Meteren was stretched out on the floor of his cabin. His sheepskin-lined windbreaker was soaked with blood.

# CHAPTER 15

"Right," Grijpstra said. "I'll keep him covered while you get the bandages."

"Can I help?" Runau asked.

Grijpstra looked at the yacht, now tied up to the botter. The surface of the lake was still calm but soon the early morning breeze would start up and small waves would be lapping against the yacht's side, flooding it slowly.

"You see if you can save your boat," Grijpstra said. "Maybe you can block the holes."

"Hey," van Meteren said.

The three men looked at the Papuan's face.

"Look in the bottom drawer," van Meteren said, pointing at the cabin's port wall. "You'll find some rubber sheeting in there I use for repairing the dinghy with, and some cleaning rags. You could twist them into the yacht's holes. She'll still leak, but not too badly."

"Go ahead," Grijpstra said to Runau.

While Runau rummaged through the chest of drawers de

Gier fetched the Red Cross tin from the yacht's cabin, staying as far away as he could from the rear of the boat.

Runau joined him, with an armful of cleaning rags.

"I'll wait for you here," Runau said. "Bandage him up and then you can come and stand on the front deck while I try to do something about the holes. It would be better if Grijpstra came as well. He is nice and heavy and can stand on the front deck with you, but somebody will have to watch van Meteren."

"I was lucky," de Gier said. His mouth twitched a little.

"You mean that you didn't shoot him through the head?"

"Yes," de Gier said. "I was aiming for his shoulder but I didn't have much time."

"Maybe you weren't lucky," Runau said. "Maybe you are a good shot. Have you had a lot of practice with the carbine?"

"Yes," de Gier said. "I try to go to the rifle range at least twice a month."

"Keep it up," Runau said. "I don't think I could have hit him in the shoulder, not even when I was in training."

"Very good," van Meteren said.

"What do you mean?" Grijpstra asked.

"You are pointing your pistol at me," van Meteren said, "and I am on the floor, bleeding. A friend of mine got killed in New Guinea because he wasn't paying sufficient attention to a wounded prisoner. The man looked harmless enough, leaning against a tree and bleeding like a slaughtered pig, but he had a revolver and he shot my friend."

"Have you got a revolver?" Grijpstra asked.

Van Meteren tried to change his position and grimaced with pain. "Yes," he said, "under my armpit, very close to the wound."

De Gier had come in. He put his left hand under van Meteren's head, lifting it a little off the floor.

Grijpstra threw him a small cushion.

"That's better," said van Meteren. "Take my revolver and then we can get the jacket off. The wound isn't dangerous, I think. The lung hasn't been touched, it may be just a flesh wound but it's certainly bleeding. Perhaps you can stop the blood."

De Gier worked quietly, bandaging the wound and fastening the gauze with metal clips. He made a sling for van Meteren's arm.

Van Meteren's teeth chattered.

"Are you in bad pain?" de Gier asked.

"It's beginning to hurt now," van Meteren said.

"Shock," Grijpstra said. "Give him one of the pills from the tin."

Van Meteren swallowed the pill and de Gier poured him a mugful of tea from a thermos flask he had found in the cabin.

"I'll be all right," van Meteren said. "I have had shock before. Very hard to control. I have been knifed during a jungle patrol, didn't see the man coming. My teeth chattered for hours afterwards. They were all laughing at me but I couldn't stop."

"To be knifed isn't very funny," Grijpstra said.

"The man who knifed me got shot in the stomach," van Meteren said. "That isn't funny either. He was dead by the time we got back to camp and he had been howling all the time he was on the stretcher. A sergeant from Ambon. Very tough fellow, a commando. Most of the Indonesian commandos came from Ambon."

Runau came back.

"How's the yacht?" Grijpstra asked.

"She won't sink," Runau said, "but our friend did a neat job."

"I am sorry," van Meteren said. He looked sorry and Runau went over and patted him on the sound shoulder.

"Don't worry, friend. The yacht is insured. A bit of welding and she'll be as good as new."

De Gier had been watching van Meteren's face. The Papuan seemed much calmer now.

"You look better," de Gier said.

"So do you, de Gier," Grijpstra said. "You've got some color in your face again. Now let's get going, we'll have to get this chap to the hospital. He isn't coughing blood so his lung is probably all right, as he says, but there is a bullet in him and it should come out. Will you take the boat back for us, Runau?"

"Sir," Runau said and left the cabin.

"Nice military fellow," Grijpstra said. "Calls me Sir and all. Does as I tell him. I wish you'd behave like that, de Gier."

"You'd be in a dinghy now," de Gier said.

Van Meteren laughed.

"How did you know I was on this boat?" he asked.

"Grijpstra's idea," de Gier said. "You remember the map you have on your wall?"

"Yes," van Meteren said, "silly of me. Very silly. Never thought of it. A maritime map. I used to look at it a lot, plan all my trips on it."

"If it hadn't been the map it would have been something else. Somebody would have caught you sooner or later. The State Police were alerted and we knew what you looked like. We found Seket as well, there's always something that connects."

"How did you find Seket?" van Meteren asked.

De Gier told him.

"I couldn't help *that*," van Meteren said.

"Didn't say you could," de Gier said.

"No." Van Meteren grinned. "Perhaps I should have controlled my greed, but I always wanted to have a motorcycle and a Harley is the biggest motorcycle you can get. Still, you have done very well. My congratulations! It would have been nice to work with you."

"Don't be so modest," said Grijpstra, who had poured

himself some tea from the thermos. "We would never have caught you. You *let* us catch you. You could have shot the lot of us, one by one, like sparrows on the roof of the gardenshed."

"I am not a murderer," van Meteren said.

There was an awkward silence.

"Let's have some breakfast," de Gier said and opened a cupboard at random.

"Where did you get the revolver?" Grijpstra asked and sat down close to van Meteren. He had put his pistol away after de Gier had removed the revolver and left it in Runau's care near the rudder, together with the rifle and the carbine. De Gier wasn't taking any risks. He had been very impressed by the Papuan. Beer in his eyes and a chair kicked to smithereeens, within a split second from the expression of infinite sadness on the suspect's face. And the sadness had been real, which made the fast reaction even more amazing. The Papuan was dangerous, even with his wounded shoulder.

"But he didn't kill us when he had the chance," de Gier kept on thinking.

"I'll tell you," van Meteren said, "but first I'll tell you where the food is. We can have breakfast together and de Gier can prepare it."

Soon there was a smell of crisp bacon and fried eggs and fresh coffee. The boat was well stocked.

"I got the revolver in Belgium," van Meteren said when he had eaten. "A Smith & Wesson, like the one I had in New Guinea. You know how I got the Lee Enfield, I smuggled it through customs. I also tried to buy a jungle knife, I lost mine just before I left and I haven't been able to find another one just like it. They aren't made anymore."

"You were homesick," Grijpstra said.

"Perhaps. In New Guinea I was somebody. I had a uniform, arms, a task in life. I served the queen. My queen. Here you laugh about the royal family, perhaps the crown is a symbol, a symbol of the past they say, but to us in New Guinea the queen was holy. We saluted every time we passed her portrait. Religion and the law are very close. I still think the queen is a sort of saint. I cried when I saw her in the street. She was all I had when I left my island. But nobody wanted me when I came to The Hauge to ask for the queen's orders. I showed them my medals and my papers. They were polite and patient, but they had no time for me. I was a strange black fellow from far away. With a Dutch passport."

"Constable first class van Meteren at your service," de Gier said.

"Exactly. Constable first class of the overseas state police. I thought it meant something. It meant nothing at all. I spoke to the soldiers from Ambon who came to Holland instead of joining the Indonesian army as commandos and paratroopers. They were treated as I was treated. But there was a difference. They had each other. I was alone."

"That's just the way you feel," Grijpstra said, "but the feeling is wrong. You are human here, just like the rest of us. We don't discriminate against colored people in Holland. You are a Dutch citizen. You have your rights."

"Yes," van Meteren said, "an old-age pension in case I manage to reach the age of sixty-five years. You gave me a job. I became a clerk. It wasn't too bad really. I like writing. In New Guinea I would tear up a report if there was one little mistake in it. I would work overtime to get the wording exactly right. It was appreciated. But nobody appreciated what I did here."

"Now, now," Grijpstra said.

Van Meteren fingered his shoulder.

"All right. I am telling you what I used to think. Since then I have changed a lot. At that time I wanted to rejoin the police, I don't think I ever stopped being a policeman. I am an expert on all arms, including the bren. I am very good with a knife, I can throw a knife too and I learned judo. But I am not just a fighter. I know the law. By heart. Call a number and I'll recite the article to you."

"More eggs?" de Gier asked. "More coffee?"

"More coffee," van Meteren said.

"You could have gone back," de Gier said, filling the mug, careful not to step between Grijpstra and the Papuan.

"I thought about going back, but I needed money. It would have taken me a few years to save up for the ticket, but I wanted more than the ticket. I wanted to return in style."

"I don't understand this about the police," Grijpstra said. "There are Indonesians in the Dutch police, aren't there? And Chinese too."

"No Papuans," van Meteren said. "Not one. They think we are cannibals. We'll eat the prisoners."

"So you came to Amsterdam?"

"Yes. And they gave me a job as a traffic warden. I have a cap again, and a rubber truncheon."

De Gier wanted to say something but van Meteren raised his hand.

"You are a nice man, de Gier. And very likely you are right. Perhaps I should have been content, after all, there are plenty of Dutchmen in the parking police. It's an honest job, very useful. Perhaps I am too ambitious. Don't argue with me. If you let me talk you'll have a confession. You can make notes if you like and I'll sign the statement. It'll save time."

De Gier didn't say anything.

'I was content, in a way. I didn't like The Hague. It reminded me of a cemetery, full of shadows. In Amsterdam I began to live again. People talk to each other here, even in the street, and there are a lot of Negroes in Amsterdam. I stopped feeling black. People thought I came from the colonies in South America, I didn't have to explain myself. And it got even better when I met Piet Verboom. The people of the Hindist Society accepted me."

"Yes," Grijpstra said. "Verboom. Tell us about your relationship with him."

"What do you think our relationship was?" van Meteren asked.

"Drugs," Grijpstra said. "You both dealt in drugs."

Van Meteren smiled.

"I wasn't a dealer," he said. "I was a bodyguard. Piet had convinced himself he wasn't a mere drug dealer. He had combined it with mysticism. Meditation and self-discipline were part of his ideas, but the whole process should be combined with drugs. Drugs accelerate the opening up of the mind. He kept on telling me that drugs were part of our evolution. And drugs, like mysticism, come from the Far East. It all sounded very logical when you listened to him. But drugs are dangerous, there are a lot of criminals in the trade. He felt safer when I was around."

"And you kept your job as a traffic warden?"

"Of course," van Meteren said. "It gave me something to do during the day. A traffic warden is a respectable person. Piet's activities were always limited to the evenings and the weekends."

Van Meteren was speaking very slowly now. The pill had begun to work. De Gier lit a cigarette and gave it to him. It was very quiet on the lake, the rhythmical muffled explosions of the diesel engine created a peaceful atmosphere. Runau had relaxed, and was steering the botter as he listened. A covey of waterfowl almost touched the mast with their wings. The coastline had become visible.

"Not a bad life, eh?" van Meteren asked. "I have spent days in the boat like this, during the weekends mostly. I have always felt very good on the water, doing nothing in particular, watching the birds and the clouds and fishing a bit, maybe."

Grijpstra had stretched out on a bench, de Gier was sitting on the floor next to van Meteren, he was scribbling in his notebook.

"How's the yacht?" van Meteren asked Runau.

"All right. The cleaning rags have done the trick. She isn't leaking anymore and I have hosed most of the water out."

"I am really sorry," van Meteren said. "I hope I haven't ruined her."

"Don't worry," Runau said. "I came of my own free will. I knew something might happen."

"Go on," de Gier said.

Van Meteren smiled. "You want to know it all, hey? You'll get it all, all you need is a little patience."

"How do you feel now?" Grijpstra asked.

"Better. That pill must have been very strong. But let me tell you the rest of it. Piet had made a few long trips. He had been to Pakistan and he had been offered hash. Piet was a good businessman. He made a plan, got the stuff into the country and kept it for a while. He didn't want to run too much of a risk and preferred selling to a wholesaler rather than directly to the consumer."

"I thought he was an idealist," de Gier said.

"He was, in a way. I am sure he believed what he preached, or perhaps it was the other way around, he wanted to make a lot of money so he thought of a highminded theory to fit his facts."

"So you hung him," de Gier said.

The Papuan's eyes fixed de Gier's.

"Yes. So I hung him. The hash was all right. I have smoked it myself. Often. Here on the lake, for instance. I don't think it does any harm. I made the contact with Beuzekom. I found him by chance. He had parked his little Mercedes bus on a sidewalk and I gave him a ticket and noticed that he had a lot of tins in the car. Ringma was with him and became very nervous when I asked about the tins. I opened one of them and they offered to bribe me but I made an appointment instead and introduced them to Piet. Piet's stuff was better and cheaper than what they had been buying so far. They bought everything Piet had to offer and asked for more. They paid cash as well.''

"How much?'' de Gier asked.

"A lot,'' van Meteren said. "Beuzekom is the most important hash dealer in Amsterdam. And he is hard to catch. He has been caught once but the man who gave his name to the police has disappeared.''

"Who financed Piet's business?'' Grijpstra asked.

"Joachim de Kater. Piet had no money, not much anyway. Short-term loans at very high interest. I was always around when there was money in the house, money or drugs. I would report sick at work or take a day off. Usually we could organize it all in one day.''

"How much were you making yourself?''

"Not as much as you would think,'' van Meteren said, "about fifty thousand a year, maybe, and free board and lodging. And that was more than Piet had intended. I made him pay me. He was frightened of me. And he needed me, of course. He wouldn't go anywhere without me. I spent the money on the motorbike and on this boat and I intended to save a hundred thousand. Take it to New Guinea with me.''

"With a Dutch passport?''

Van Meteren laughed.

"I may be a clown here but in New Guinea it would have been different. It is a very big island and I know it well. I would have found a nice spot and I had made some plans. Wild plans. I might have become a pirate, an admiral with thirty or forty canoes under me, each canoe with a crew of thirty cutthroats. I could have been a king.''

"King Doodle the First,'' de Gier said. "But why did you read all that Dutch history?''

"Curiosity,'' van Meteren said. "I lived here and I wanted to know where I lived. I read about your tribal wars and about the Romans, and the Spanish, and the French, and the Germans. Your history isn't all that different from ours.

Our wars are still tribal but there is only a difference in scale. I have been studying your methods.''

"And what did Piet make out of it?" Grijpstra asked.

"More than I did. But he was spending a lot. He was eating in expensive restaurants and spending money in the red quarter. And some of it went into the house at the Haarlemmer Houttuinen. The Society was making some money, but not enough for all the building going on. A new roof alone cost him fifty thousand.''

"And Joachim de Kater kept on lending money?"

"Sure. He was making a fortune without lifting a finger. He took the risk that Piet wouldn't repay the loan but he always insisted on guarantees and Piet was using the house as security, and that other house he owned in the south.''

"Did Piet have anybody else working for him?"

"No," van Meteren said. "I was his only assistant. He didn't believe in having a lot of people working for him. The Hindist Society was also run with the absolute minimum in manpower. He was a good merchant, he didn't believe in spending his profit on wages. He also didn't believe in sharing his secrets.''

The Papuan groaned. Grijpstra got up and climbed onto the small roof of the cabin. A thin ragged fog seemed to protect the botter.

"Beautiful," Grijpstra thought. "A pleasure trip. Perhaps I should hire a boat and take the children for a day on the lake.''

He sighed and climbed down into the cabin again.

The Papuan had closed his eyes but opened them again when he heard Grijpstra come in.

"It was, in a way, a pleasant, easy business," he said. "Beuzekom was a dangerous man perhaps but he knew I carried a revolver and he was always very polite. When the casks had to be handed over I made him and Ringma do all the carrying. I watched them, and that was all. Piet liked that.

"You are my nice sweet Papuan,' he would say. He also used to call me his 'pet tiger.' "

"But you killed him," de Gier said.

"Yes," van Meteren said. "I waited for the right moment. I had to kill him, but it had to be a good kill."

"*Had* to kill him?" Grijpstra asked.

Van Meteren nodded.

"Perhaps your people in The Hague were right when they refused to accept me into the Dutch police. Perhaps I am still wild. You see, a Papuan chief is killed when his policy of government is wrong. Nobody can judge a chief, he is too powerful. So he is killed at the right moment. The killing is hardly discussed. The tribe decides, but quietly. A certain atmosphere forms itself and everyone agrees. Then one or two men kill the chief, the men who are closest to him. But, it's hard to explain that to you perhaps, those men aren't the killers. The *tribe* kills."

The detectives stared at van Meteren.

"Do you understand?" he asked.

"A little," de Gier said.

"Perhaps I can make it a little clearer," van Meteren said. "A Papuan has no individual face, you see. He has a name and people know him by that name, but the name is only for convenience. In reality he has no name, no face, no individuality. He belongs to the tribe, and that's all. He is part of a whole."

He looked at the detectives who were still staring at him.

"I met with a tribe once who had never been in contact with either the Dutch or Papuans who were working for the Dutch. One of my patrol had a mirror in his pack and he gave it to one of the tribe's warriors. The warrior was a tall, powerful man with a big nose and a bleached bone had been stuck through the nose. He looked into the mirror and laughed. I asked him why he laughed. He said he had seen a funny fellow who lived in the water."

"What happens if you take a photograph of a group of Papuans and then show it to them?" de Gier asked.

Van Meteren smiled.

"You have understood, I see. Each one will recognize all his friends."

"Except one man," de Gier said. "There'll be one man on the photograph he won't recognize."

"Exactly," van Meteren said.

Runau came into the cabin, they had more coffee and lit cigarettes.

"So you waited for the right moment," Grijpstra said.

"Yes. Thérèse had thrown a book at him. The book hit him on the temple with such force that he became dizzy. When I came into the room he was sitting on the floor, stunned, with his head in his hands. I ran to his mother's room and made her give me a Palfium pill. She always had a little jar full of those pills. The doctor prescribed as many as she wanted. The pills might be bad for her, but she was old. With a pill in her stomach she would be quiet for a few hours. She is a very difficult woman to handle."

"Yes," de Gier said.

"Did Piet know you were giving him a drug?" Grijpstra asked.

"Perhaps, but he didn't have time to think. I told him to swallow the pill and he swallowed. He didn't have much resistance, he wasn't used to drugs. He would never drink more than two beers or one whisky at a time and even when he smoked hash he would stop after the second cigarette. The pill made him very weak, perhaps he was hardly aware when I hung him."

"But why did you want to kill him?" de Gier asked. "You had been helping him with his business so you must have approved of what he did. Were you after the seventy-five thousand guilders?"

"He didn't have the money," van Meteren said. "He had already spent it."

Grijpstra shook his head and looked as if he were going to say something but de Gier stopped him, touching his arm.

"What had he done with the seventy-five thousand, van Meteren?" de Gier asked pleasantly.

"He had bought heroin," van Meteren said. "Beuzekom was always asking for heroin. Piet didn't have any contacts, he could only buy hash. When Beuzekom kept on asking for heroin Piet contacted Joachim de Kater. Joachim and Beuzekom didn't know each other, Piet always saw them separately. Joachim was interested in the heroin idea. Heroin is very expensive and not as voluminous as hash. Heroin is like gold dust, it's probably the most profitable commodity in the world. Piet told Joachim that he hadn't been able to locate a source of supply, not even in Marseilles, and Joachim became tempted to locate a source himself. He thought he might have a better chance than Piet, and he was right. Joachim de Kater is a member of the establishment, and he had a second asset, he knew his way about in France. I believe he spent a few years in France as a young man, taking a course at the Sorbonne University."

"We had Joachim checked out," Grijpstra said, "but we didn't find out that he had lived in France."

Van Meteren smiled.

"Joachim was a bit like Piet. Very quiet, very secretive. He never boasted. People who don't boast are very remarkable."

"And dangerous," Grijpstra said.

"And dangerous. Joachim found heroin and sold it to Piet. But Piet had to pay in cash. Joachim wasn't going to lend him the merchandise. So Piet mortgaged his two houses, gave Joachim the money and received the heroin."

"Cash on the barrelhead," de Gier said.

"Ahoy," Runau shouted and the detectives joined him. A low gray speedboat was approaching the botter. Two policemen, carbines at the ready, stood on the forecastle. The boat was approaching them at speed, its bow cutting the silent lake and causing a high sparkling white wave.

"Cut the engine," de Gier said to Runau, "or they may fire at us. We have had enough action today."

Grijpstra went back into the cabin.

"We have company," he said to van Meteren. "You'll be in the hospital soon. So *you* have the heroin now, haven't you?"

"The lot," van Meteren said, "and it will never reach the users. Heroin is the end of everything. Piet wouldn't believe me when I tried to tell him. Hash is all right perhaps but I saw a lot of heroin addicts when I walked the streets as a traffic warden. They were all dying. Heroin is the evil spirit itself, it goes straight into the blood and it will never let go. It makes puppets out of us, crazy puppets who won't last."

"That's why you hung him?" Grijpstra asked. "Why not tell us?"

"You would have jailed him for a bit," van Meteren said. "The police can't change the law. I could, but no judge will believe me when I say that I killed him to stop him."

The police boat touched the botter.

"What would you have done if we hadn't caught you?" Grijpstra asked.

"Waited for at least a year, sold the botter and the Harley and gone back to New Guinea."

"As King Doodle the First?" Grijpstra asked. "Would you have become a king? Or an admiral of a pirate fleet of war canoes?"

Van Meteren smiled.

"Perhaps. I might have become a hermit, who knows. There are a lot of small islands in my country. I might have retired and lived with the animals."

"And the heroin?"

"I would have destroyed it. But I always reckoned with the chance that you might catch me so I kept it for the time being. It may still serve a purpose."

*       *       *

"Morning," said the policeman who entered the cabin. "Is that fellow the prisoner?"

"He is," Grijpstra said.

"Wounded, is he? We'll let him stay where he is and you can follow us. I'll radio for an ambulance. We'll be in the harbor within half an hour. They can take him straight to the hospital."

"Thanks," Grijpstra said.

"We have looked everywhere for your boat," the policeman said, "and all we found were fishermen, cursing us because we were disturbing the fish with our bow wave."

"It's a hard life," de Gier said.

Grijpstra looked at the water policeman, a strong healthy looking giant with a suntanned face.

"What a life," Grijpstra thought, "play around on the water all day."

Van Meteren laughed, he had read Grijpstra's thoughts.

# CHAPTER 16

The chief inspector sat behind his desk, watching his cactus, which showed signs of growing a branch. The future branch was still no more than a slight swelling and might be a mere bump, some sort of infection, a wound perhaps, but it might also be a bud. Perhaps the cactus was trying to develop a flower. The chief inspector was considering whether he should cut it off. The bump, wound, growth or bud was spoiling the straightness of his plant.

He shook his head irritably. Perhaps the growth would be interesting. He closed the small penknife that had been lying on his desk for some time and put it back into his pocket.

The room was stuffy, filled with a damp heat being wafted in through the open windows by a listless draft that might, later in the day, develop into a breeze. The heat had a slight smell of a hospital.

The chief inspector opened his nostrils and breathed deeply.

The smell made him think again of the Papuan who had been sitting at the other side of his desk, a little while ago. The Papuan had been flanked by his two captors. He brought some order in his thoughts.

"They caught him." he thought. "They had to shoot him to catch him but they merely winged him. Good work. An insignificant wound that is healing already. And they took him here. An arrested murderer. Took a long time though, three weeks is a long time. But he was clever. An intelligent man. And a dangerous man, no doubt about it. A trained killer, properly trained. And now they say he is trustworthy."

He closed his eyes and the orderly thoughts flaked off into a hazy pattern of hardly connected and only partly formed images. Papuans, he thought, wild men from the early ages. He saw the wild men from the early ages who once populated the swamp that, now, today, was called Holland. Powerful small men, bearded and low-browed, huddled near their campfires, exhausted from a buffalo hunt or an attack on a competing tribe's close-by village.

"Then the Romans came," the chief inspector thought. "In New Guinea the Dutch came. Some of our wild men must have joined the Roman army and some of them must have seen Rome. And now a Papuan has come to Amsterdam."

He got up and looked out of the window.

Grijpstra had made a proposition, a proposition inspired by an idea of the Papuan. The Papuan had lost his rights, he had been arrested, a prisoner's requests are of little consequence.

He looked at his cactus agin, the enormous green phallus, the thorned phallus.

He had been requested to release a murderer, for a limited period of time of course. But a free man can escape. He turns a corner, he runs, he catches a streetcar or jumps on a bicycle. There are a lot of bicycles in Amsterdam.

He picked up his phone.

"The commissaris is ill today, sir," a girl's voice said. The chief inspector put his hand over the phone, swore, took his hand off the phone, thanked the girl, and rang off.

He dialed again.

"My husband is suffering of an attack of rheumatism, he is in the bath. It eases the pain, he says. Can I give him a message?"

The chief inspector thought.

"I really have to speak with your husband, madame," he said.

"One moment."

The chief inspector waited.

"Could you come here?"

"Right away," the chief inspector said. "I'll be with you in fifteen minutes."

The chief inspector sat on a wooden footstool and looked at the commissaris' head. He had placed himself in such a position that he couldn't see more than the commissaris' head. The commissaris was in his bath, stretched out on his back, hands folded on his small, round, old man's belly which, if the chief inspector could have seen it, would have reminded him of an old-fashioned pith-helmet. "Well?" the commissaris asked.

The chief inspector spoke for some ten minutes. The commissaris interrupted him only once. He wanted one of his small cigars, from a box which the chief inspector found on the bathroom floor. The chief inspector lit the cigar and placed it carefully between the commissaris' thin bloodless lips.

The commissaris inhaled, puffed, and began to cough. The chief inspector removed the cigar.

"All right," the commissaris said.

"All right," Grijpstra said and put the phone down.

De Gier jumped from his chair.

"They agree?" he asked unbelievingly.

Grijpstra nodded.

"But if anything goes wrong the case is all ours again."

De Gier laughed.

"What would you expect?" he asked.

Grijpstra smiled. "I didn't expect them to agree."

"No," de Gier said. "I didn't expect them to agree either but perhaps they should have agreed. The police have always used methods like that."

Grijpstra nodded, and rubbed his chin. The tough short hairs bristled against the inside of his hand. He hadn't shaved that morning and he hadn't had time to sneak off to the upstairs toilet where he kept an old tin containing a much better razor than he had at home, and a tube of shaving cream. Mrs. Grijpstra didn't approve of shaving cream, ordinary soap is much cheaper.

"You haven't shaved," de Gier said.

"No," Grijpstra frowned and a deep line formed between his eyebrows.

"Faulty discipline, hey?" de Gier asked.

"Yes yes."

"But you should shave. Why didn't you? Did you over-sleep?"

"I like shaving," Grijpstra said, "but they shouldn't shout at you when you are shaving."

De Gier nodded. "You are quite right. They shouldn't."

"Because if they shout at you," Grijpstra explained, "you may become a little annoyed, and throw your brush on the floor."

"And leave the house," de Gier said, "and bang the door."

"*Now* I'll shave," Grijpstra said. "I'll be a little while. I'll have to get some hot water from the canteen. You go and fetch van Meteren. I hope he slept well. The doctor should have come and seen him meanwhile. He is a strong chappie all right, a little heap of misery yesterday and full of beans today according to the guards.''

"He had a good cell," de Gier said, "and I saw to it that they looked after him. Clean sheets, extra pillows, cups of tea, and the drunks next door were taken downstairs. I think he had a long quiet night.''

De Gier was back within half an hour with van Meteren, who lit one of Grijpstra's cigars, drank the coffee that de Gier fetched, and looked through the telephone book that he found on de Gier's desk.

"Hello," van Meteren said, "is that you, Mr. de Kater? This is van Meteren.''

Grijpstra had pressed a switch and a microphone attached to the telephone made de Kater's voice audible to the detectives.

"Morning, Mr. van Meteren," de Kater's civilized voice was saying. "How are you? I hope you found a good room?''

"Certainly. Close by, too. I am living around the corner from my old address, on the top floor of an old house on the Brouwersgracht, I am quite comfortable here.''

"I am glad to hear it. I am sorry about having had to ask you to move but you will understand that I bought the house at the Haarlemmer Houttuinen to sell it again, and an empty house is easier to sell. What can I do for you, Mr. van Meteren?''

"A small favor Mr. de Kater. I am planning to leave the country in the near future and I need a little money. I worked it out and I could use some twenty thousand, in small notes, twenty fives and hundreds perhaps.''

"Yes?" de Kater asked politely.

"Yes, and I thought that you might be able to help me. Piet Verboom gave you a much larger sum, not so long ago and I am sure that you didn't bank the money. That money should still be around and available, I thought.''

The microphone was quiet and Grijpstra and de Gier studied the small gadget, made of gray plastic.

"It's covered by a grid," de Gier thought, "like the town's sewers are. There are rats under the grids of the town's sewers."

"Quite, quite," de Kater's voice said. It didn't sound as civilized as before. It sounded hoarse as well. "Yes, yes." Grijpstra sucked his cigarette, de Gier had closed his eyes. Van Meteren's voice sounded very pleasant and relaxed, as if he were talking to a friend or a very close acquaintance.

"The amount isn't all that large," van Meteren said.

"Perhaps not," de Kater said, "but I was thinking what you would be prepared to do in exchange."

"Oh, I'll do something in exchange all right," van Meteren said.

"What?"

"I'll explain it to you. You delivered some merchandise to Piet Verboom, shortly before Piet died, as you will remember. The merchandise was paid for and the money was received by you, and the transaction came to an end, a satisfactory end to all parties concerned. But the goods still represent a certain value, perhaps more than Piet paid at the time, for prices are rising."

"Yes, you are right," de Kater said. There was a slight tap, followed by the sound of de Kater breathing in.

"He lit a cigar," Grijpstra thought, "a nice long fat cigar."

"And I thought that you might be interested in buying the goods back again," van Meteren said.

"For twenty thousand guilders?" de Kater asked.

"Yes, indeed. A small part of the value, but the goods aren't altogether mine, although I might say that I have inherited them."

"Ha," de Kater said. "If you have possession of the goods you could say that you are the owner as well. Why didn't the police find the merchandise?"

"They didn't look in the right place."

"Quite," de Kater said, "but tell me, why sell them to me? Supposing of course that you have them. You were Piet Verboom's assistant, surely you know who he intended selling the goods to, and if you do know, why, you can get the right price, I suppose."

Grijpstra looked up. Van Meteren raised a hand and smiled.

De Gier's eyes were still closed.

"I know the buyers," van Meteren said, "but I am not going to take the risk of approaching them. Piet's death woke the police and they are sniffing around everywhere."

"I see."

"And I am in somewhat of a hurry," van Meteren said. "I want to leave the country. The police are sniffing around me too, or they were, rather. I think they have stopped suspecting me and they stopped shadowing me."

"You are sure?"

"Absolutely sure."

"You were in the police yourself, weren't you?"

"I was," van Meteren said, "and I know when I am being shadowed. Any Papuan knows, he needs no police training for *that*."

"Twenty thousand," de Kater said

"Twenty thousand."

"Well, your idea interests me. When and where, Mr. van Meteren?"

"Tonight, in your own property, the old house in the Haarlemmer Houttuinen, nine o'clock. I'll meet you in the street outside."

"And you will have the goods with you?"

"No goods, no money, Mr. de Kater." The silence returned. De Gier opened his eyes and stretched. Grijpstra screwed the stub of his cigarette into the ashtray. He was using a lot of force and the paper of the cigarette disintegrated and mixed with the tobacco grains. Van Meteren's eyes glittered.

"I don't like to rush into things," de Kater said, "but I am rather interested. If I don't show up tonight you may ring me again."

There was a click and the line died. Van Meteren carefully replaced the receiver on the hook.

"Do you think he will come?" Grijpstra asked.

"Sure," van Meteren said. "His greed will drive him straight into our hands. He'll be there tonight and you can grab him with the heroin under his arm."

"I'll take you back to your cell," de Gier said.

Grijpstra was shaking the Papuan's hand. "See you tonight. Christ Almighty, if we pull this one off it will be medals for everybody."

"I already have two medals," van Meteren said.

## CHAPTER 17

De Gier squatted between the bushes that grew against the side of the railway-dike on the other side of the Haarlemmer Houttuinen and watched the front door of number 5 and his watch at intervals of about five seconds. Two other detectives had hidden themselves close by. They were sitting on dog turds and both were complaining. De Gier had managed to keep himself clean but his legs hurt and he was squatting down with some difficulty.

"Bah," de Gier whispered to himself. Their position wasn't ideal. They were on the wrong side of the railway dike's fencing and he doubted that they would be able to get through the hole, which he had cut in the fence's chicken wire, quickly enough. But there had been no other place. He hoped the youth-gangs that were bound to roam the area wouldn't discover them. Fortunately the street was empty, only an occasional car passed.

De Gier studied the lonely pedestrian on the sidewalk on

the other side of the street. He had recognized the chief inspector, dressed in an old worn duffelcoat and talking to his Alsatian, a young dog that by wagging his tail and barking, was asking to be released from his leash. De Gier looked at the chief inspector with admiration. The chief inspector shuffled along, dragging his feet, and seemed some twenty years older than his real age.

"You see that fellow over there?" he whispered to the detective next to him.

The detective looked.

"I see him. The old chappie with his dog. There was another man some minutes ago, with two dachshunds. Anything the matter with him?"

"That's the chief inspector," de Gier whispered.

The detective looked again.

"You are right. What's with his hair? Is he wearing a wig?"

"No," de Gier said. "Why would he be wearing a wig?"

"He looks different," the detective whispered.

De Gier produced a small pair of binoculars, his private property for which he had paid a lot of money once. The chief inspector's hair did appear different, curly, not slicked down with fat as it usually was.

"Must have washed and ruffled his hair," de Gier thought. "Very effective. Goes with the old duffelcoat and the shuffling gait. He looks like one of the old unemployed characters who live around here, by themselves mostly. Misfits, drunks, potential suicides.

He looked at his watch again, five to nine. Van Meteren had arrived and was waiting near the front door of number 5, leaning against the wall. The chief inspector had allowed the Alsatian to drag him away. Around the corner an old car should be parked with two detectives in the front seat, and two uniformed constables were supposed to patrol the Haarlemmer Street. The Haarlemmer Street is regularly patrolled by cops on foot so de Kater, if he would be coming through there, shouldn't be unduly suspicious. They might catch him later though, should de Kater, in a panic, want to escape through the back of the house in the Haarlemmer Houttuinen, for the two streets are parallel and the gardens connect.

And then there was Grijpstra, of course, hidden in the courtyard of the house, together with a young burly detective who could walk up a gable and who had shown them a diploma from a mountain club to prove it. They had tried to think of everything.

The detective put his hand on de Gier's arm. "Is that our man?"

Joachim de Kater had appeared, striding along energetically, carrying an obviously empty suitcase and twirling an umbrella. He waved at van Meteren and the two started talking to each other. They seemed to agree after a while and de Kater opened the front door with his key. The door opened, and closed. The street became quiet again. The chief-inspector's Alsatian lifted his leg and pissed against a lamp post. The chief inspector waited patiently for the dog to finish.

"And now?" the detective whispered.

"Quiet," de Gier snapped.

De Gier tried to imagine what was happening inside the house. The heroin was hidden in the Buddha statue that throned in the corridor, the cheap copy that Piet Verboom had once bought in the Paris flea market. De Gier knew now, because van Meteren had explained it to him, that the statue was hollow. Metal statues, even if they are hollow, cannot usually be opened and the detectives who had searched the house hadn't thought of forcing the Buddha's head off the body.

De Kater had become the rightful owner of the house and its contents. According to Constanze he had inserted a clause into the contract that stated that anything in the house, whether furniture, ornament or whatever, came with the house. The statue was his, and the heroin inside the statue was his as well, but he hadn't known that the heroin was inside the statue.

De Gier sighed. He had thought about the statues when Constanze had been telling him about the sale of the house. He sighed again, thinking of Constanze's body and of the long leg that she had put on top of his own. He thought of the firm warm breasts and the soft slightly hoarse voice. And now he was here, squatting under a bush, with a branch scratching his neck and dog shit all around, and next to a bad-tempered detective.

He might have deduced that the Buddha statue was hollow but he had only thought of the sudden popularity of Eastern religions that would influence the price of the statue. He had thought that Piet Verboom and Joachim de Kater were clever people and that buying at the right time and selling at the right time seemed a more intelligent way of filling one's time than the detection of crimes. The original of the statue, according to Constanze, stood in a temple in Ceylon. A famous statue, several times stolen and returned again, and often copied. All the copies would be hollow, de Gier thought. Saves bronze and bronze is an expensive metal. Piet had discovered the hollowness of the statue when he studied its head, which hadn't been screwed on properly. A plumber had unscrewed the head, using a special oil and as little force as possible and the statue had been cleaned out and become a container. A container of the powder that leads the user straight to heaven. But a very temporary heaven and after a short while the user drops through a hole in its floor, straight into hell, and eventually the hell becomes permanent.

De Kater would now be standing next to the statue, impa-tiently waiting for van Meteren who would be giving him the small sealed bags, one by one, carefully of course, for he was handling very special merchandise. And the bags would be going into de Kater's suitcase. But they wouldn't stay there. Their contents would find their way into the blood of some of the young people of Amsterdam, the blood of simpletons, looking for higher spheres.

"But not this time," de Gier thought, and felt a wave of contentment. The feeling surprised him.

"Careful now," de Gier thought. His leg hurt because of a muscle knotting itself into a hard ball. He massaged the leg. "Easy now, soon you will be a dedicated police sergeant, motivated, complete. Complete with a sense of purpose."

He was muttering to himself.

"Pardon?" the detective asked.

"Nothing," de Gier said, "just stay put. We'll catch him when he leaves the house."

"Don't we want the black fellow?" the detective asked.

"We've got him already."

"An informer?"

"Sort of," de Gier said.

"He better watch it," the detective said, "if he shows himself as openly as that he won't last. We'll fish him out of the canal soon."

"Not him," de Gier said.

The door opened and de Kater became visible. He was holding on to the suitcase. It didn't seem heavy.

"Heroin is pretty light," the detective whispered. "If that suitcase is full he is carrying a hundred thousand guilders at least."

"Up," de Gier said.

"Now," de Gier shouted.

It was easy. De Gier, followed by his two assistants, sprinted across the road. There was no traffic. De Kater saw him and dropped the suitcase. He ran toward the old dented car and the two detectives opened the doors and rushed at him. De Kater turned and ran toward the chief inspector. He had dropped the umbrella as well. Nobody seemed very concerned about the pistol in de Kater's right hand. One of the detectives behind him fired, pointing his pistol at the moon. De Kater dropped his weapon and surrendered to the chief inspector and his dog who was showing his teeth and growling. The chief inspector hadn't moved, he had merely told de Kater to stop, in a pleasant voice.

"Some show," de Gier thought when he put his hand on the shoulder of the criminal. "Six men and one dog."

De Kater began to cry. Nobody was surprised. Suspects, at the moment of arrest, often cry. Fear, or a feeling of release, or both. Or shock perhaps.

"Easy now," de Gier said, "we won't hurt you. Do you have a license to carry a firearm?"

"No," de Kater sobbed.

"And can you tell us what you have in your suitcase?"

"Heroin," de Kater sobbed.

"You better come with us," de Gier said.

# CHAPTER 18

The two detectives who had been in the old car took charge of de Kater and drove off. Van Meteren appeared in the open door, grinning.

"Neat job," the chief inspector said, "very neat, van Meteren."

"It was a pleasure, sir." The Papuan laughed. "I don't think he suspected anything at all."

"Thanks to you," Grijpstra said. "I was very close to you, you know. I had sneaked into the back part of the corridor but you couldn't see me, it's very dark in there. I overheard the last part of your and de Kater's conversation. Perfect acting on your part, congratulations."

"Yes," van Meteren said, "I heard you, I thought de Kater would hear you as well but he was concentrating too much on the money, and on the dope, of course."

"Did he pay up?" the chief inspector asked.

Van Meteren patted his jacket. "The lot. He tried to pay less but I wouldn't have it. He was armed although he didn't say so, but I think that he must have suspected me of being armed as well.''

He produced a fat brown envelope and gave it to the chief inspector.

"Here you are, sir, notes of a hundred guilders. He said he didn't have smaller notes. Twenty thousand, I counted the amount very carefully.''

The chief inspector slipped the envelope into his inside pocket.

"Thanks.''

"That's a lot of cash to carry around,'' one of the detectives said, "and a gun as well. That's the trouble with these sugar merchants, they all carry pistols nowadays. They have become proper highwaymen and before you know they put a hole into you and off you are for a few months, eating porridge and mashed vegetables in a dreary little hospital room.''

"Part of the game, mate,'' Grijpstra said kindly. "Are we going home, sir?''

"Might as well,'' the chief inspector said.

"A moment,'' van Meteren said. "If you don't mind I would like to talk to you, sir, and to Grijpstra and de Gier. In the house, perhaps.''

"Sure. I would suggest that the other three have a quiet beer in the Haarlemmerstraat. There is a reasonable pub on the corner, run by Aunt Jane, that fat lady with the red hair. I'll meet you later in there, and we can have a final beer together.''

"Sir,'' the detectives said.

"So?'' the chief inspector asked. They were standing in what had once been the bar of the Hindist Society. Van Meteren faced them from behind the bar and the police officers, after looking around, settled themselves on bar stools.

"Three beers,'' de Gier said.

"Sorry," van Meteren said, "no beer, but there is some coke and lemonade here and I can clean a few glasses."

"That'll be nice," Grijpstra said.

Van Meteren washed and wiped four glasses and opened four bottles of cola.

"The place is still complete," de Gier said.

"Not quite. The draft beer has been taken out; it won't keep, I think," van Meteren said, "but the furniture and everything is still here. De Kater could probably have sold the lot for a good price, he might have auctioned it. There are a lot of new pubs opening up in town."

"Silly man," the chief inspector said, "a silly man taking a silly risk. But we have got him now. A pity we can't grab the other two but they won't last either. They are bound to slip up one of these days and we can catch them like rotten plums falling off the tree."

"Brr," de Gier said. "I don't like this stuff."

"Spit it out," van Meteren said. "I have some soda here. The other two, you say, sir. I would like to talk about them."

He opened another bottle and gave it to de Gier. "Here, have another glass as well."

"You mean Beuzekom and his friend?" the chief inspector asked.

"Yes sir. Perhaps you won't catch them. I got to know them and especially Beuzekom is very intelligent. They won't stay in the game, not when he feels that he has made enough. They'll go to Spain and dabble in real estate and become respectable. If you want to catch them it should be right now."

"We'll have to be quick," Grijpstra said. "The newspaper vultures haven't smelled anything yet but they will soon and once they honk the news around Beuzekom and Company will go into cover and we'll never flush them."

"There is my arrest as well," van Meteren said. "They might not find out about de Kater until you want them to find out but that chase on the IJsselmeer was quite spectacular, spectacular enough to make headlines.''

"Not yet," the chief inspector said. "I have seen the papers. You got into the harbor of Monnikendam at the right time. The vultures were all fast asleep. What we did here tonight is dangerous, however. The newspapers have patrols in the city and they pay for every tip, in case the patrol misses out. If somebody in the neighborhood noticed the commotion the game is up.''

"So we'll have to be quick," van Meteren said. "I am glad you agree. I suggest that I phone Beuzekom now. He should be in. It's Sunday. He drinks on Saturday and rests on Sunday. I'll ask him to come here. We still have the heroin, it can go back into the statue. We can play the same game.''

He took a sip and watched the three men on the other side of the bar.

De Gier began to grin.

"You like the idea, de Gier?" the chief inspector asked.

"Yes sir. A lovely idea, too good to work almost. Twice in one evening, what a beautiful thought.''

"Grijpstra?''

"Lovely," Grijpstra said.

"We don't have enough men for a proper trap," the chief inspector said.

"I'll fetch the beer drinkers.''

"Right, de Gier. Perhaps I should telephone the commissaris first.''

The chief inspector walked to the phone, but hesitated. "Perhaps not. He is sick. And he approved the first trap.''

Nobody said anything.

"Right," the chief inspector said.

"I'll fetch those jokers in the pub while you phone Beuzekom," de Gier said to van Meteren.

"Yes, but get them quickly. If Beuzekom answers I'll tell him to come right away. Fetch the others but don't come in while I phone; I'll tap on the window when I am done."

"Go ahead," the chief inspector said.

De Gier left and van Meteren dialed the number; he knew it by heart.

"Beuzekom," the phone said.

"Evening Beuz, this is van Meteren."

"Ha," Beuzekom said, surprised, "good to hear your voice. Haven't seen you for a while, how are you? Still in business or has everything died since Piet left us?"

"Still in business Beuz, and how are you two?"

"Well, what can I tell you? We are all right, I suppose, but Ringma has been annoying me lately. He mopes about all the time. We should go on holiday but we have been spoiled. Holidays cost a lot of money these days, the sun has become expensive when you are used to four-star hotels."

"You sound as if business has been bad."

"There's always the small trade," Beuzekom said. "There have been some supplies but some of it is rubbish, it looks all right but it isn't and it is hard to see the difference. If they get any cleverer I'll have to hire a chemical engineer and install a laboratory. They can even imitate the smell now."

"Did they fool you?"

"Not yet, but they will one day."

"And the real business?"

"Sugar, you mean?" Beuzekom asked. "Yes, well, nothing doing. Can't get it. Whatever happened to that lot Piet was going to give us? He didn't take it with him so it must still be around."

"Yes," van Meteren said.

"You are serious? Is that why you phone me?"

"Yes."

"Splendid," Beuzekom said. "Excellent fellow! You know I am in the market. What's your price?"

"You are lucky," van Meteren said. "I've got it and it's

for sale. I never read the papers so I don't know about inflation, you can have it at the same price.''

"The price Piet wanted?"

"Yes."

"Same quantity, same quality?"

"Yes."

"One hundred and twenty thousand?"

"That's it."

"One hundred and twenty thousand," Beuzekom said softly.

"Yes. You can bring it now and I'll give you the goods. But only if you come *now*. I am sitting right on top of the goods and you should be sitting right on top of the money. You had it then and I am sure you haven't spent it."

"Why right now?"

Van Meteren laughed.

"I don't want you to bring all your friends. I am alone."

"Alone with a head full of tricks and a forty-five revolver under your armpit," Beuzekom said. "I know you, you old jungle nigger. I have never underestimated you. Even without a gun you can tie me into knots."

"I am not a nigger," van Meteren said, and stopped smiling at the telephone. "I am a Papuan."

"Worse," Beuzekom said. "I just read a book about you guys. You decorate your huts with the skulls of your enemies."

"I don't want your skull," van Meteren said. "Are you coming or aren't you coming?"

"Can I bring little Ringma?"

"Yes."

Beuzekom breathed deeply.

"Right. We'll come. Right now. Where are you?"

"Haarlemmer Houttuinen number five."

"Are you still living there?"

"No, I moved but I am here now and if you are here within a quarter of an hour the deal is on."

"We'll come, Mr. Papuan," Beuzekom said slowly, "but no tricks! If you try, Ringma and I will try to get you. Maybe we'll fail but I swear we'll try."

"I have never given you any reason not to trust me," van Meteren said.

"True. You are a nice man. A friend. We'll be there."

"See you," van Meteren said and rang off.

"He is coming right now," van Meteren said to the chief inspector.

"You look exhausted," the chief inspector said. "Right now? That's too quick, maybe. Where is de Gier?"

Van Meteren looked out of the window and made a sign.

De Gier and the three detectives came into the bar.

"O.K.," the chief inspector said. "I'll take Hector into the street for a little walk. De Gier takes his old position in the bushes and his two colleagues go with him. No. De Gier can go by himself and the other two can hide behind some of those parked cars. We should be able to get at our friends from as many directions as possible. Beuzekom is dangerous and Ringma probably too, and they'll be armed. They won't cry like de Kater."

"They can be as dangerous as they like," the young burly detective who could climb gables said. "It saves money, now I don't have to go to the pictures."

"Yes, yes," said the chief inspector. "Grijpstra, take Tarzan here to the courtyard and restrain him. He'll be yelling and prancing around in a minute. We don't want an adventure, we only want an arrest. Van Meteren stays here."

"Yes sir, " everybody said.

De Gier was back in the bushes. The same branch was scratching his neck and the dog turds smelled worse than before for he had walked right through them this time. He was muttering to himself again but he was smiling as well. Like Tarzan, he was enjoying himself.

"I hope he attacks me," he thought. "I'll trip him up and

break his nose. That beautiful nose in the handsome face.''
He saw the arrogance on Beuzekom's face again. ''He can
bleed a little this time.''

He was watching the road now. There had been an accident somewhere and the traffic was thick and slow. He
couldn't see the other side of the street.

''But I'll only go for him if he provokes me,'' de Gier was
saying to himself.

The traffic was moving now. He saw the chief inspector.
Hector had seen a cat and was barking and the chief inspector
was trying to shut him up.

''There they are,'' de Gier thought.

Beuzekom drove his Mercedes bus onto the pavement.
The two dealers walked to the front door and rang the bell.
The door opened straight away. Beuzekom, like de Kater,
was carrying a suitcase.

Ringma was looking around him.

Van Meteren made an inviting gesture and Ringma followed his friend.

Three minutes passed before de Gier heard the shot. He
leaped through the fence and ran across the street. A city bus,
trying to avoid him, pulled over and nearly hit a car coming
from the other direction. Both cars were sounding their horns
but de Gier didn't hear them. Together with the two other
detectives he kicked the door, which swung open, squeaking
on one hinge.

Ringma was in the corridor, leaning against the wall.
There was a pistol in his hand but it pointed at the floor. One
of the detectives tapped Ringma's wrist and the pistol fell and
was caught by the detective's hand. Beuzekom was on the
floor, groaning and holding his hands between his legs.

''The bastard. He kicked me in the balls. I never thought
he would. He was smiling at me when he did, smiling and
talking.''

"Where is the heroin?" Grijpstra asked.

"Here," Beuzekom groaned, "in the suitcase. He gave it to me. It came from the Buddha over there and when I had it all and he had the money he kicked me."

They went through his pockets and de Gier took his pistol.

"Where is van Meteren?" the chief inspector asked.

Ringma, who hands had been handcuffed, pointed with his head.

"Through there, that door on the side."

"No," the chief inspector said.

# CHAPTER 19

"Well, well," the commissaris said, "you had a busy evening."

"Yes sir," the chief inspector said. "It's a pity, sir."

They were sitting in the back garden of the large house which the commissaris rented in the old city. The evening was warm and they could hear people in the other gardens around them, enjoying the breeze. The commissaris' wife had brought a tray with a stone jar of cold jenever and two small glasses and a tray of mixed nuts. The two officers were smoking the commissaris' small cigars. The commissaris was rubbing his right leg. He had spent the day in bed and his wife had massaged his legs with a special ointment and he felt much better, but his face still twisted at times when his legs suddenly shivered.

"Who fired the shot?" the commissaris asked.

"Ringma, sir. When van Meteren kicked Beuzekom

Ringma fired to protect his friend, or perhaps to revenge him.''

"Friend and lover," the commissaris said. "A kick in the balls you say. It is easy to kill a man that way. But Beuzekom was still talking?''

"Yes, van Meteren meant to stun him temporarily, I think. I spoke to the doctor who saw Beuzekom and his condition is reasonable, he doesn't have to go to the hospital. It'll be painful for a while, the doctor said.''

"Your health," the commissaris said and raised his glass.

"Your health," the chief inspector said and emptied his glass in one go.

The commissaris refilled the glasses.

"So van Meteren meant to cause a sudden commotion so that he could escape without anyone paying any attention. He knew that the police could come in any minute.''

"Yes sir. He had to do it while they were still inside and while we were still in hiding. If we had come in to arrest the two men, or if we had waited until they were in the street, we would still have been able to watch him. And he had to think of his two clients as well. They were both armed and aware. He had to shake them.''

"Clever," the commissaris said. "He probably provoked Ringma's shot as well. It would shake *you* and you would be rushing around trying to get the pistol and he would have more time.''

"You said he disappeared through a side door?" the commissaris asked.

"Yes. The door opens into a narrow corridor that leads right to the back of the house and another door, but it also leads to some stairs and into a cellar that has two exits into the courtyard, a door and a window that doesn't close properly. These old houses consist of corridors and stairs and doors, you can go around and around for ever unless you know the way. Van Meteren knew the way.''

"I can imagine it easily enough," the commissaris said.

"Van Meteren sneaking out quietly while you were rushing about upstairs, disarming and questioning our two friends. By the time you woke up he must have been in the street, well away, waiting at a tram stop somewhere probably."

"And with one hundred and twenty thousand guilders in his pocket," said the chief inspector.

The commissaris began to laugh.

"The working capital of Beuzekom and Company, representing a thousand clever tricks and a whole heap of illegal and immoral activity. Not bad, hey? Not bad at all."

The chief inspector scooped a handful of mixed nuts from the dish and filled his mouth with it.

"Not bad," he said.

"Beg pardon?" the commissaris asked.

The chief inspector pointed at his mouth and began to chew.

"Easy," the commissaris said. "Don't choke on those nuts. My wife did the other day and I had to whack her on her back. She was getting blue in the face. Terrible."

The chief inspector finished chewing, swallowed, and drank a little more jenever.

"Have another glass," the commissaris said, and poured from the stone jar his wife had left near his chair. "What about the two uniformed constables in the Haarlemmer Street. Didn't they see him?"

"Yes sir. That was the worst of it all. They did see him and they let him go. They thought he was one of us. It seemed he waved at them but perhaps they put that in to make us feel even more ridiculous."

"You hadn't told the constables that van Meteren was a prisoner, or a suspect anyway?"

"No sir." The chief inspector scooped another handful of nuts from the dish.

"My fault, sir. They didn't know so they can't be blamed. All my fault. I thought nothing could happen with half a dozen plainclothes detectives around van Meteren at all times.''

''No,'' the commissaris said.

The chief inspector looked at the commissaris.

''Not your fault,'' the commissaris said. ''I don't think we can talk about blame. Van Meteren is a policeman, a real policeman. I kept on having the idea that he was one of us, even after he had been arrested and was facing us as a suspect. And if you think that someone belongs to you, that he is part of the same group, you don't pay special attention to him.''

When, about an hour later, the jenever was running out the commissaris mentioned the term ''force majeure.'' The chief inspector felt pleased but didn't pursue the subject.

The conversation had changed its course. They were discussing the Papuan's chances.

''He may have stolen a car and crossed the border to Belgium,'' the commissaris said. ''The small roads aren't checked anymore. You can drive straight through nowadays, even the main routes are easy.''

''And he has got a lot of money,'' the chief inspector said. ''He can buy any passport he likes and take a plane to Indonesia from Paris, or to Hong Kong, or to Singapore. Interpol has been informed and he may be caught in a foreign airport but the chance is slim.''

''He isn't in a hurry,'' the commissaris said. ''Maybe he is taking a roundabout way, perhaps through the West. He can pose as a Negro and go via Surinam, Dutch Guinea in South America.''

''We thought of that, the police in Paramaribo have been alerted.''

''If we can think of it he can guess our thoughts,'' the commissaris said. ''No. He'll pick an original way, the man is intelligent, very intelligent. I think he'll make it. He'll be in his own country soon. New Guinea. They call it West Irian now, I think. There must be a few million Papuans running about over there and he can lose himself in the crowd, stick a bone through his nose and a couple of feathers in his hair. Didn't you say that he may want to become a hermit on an island?''

The chief inspector was looking at the sky.

"Or a king? De Gier was telling me about King Doodle the First. A powerful native king with a fleet of war canoes. I have seen pictures of those canoes, big boats, forty warriors to the boat. They go in for piracy and quick fights and they eat their victims. Long pig. Campfires. Drums. Full moon. Getting drunk on palm wine. Maybe it's a good life.''

"Yes," the chief inspector said. "Or he may have become influenced by his sojourn over here and try to create a socialist state.''

The commissaris shifted his legs slowly.

"No, no," he said, "I think he is too clever to go in for power. Power weighs you down, there's nothing worse than becoming important. I would rather imagine him as a hermit, sitting by himself on a small island; there must be thousands of islands over there where no one ever goes, no one to bother him and all space and time for himself.''

"And what would he be doing with himself over there?'' the chief inspector asked. "Masturbate and go crazy?''

The jenever came to an end. The chief inspector asked the question again.

"Well," the commissaris said, "there have been hermits before in the world and there must be quite a few around right now. They are not crazy, you know. They meditate, that's what they do. They find a quiet spot and sit on it, and they breathe in a certain way and keep their backs straight and concentrate. Wasn't he doing that here as well? That Hindist Society was some sort of a meditation thing, wasn't it?''

"That Hindist Society was all balls," the chief inspector said. "Nonsense, another way to make money ."

"Everything is nonsense," the commissaris said slowly. The chief inspector hadn't heard him.

"Force majeure," the chief inspector said. "You said that just now. Force majeure makes us blameless. We did our best but something happened that we couldn't have foreseen. Caused by a power beyond us. Force majeure means an act of God."

"Ah yes," the commissaris said. "God."